Praise for t
T. C. LoTempio

"Nick and Nora are a winning team!"

—Rebecca Hale, *New York Times* Bestselling author

"A fast-paced cozy mystery spiced with a dash of romance and topped with a big slice of 'cat-titude.'"

—Ali Brandon, *New York Times* Bestselling author

"Nick and Nora are the purr-fect sleuth duo!"

—Victoria Laurie, *New York Times* Bestselling author

"A page-turner with an endearing heroine."

—*Richmond Times Dispatch*

"Excellently plotted and executed—five paws and a tail up for this tale."

—*Open Book Society*

"Nick brims with street smarts and feline charisma, you'd think he was human . . . an exciting new series."

—Carole Nelson Douglas, *New York Times* notable author of the Midnight Louie mysteries

"I love this series and each new story quickly becomes my favorite. Cannot wait for the next!"

—*Escape With Dollycas Into a Good Book*

"I totally loved this lighthearted and engagingly entertaining whodunit featuring new amateur sleuth Nora Charles and Nick, her feline companion."

—*Dru's Cozy Report*

Books by T. C. LoTempio

Nick and Nora Mysteries

Meow If It's Murder
Claws for Alarm
Crime and Catnip
Hiss H for Homicide
Murder Faux Paws
A Purr Before Dying

Urban Tails Pet Shop Mysteries

The Time for Murder Is Meow
Killers of a Feather
Death Steals the Spotlight

Cat Rescue Mysteries

Purr M for Murder
Death by a Whisker

Death Steals the Spotlight

Urban Tails Pet Shop Mysteries

T. C. LoTempio

BEYOND THE PAGE
PUBLISHING

Death Steals the Spotlight
T. C. LoTempio
Copyright © 2023 by T. C. LoTempio.
Cover design and illustration by Dar Albert, Wicked Smart Designs

Beyond the Page Books
are published by
Beyond the Page Publishing
www.beyondthepagepub.com

ISBN: 978-1-960511-17-1

To the real Princess Fuzzypants and her human, Susan

Acknowledgments

This book wouldn't be possible without the efforts of my editor, Bill Harris, who always strives to make my books the best they can be. Also thanks to my agent, Josh Getzler, and his able assistant, Jon Cobb!

Extra-special thanks go to Susan Johnston and her beautiful Maine coon cat, Princess Fuzzypants, who allowed me to make a character out of her! It just goes to show that when you have a writer for a friend, no one is safe . . . not even a cat.

And as always, I thank all the loyal readers who support Shell and company.

One

"Shell, dear, I need to order some of that Shiny Coat Shampoo for my darling Priscilla. Oh, and by the way, is it true your mother's gotten Steven Spielberg to direct the Fox Hollow Players' fall production?"

My hand paused in midair and I nearly dropped the pencil I was holding. The woman at my counter was Minerva Sparks, assistant librarian at the Fox Hollow Library. She was also a good customer of Urban Tails, the pet shop I'd inherited from my late Aunt Tillie. I knew Minerva had a reputation as a notorious gossip, but this tidbit really floored me.

"I-I don't think so," I stammered. "Where in the world did you hear that?"

Her fingers fiddled with the package of catnip balls on the counter. "Oh, Jessie Longacre heard it from Sally Peabody, who heard it from Viola Kizis. Viola said Garrett told Angelina Monroe Clarissa landed a big-name director for the production of *Our Town*. She didn't mention a name, but what name's bigger than Spielberg, really? And I haven't heard he's got anything new coming out now."

"My mother hasn't mentioned anything about that to me," I said. And that was the truth. She hadn't said a word about finding any director, let alone Spielberg, when I'd spoken to her over a week ago. I should mention that my mother and I have never been particularly close, most likely due in part to my career choices over the past few years.

In my previous life in LA I'd been Shell Marlowe, the star of *Spy Anyone*, a popular cable TV show about two married spies. Needless to say that career choice didn't sit well with my mother, a classically trained Shakespearean actress. When the show was canceled, I wasn't certain what my future held, but then fate stepped in: my Aunt Tillie died and not only left me her Victorian mansion, but her pet shop business as well. I wasted no time in relocating to Fox Hollow, Connecticut, and taking back my real name of Shell McMillan. My mother hadn't been crazy about my work on the spy show, and she was even less thrilled with my running a pet shop. No one had been more surprised than me, though, when she'd showed up at the shop's grand opening to "support her daughter"—and the shocks just kept on coming. Not only had she volunteered to take on the role of temporary theatrical manager for the Fox Hollow Players, she'd become a silent partner in Secondhand Sue's, the antique shop owned by my friend Sue Bloodgood. I'd considered backing Sue as well, but you know the old saying: you snooze, you lose. And there was no way in hell I was going into any sort of business venture with my mother.

Minerva's nasal voice broke into my thoughts. "Well, no matter who she gets, its got to be better than Perry Halloway. The man is a dolt." Perry Halloway was Fox Hollow High's English lit teacher. She rolled her heavily made up eyes dramatically. "You should have seen last year's production. They did *Death of a Salesman*. Now don't get me wrong, Perry is a brilliant teacher, but truthfully, Ian Lewis would have been a better choice for director."

I frowned as I stuffed the catnip balls she'd purchased into a bag. "Isn't Ian Lewis the high school janitor?"

Minerva picked up the bag and shot me a triumphant smile. "Exactly," she said.

As she swept out of the store, I reached beneath the counter for my iPhone. I pressed the speed dial button for my mother and, as I expected, the call went to voicemail. I left a message. "Mother, this is Shell. Give me a call when you get a chance. There's a crazy rumor going around that you've gotten Spielberg on board to direct the Fox Hollow Players."

"Clarissa knows Spielberg?"

I turned around at the sound of my former costar's voice. Gary Presser had come to Fox Hollow to help out when I'd been suspected of murder a short time ago. I'd thought he'd return to LA once the culprit was behind bars; instead, he declared he'd been won over by the town and a simpler way of life and had decided to stay on. While he searched for the perfect apartment, he was staying with me. He didn't seem to be in too much of a hurry to leave, and I had to admit the arrangement suited me just fine. Gary, believe it or not, was a regular Felix Unger around the house and my two cats, Purrday and Kahlua, had become enormously fond of his cooking. As had I—although I'd never admit that out loud.

I looked straight into his big blue eyes. "I greatly doubt it. Mother doesn't know half the famous people she says she does. And I'll bet a month's Urban Tails receipts she never met Steven Spielberg."

"Thinking of Clarissa rubbing elbows with Spielberg is a bit frightening—for Spielberg," Gary remarked with a chuckle.

"Poor Garrett. He had no idea what he was in for when he asked Mother to help out with the theater group." Garrett Knute, a retired accountant who served on the Fox Hollow Museum board of directors, was also the founder and manager of the Fox Hollow Players. He'd developed a bit of a crush on my mother when she was here, and my mother had played that to the hilt. As far as anything developing between the two of them, though, I felt reasonably sure that was a long shot. My parents' divorce had soured my mother on the idea of romance and men in general, and Knute, at sixty-plus, was a confirmed bachelor.

Gary moved behind the counter. "The person I really feel sorry for is Sue Bloodgood. Sure, it's all roses now, but wait till your mother starts bossing her around about the antique shop. She'll be ready to dissolve the partnership like that." He snapped his fingers in the air for emphasis.

"I'm not so sure," I said. "Sue's wanted to expand into more upscale items for a while, and my mother is very knowledgeable about antiques, which is just what Sue needs if she truly wants to expand her business. Plus, Sue's not exactly a shrinking violet. She's more than capable of standing up to my mother. I doubt that'll happen though," I added on a sigh. "The only person my mother seems comfortable bossing around is me. I think it's more likely she'll get bored after a while and want out."

Gary rubbed his hands together. "And once that happens she'll be looking for an out. That will be your chance. I know you wanted to back Sue too."

"I've always loved antiquing," I admitted. "I used to go to auctions with my Aunt Tillie in the summers when my parents would drop me off here for a few weeks. Of course, I'm not as well-versed as Mother, but I think I'm pretty good."

"You're very good," Gary said. "Only thing, though. If you went into business with Sue, would that be considered a conflict of interest? You know, considering your relationship with her brother?"

I felt my cheeks start to redden. Sue's brother, Josh Bloodgood, was a homicide detective I'd recently started dating. We'd first met when I was the number-one suspect in the aforementioned murder investigation. Our relationship had gotten off to a slow start, but over the past few weeks it had gained quite a bit of momentum. "I don't see how," I murmured. "Anyway, I'm perfectly happy managing Urban Tails." Then, seeing the twinkle in Gary's eye, I swatted him on the arm. "Oh, you! You're teasing me."

"Yeah. Even you have to admit, you make it easy," he said with a laugh. He looked past my left shoulder. "Isn't that right, kids?"

3

I glanced over my shoulder at the window, where my two cats, Purrday and Kahlua, were lounging in the midafternoon sun. Kahlua had come to Fox Hollow with me from LA. She was a pedigreed seal point Siamese, a gift from my mother because, as she'd put it, no daughter of hers was going to have a mutt for a pet. Purrday had been my Aunt Tillie's cat. A stray when she'd found him, he was also a pedigreed Persian, albeit one that had been through the wringer, as they say. Abandoned at a young age, he'd had to learn to fend for himself, and it had cost him his left eye. He was still a beautiful cat, though, with his long, silky white fur. My mother kept threatening to get him a velvet eyepatch, but so far that hadn't happened, much to my relief. I had the notion that Purrday would be none too happy about that gift.

Both cats raised their heads at the sound of Gary's voice. Kahlua opened her mouth in a large, unlovely cat yawn, then put her head back down on her paws. Purrday simply flopped over on his back and lay, all four paws up in the air.

The bell above the shop door tinkled, heralding the arrival of a new customer. I looked up and saw that it was Melanie Foster. Melanie was a waitress at Tasty Bites, the local sandwich shop. I'd had several conversations with her, and we'd bonded over the fact that we were both originally from California. Melanie was also the owner of Lottie, a beautiful tan and white King Charles Cavalier spaniel. She walked over to the counter, her pretty face split in a wide smile.

"Hey there," she said. "So . . . I heard your mom landed Spielberg?"

"Oh, no," I groaned as Gary started to laugh. "You've been talking to Minerva, I assume."

Melanie laughed, a high, tinkling sound. "Oh, don't worry, Shell. No one ever believes anything Minerva says. I mean, wouldn't it be something if Spielberg actually did come to our little town? After all, you guys did," she added, throwing a flirtatious glance Gary's way.

"It sure would. It would definitely insure Quentin Watson would be hanging around your rehearsals, hoping for a juicy tidbit for his gossip column." Watson was the editor and owner of the *Fox Hollow Gazette*. He and I had butted heads on more than one occasion.

Melanie wrinkled her pert nose. "That's something we can do without. We've got enough drama going on without that. That is, if we even have a production."

"Why, what do you mean?" I asked.

Melanie leaned in closer to the counter. "Not even Minerva knows this yet. Emmie Winfield bugged out of the production yesterday. Said it was too much, what with her taking extra courses at the university this year and all. She's got Professor Clowder for two classes, and she doesn't want to get D's. He's a tough marker."

"Oh, no," I cried. "That's a real loss. Wasn't she playing one of the main characters?"

Melanie nodded. "Emily Webb. Garrett was none too happy about her decision, but what could he do? Now he's got to scramble to find someone, because Greta Poole, her understudy, quit too."

I could understand Greta up and quitting. She worked part-time at Secondhand Sue's and called in sick more often than not. She was a bit flighty and what I'd call irresponsible. The only reason Sue didn't fire her was because she was friendly with Greta's mother. "That's too bad. Didn't Greta have a small role as well?" I asked.

Sue nodded. "Yes, the part of Rebecca Gibbs. Garrett was pretty much beside himself, I can tell you that. He even asked me if I'd want to do either role."

I looked at her, surprised. "I didn't realize you were a member of the group."

"Oh, I'm not," she said quickly. "I confess, I did try my hand at acting once, but it didn't work out. I guess I'm just not as talented as you, Shell."

"There are some who might disagree with you on that. My own mother, for instance."

"Oh, I doubt that." Melanie waved her hand carelessly. "Anyway, I told him thanks but no thanks. I had enough to do, since Benny put me in charge of catering the food for the cast and crew."

"I wonder if the show will be canceled now," I mused.

"I doubt it. Garrett doesn't want to. A lot of tickets have been sold. I'm sure he'll find someone. Either that or he'll put a wig on and do the parts himself."

The thought of Garrett Knute wearing makeup and a skirt made us both giggle. Melanie glanced at her watch. "I'm on my break, so I can't stay too long. I was wondering if you had any of that King Dog Chow. Lottie just loves it."

"Sure, we just got a shipment in. It's in aisle three, I think. I'll show you," Gary offered.

As Gary and Melanie walked off, I heard my cell ping with an incoming text. I picked up my phone and saw that it was from my mother: *Got your message. Everything under control. Will be back in Fox Hollow soon. All problems solved.*

I frowned at the screen. All problems solved? What did that mean, exactly? I slid my phone back into my purse and another thought occurred to me. Had Garrett contacted her about his actress problems as well?

"Oh, no," I muttered. "You'd better not be thinking of pressing me into service, Mother, because I'll have to respectfully decline." Then another thought struck me: was my mother planning to take over one of the roles? I knew she was familiar with that play, having done it in summer stock several times. At fifty-eight, she was still a stunning woman, albeit a bit old to play either of those parts–although God forbid I ever come out and say that to her!

Purrday suddenly let out a low growl and jumped down from his perch on the windowsill. He raced into the storeroom like his tail was on fire. His sudden action didn't seem to faze Kahlua, who stretched and flopped over on her side on the windowsill.

"Purrday," I called after the cat. "What's the matter, fella?"

A loud yowl was his response.

I jumped up and hurried into the storeroom, where I found Purrday on his hind legs, scratching like mad against the back door.

"Stop that," I admonished the cat. "Gary won't be happy to see you scratching up the door he just finished varnishing."

The cat ignored me and continued to claw at the wood. I walked over and attempted to pry him away from the door, and my action was met with a low growl.

I backed up, my hands in the air. "Okay, okay. But what's got you so excited?"

Purrday butted his head against the door.

"Is something out there?" I asked, then bit my lip. It was almost as if I expected the cat to answer me.

In a way he did. He butted his head against the door again and let out a plaintive merow.

I walked to the door, threw back the lock and opened it a crack. I didn't see anything outside. I felt something furry brush my ankles and I looked down to see Purrday squeezing himself through the crack. He took off like a shot around the left side of the store.

"Purrday, get back here."

I raced across the large yard after the cat. I rounded the corner and paused. Purrday was nowhere in sight. Swell. Then I heard a sharp merow coming from the bushes at the far end of the property. I hurried in that direction. As I got closer, I saw Purrday's bushy white tail swishing impatiently to and fro.

"Purrday, for goodness sakes. What's gotten into you?"

I approached the bushes, and Purrday moved back a step. His paw snaked out, touched my ankle. "Merow," he said. This time he sounded more insistent.

"You want me to look here?" I asked. The cat inclined his head. I bent down and parted the bushes, and I let out a gasp of surprise.

Stretched out on the ground, one paw tangled in a vine, lay another cat. For a few moments, all I could do was stare. The cat was certainly beautiful. Her hair, although a bit matted, was long and silky, a beautiful red color. Her eyes were a brilliant gold color, and they were fixed right on me.

"What's the matter, girl?" I asked. The cat was lying on her side, and the vine was wrapped around her front left paw pretty snugly. I started to tug at it, but the cat let out a meow, this one on the loud side. I'd just decided to go back into the shop to find something to snip the vine with when I heard a voice behind me.

"Whoa! What do we have here?"

I looked over at Gary, who'd followed me. "This is what had Purrday so upset," I said. I pointed to her paw. "Somehow she got herself tangled up in that vine."

"Yeah? Well, let's see if we can get you free, little lady." Gary dropped to his knees and pulled his Swiss Army knife out of his pants pocket. In two deft strokes, he'd cut the offending vine. The cat meowed and tried to sit up. I saw her wobble a bit, but finally she rose to a sitting position. The offended paw she held slightly aloft.

"I think she injured that paw," I said. "Maybe I should give Gretchen a call." Gretchen Walker was Fox Hollow's resident vet. As soon as I mentioned her name, Purrday let out a low growl. He obviously remembered the exam and accompanying rabies shot Gretchen had given him recently.

I looked at the cat. "Now, be nice," I admonished him. "Your friend here needs medical attention." I leaned forward and scooped the cat up in my arms. She made no sound of protest, but rather snuggled closer to my chest. "Well-behaved," I observed. "Probably someone's pet that got away."

Gary reached out and patted the cat on the head. Her tongue snaked out, licked at his fingers. "She looks valuable," he remarked. "She's very pretty. I've never seen a cat quite that large, though. She's bigger than Purrday."

The cat definitely was an armful. "I bet she's a Maine coon," I said. "They're the largest breed of cat. We can look it up later though. Right now I want to get her inside and then call Gretchen."

I walked back to the pet shop, Gary and Purrday beside me. We entered through the back door and I laid the cat down on the blanket that Purrday and Kahlua usually took afternoon naps on. The cat purred like a motorcar through all this, only letting out a loud meow when I touched the injured paw. Gary went back out front to mind the shop, and Purrday stretched out next to his new friend while I placed the call to Gretchen. Fortunately the vet was in. She'd just finished up with a hamster and was just about to go to lunch. She said she'd drop by within a half hour. I hung up and then got out two bowls. I filled one with water, the other with some kitty chow that my own cats were fond of. I went over to the blanket and laid the bowls in front of the cat.

"You must be hungry and thirsty," I said.

The cat struggled to a sitting position and leaned her nose toward the bowls. She sniffed at both, then started to lap up the water. When she'd finished, she turned her attention to the other bowl. Before she hunkered down to eat, she turned her head to look at me and let out a soft meow.

I smiled. "You're very welcome."

I left Purrday to watch over his new friend and went back out to the main shop. Gary had just finished ringing up a sale of birdseed for Polly Hodgins's parakeet. Polly saw me and gave an enthusiastic wave. "Shell, have you heard the news?"

I sighed. "Yes, but I'm pretty sure there's no truth to it. I greatly doubt my mother knows Spielberg that well."

"Spielberg?" Polly's brows drew together. "I thought it was Scorsese?"

I bit back a groan. "Him either."

After a bit more small talk Polly took her package and left, and I cut Gary a sidelong glance. "This is going from bad to worse. I wonder if Mother managed to get anyone at all."

"Oh, I'm sure she got *someone*," Gary said. He held out his SmartPhone. "I was looking up Maine coon cats on the internet. You were right—they're the largest breed of cat." He pointed to some photos. "Sure looks like the one you found."

I took the phone and read the article. "Largest breed, soft and silky coat, lion-like ruff around the neck. Yep, it certainly sounds like that cat."

The shop bell tinkled, and Gretchen, black bag in hand, walked in. "I got here as fast as I could," she said. "Where's the patient?"

I took her into the storeroom. When Gretchen laid eyes on the cat, she let out a little gasp. "Ooh, a Maine coon. And what a beautiful one at that! Look at that long, silky red hair!"

I explained what had happened. Gretchen carefully examined the cat, speaking softly to it the whole time. After a few minutes she rose and turned to me. "I don't think it's too serious. The paw doesn't feel swollen. The vine was wrapped tightly around it, you said?"

I nodded. "Gary had to cut her free."

"If she was like that for a period of time, it's possible the paw is just sore. Watch her for a few days and if you see her limping or favoring that paw, then bring her in for some X-rays. In the meantime, I've got some medicine back at the office that should help."

"Great. I'll ask Robbie to pick it up on his way in for his afternoon shift." Robbie was Robert Grant, my young assistant manager. "I'm certain she's someone's pet. She's too well-behaved to be a stray."

"She certainly looks well cared for." Gretchen bent down and started feeling around the cat's shoulder blade. "I don't feel a microchip," she said. "They're usually imbedded in the right shoulder blade. My scanner's out for repair, but when I get it back I can scan her to be sure."

"That would be great. Thanks so much, Gretchen."

"No problem." She leaned down and gave the large cat a pat on her head. "Anytime."

After Gretchen had left, I knelt down beside the cat. "Well, at least your injury doesn't appear to be serious," I said. I reached out to stroke her soft fur, and the cat started to purr loudly. "I bet someone is really missing you, though. We'll have to try and find your owner. In the meantime—I can't keep calling you cat."

"Uh-oh. That's a mistake."

I jumped up and whirled around to face Gary. "Geez, did you have to sneak up on me?"

"Sorry." He held up both hands. "I just think naming the cat might not be a good idea. I know you. You'll get attached to her, and when the time comes to give her back to her owner . . ."

"Give me some credit, will you? It's the right thing to do," I said. I looked back at the blanket. Purrday was giving his new friend a bath. "I think if anyone would be upset at having to give up this cat, it's Purrday. He's really taken a liking to her."

Gary cocked his head and studied the two cats. "Hm, that he has. I wonder what Kahlua will have to say about her."

I'd forgotten about my other cat. The Siamese wasn't exactly welcoming when it came to other felines. It had taken her a bit to get used to Purrday. "I'll cross that bridge when I get to it," I said. "For right now, though, I'm going to have to leave her here in the shop. I think it would be a bit much bringing her home. She needs to rest that paw, and I'm not sure how Kahlua will react to another female cat in the house."

"Not to mention Clarissa," Gary pointed out. "I assume she'll be staying with us when she returns?"

"Probably," I said and sighed. "I'm sure she'd have something to say about three cats in the house, although it's certainly big enough for everyone. Anyway, for now I'm going to make a corner for the princess here in the storeroom."

Gary raised a brow. "The princess?"

I felt color rise to my cheeks. "Well, you have to admit, she looks like royalty. I figured Princess is as good a name as any."

"Just Princess? If you're going to name the cat, then give her a decent one." Gary walked over and looked down at the cat. "She's got such large furry paws. How about Princess Fuzzypaws?"

I wrinkled my nose. "Fuzzypaws? That sounds weird. Fuzzyhead?"

Gary crossed his arms over his chest and frowned. "Oh, yeah, that's so much better," he grumbled.

I sighed. "Okay, then, how about Fuzzypants?"

At the last suggestion the cat lifted her head and let out a loud meow.

Gary burst out laughing. "I guess that's settled. Princess Fuzzypants it is."

I crossed to the desk and picked up my phone. I walked back over to the cat and took several pictures in quick succession. "That should do it," I said. "I'll make up some flyers we can tack up around town, and on my lunch hour I'll go down to the *Gazette* and put an ad in the paper." I paused. "If someone is going to claim her, best they do it before Purrday becomes too attached."

Gary shot me a knowing look. "And you, too."

• • •

Shortly after twelve I made my way down to the *Fox Hollow Gazette*'s offices. I pushed through the front door and walked straight through the cozy foyer-type waiting area to the reception desk, a wooden, circular affair with a computer and stacks of papers on either side. The receptionist, the fiftyish June Reagan, looked up and peered at me over the rims of her granny-style wire-rimmed glasses.

"Well, well, Shell McMillan. What brings you here?"

"I need to place an ad in the paper," I said.

June pushed a pad in front of her and plucked a pen out of the cup beside the computer monitor. "Okay, what sort of ad? Advertisement for Urban Tails?"

"No, Lost and Found." As June raised an inquiring eyebrow, I added, "Purrday found a stray cat behind the pet shop. She looks like a valuable cat, and she's very well-behaved. I'm thinking she's someone's lost pet."

"Was she wearing a collar?"

"No."

"Microchipped?"

"Gretchen didn't think so."

June sniffed. "Most pets today are microchipped, especially if they're pedigreed. If this one's not, then maybe she was stolen from a breeder or something before she could be."

"Good point." I resolved to look up breeders of Maine coon cats when I returned to the shop. "In the meantime, though, I'd like to place the ad, just in case."

I dictated a short ad to June, then pulled out my phone and showed her the pictures I'd taken. "She sure is beautiful," June declared. "I bet her owner is really missing her. We'll run the ad starting tomorrow. Then, if that doesn't bring any results, we can always do a feature story in our Pet Corner section."

I sent June the photos of the princess and then turned to leave. As luck would have it, Quentin Watson chose that moment to return from his own lunch. "Well, well, Shell McMillan," he boomed out. "Has your mother returned with her famous director yet?"

Of course, I should have figured Watson would have heard the rumor. He prided himself on knowing everything that went on in Fox Hollow. As he put it, he had sources everywhere.

I gritted my teeth. "Before you say another word, I haven't heard from my mother since she went back to LA. I have no idea who, if anyone, she might be bringing back with her."

Watson let out a snort. "Don't worry, Shell. I greatly doubt your mother is bringing either Spielberg or Scorsese back here."

"Thank you," I said.

I was halfway to the door when he called after me, "My money's on Ron Howard."

I whirled around and gave the newsman a black look. "Very funny."

Watson was still chuckling as I hurried out of the *Gazette* office. After taking a few calming breaths, I went over to Tasty Bites, where I ordered a roast beef on rye with mayo to go. Melanie wasn't around, so Sharon Callahan filled my order. She wasted no time informing me that she'd heard from a reliable source that Quentin Tarantino was the director of choice. I beat feet out of there as fast as I could and headed up the block to my own shop. As I approached I noticed a long black limo parked out in front. I quickened my steps and hurried through my shop's front door . . . and then stopped dead.

My mother stood beside the front counter, arms folded across her chest, tapping one Gucci-shod foot impatiently. What's more . . . she wasn't alone.

Two

My mother glanced up, saw me, and rushed over. "Crishell!" she cried, enveloping me in a huge bear hug. "It's about time! We were wondering where you were."

I extricated myself from her grasp, which I felt pretty sure she'd done more for show than anything else. "I-I had an errand to run," I stammered. "Didn't Gary tell you?"

My mother glanced over toward aisle five, where Gary was busy helping a customer with gerbil food. "He did mumble something about you being right back," she remarked. She reached out and squeezed my arm. "I've got the most marvelous news! Come and meet my guests."

I walked back with her to the counter, where two other people, a man and a woman, stood. Their backs were to me, but as my mother called out both turned around. One of them I recognized immediately. "Tim Scott," I cried. "What are you doing here?"

The man's face split in a wide grin. "Doing your mother a favor, what else? I'm so glad to see you, Shell."

I stepped forward to give the man a hug. I hadn't seen Tim Scott since the wrap party for *Spy Anyone*. He'd been Patrick's right hand, performing all the duties a good assistant director did: tracking daily progress against the production schedule, arranging logistics, preparing call sheets, maintaining order on the set. He looked exactly as he had the last time I'd seen him. Tall and thin with streaks of silver in his blonde hair, dark eyes and a lined, craggy face. He slid his wire-rimmed glasses up on the bridge of his nose and looked me up and down. "I see small-town life agrees with you. You haven't changed a bit, and neither has Gary."

"Thanks. You look good too. So, what have you been up to?"

Tim shrugged. "Stock plays, mostly. Some independent TV shows." He paused and shifted his weight from one foot to the other. "I don't know if you heard, but after he turned down doing the *Spy* reboot, Patrick got hired by Imagine Pictures to direct a film over in France."

I knew why Tim seemed embarrassed—Patrick was Patrick Hanratty, the former director of *Spy Anyone*, and my former fiancé. Considering how things had ended between me and Patrick, he probably felt a bit uncomfortable

13

mentioning him. I swallowed. "That's a swell opportunity for him," I said. "I wish him nothing but the best." Much to my surprise, I found I meant it.

A look of relief crossed Tim's face. "It sure is," he said. "Anyway, right now I'm between jobs, so when your mother tracked me down and explained the bind this theater group was in, well, I figured it was the least I could do, especially after she said how much it would mean to you."

I gave my mother a sharp look, but she was the perfect picture of innocence. I sighed. "That was sweet of you, Tim."

"And of course, when Garrett texted me about his actress problem, well, I couldn't let that go," my mother interrupted. She turned to the woman who stood just off to the left of the register. "We were very lucky to get Taylor Tyson."

I smiled at the girl. "I thought you looked familiar," I said. "You had a small role in the next-to-last episode of *Spy Anyone*, didn't you?"

Taylor nodded. "Yes. Only I'd call it more of a miniscule role. I was on-screen for what, two minutes? I slipped you a file, I believe, that was under my raincoat." She tossed her dark, wavy hair so that it cascaded over one shoulder. Her dark blue eyes twinkled as she looked at me. I judged her to be about ten years younger than I was, which would put her in her late twenties. There was something I found very likeable about her, but I just couldn't pinpoint it. Maybe it was the genuine warmth in her smile, or the interest in her gaze.

"Taylor has done several commercials, and she just ended a run in a Las Vegas production of *A Midsummer Night's Dream*," my mother informed me. "She's done a lot of Shakespeare, as a matter of fact, and she's very good. She's also between jobs at the moment."

Taylor nodded. "So when Raymond and your mother approached me about filling in for the role of Emily in *Our Town*, I just couldn't say no."

I frowned. "Raymond?"

"Raymond Terrill," Tim supplied. "Your mother managed to convince him to help out as well."

I'd heard of the man. He was a noted Shakespearean stage director and rumored to be very difficult to work with. Before I could make a comment, the shop door opened and a tall man walked in. "There you are," he boomed. "My driver had a devil of a time finding this place. Talk about backwater towns—and a pet shop, no less."

Tim nudged me. "That's Terrill," he whispered.

14

Terrill swept across the room and paused before my mother. He bowed low, took her hand, and planted a soft kiss on her upturned palm. "I would only do this for you, my dear," he said.

My mother actually blushed. "Oh, really, Raymond," she said. Her simpering tone was worthy of the best Scarlett O'Hara impersonation. "You flatter me."

I took a moment to study the man. He was taller than Tim, six-three at least. His dark brown hair was on the longish side, streaked with white at the temples. His goatee also had a few silver hairs. I detected a hint of a British accent in his voice, but whether it was real or affected I had yet to determine. A mental image of the actor Vincent Price came to mind. He turned and fixed his piercing brown gaze straight on me. "And this is your lovely daughter. Shell Marlowe needs no introduction." Before I could say a word, he'd grabbed my hand and planted a kiss on my palm as well.

"It's nice to meet you, Mr. Terrill," I said. "And so nice of you to do this for the Fox Hollow Players."

Terrill waved his hand. "Not a problem, my dear. I'm between engagements, so when your mother approached me, how could I refuse?" His tone, however, indicated to me that he probably wished he had. Terrill didn't even bother to hide his distaste as he looked around Urban Tails. It was obvious small towns held little appeal for him, and I hoped for my mother's sake that he would last out the performances.

Terrill glanced at Tim and Taylor. "Have either of you been over to the theater yet?"

"We were going there now," my mother said. "I just wanted to stop by and see Crishell first. And Gary too," she added as he approached.

Gary shifted the bag of gerbil food he held in one hand and smiled at my mother. "Clarissa. Nice to see you again." He turned to Tim and said with a smile, "Well, old friend, we meet again."

Tim laughed. "Yes, and who would have ever thought I'd find Gary Presser, the idol of millions of women, ringing up gerbil food."

Gary grinned. "If anyone had told me six months ago I'd find small-town life refreshing, I'd have said they were full of it, but . . ." He shrugged. "Hey, life happens."

Gary stepped behind the counter to ring up the sale and we moved off to the side to make room for the customer. She wasn't a regular, but she'd stopped in several times and was around my age, a redhead with creamy skin and a decent figure. I noticed Terrill eyeing her as she paid for her purchase, and his gaze followed her as she walked out the door. When the door had closed behind her, he dragged his gaze to Tim. "I thought Noelle was coming too," he said.

"She is," Taylor piped up. "She had to take a later flight. She'll be here tonight."

Terrill's brows drew together in a deep frown, then he waved his hand. "Still irresponsible, I see. Good thing her part is a minor one."

Terrill took my mother's arm and led her away. As they huddled together in conversation I whispered to Tim, "Who's Noelle?"

"Noelle Boyd," he answered. "She's done a bit of television, *Law and Order* and a few Hallmark movies. She just ended a run in the road company of *Rent*."

"I'm not familiar with her work," I admitted.

"That's not surprising. It's been rather . . . sporadic," said Tim. "She had an audition this morning, that's why she had to take another flight." He paused. "I was surprised when your mother said she'd asked her to help out. Noelle is . . ."

But whatever Tim was about to say was drowned out as Raymond Terrill and my mother came over to us. "All right, people," Terrill boomed. "Let's get going and see this theater. I want to get it all over with *now*."

And with that announcement, Terrill turned and strode out of the shop. Tim cast me an apologetic look, and then he and Taylor quickly followed. My mother hung back and squeezed my hand.

"I know he seems a bit much, dear, but that's how these artistes are! And Raymond is an excellent director. I was lucky to secure his services." Translation: *I had to use all my charm to convince him to come to this backwater town to help out.*

I hoped Garrett Knute would be similarly impressed, but I had my doubts. "Will you be coming back to the house later, Mother?" I asked. "I could have Robbie help with your suitcases."

She looked at me in surprise. "Oh, didn't Olivia tell you?"

I frowned. "No. Tell me what?" Olivia Niven, the owner of Niven's Dance Studio, was one of my best friends in Fox Hollow. She and Gary had been dating off and on. The past few weeks, though, she'd been busy getting together a recital so we hadn't seen too much of each other.

"One of her friends, Joannie Adams, is a realtor, and she's secured a lovely little bungalow for me to stay in. Rent with an option to buy."

I swallowed. "Rent to buy? Wow . . . that's great." I made a mental note to have a long confab with my bestie later.

"I just didn't feel right sponging off of you, dear," my mother added, with a pointed glance Gary's way. "I feel better with a place I can call my own. After all, this Fox Hollow thing with the antique store could turn out to be permanent. I wanted to keep my options open." She made a show of looking at her watch. "I'd better get going. I don't want Raymond's good mood to dissipate. I hope Garrett is on time."

She blew me an air kiss and turned on her Gucci-shod heel. Gary leaned over and whispered to me, "If that was Terrill's good mood, I shudder to think what his bad one is like."

"Me too," I agreed. "But Mother seems to like him so I'm willing to give him the benefit of the doubt."

I started to turn away when I saw my mother pause in front of the door to whip out her cell phone. She looked at the screen, frowned, then turned abruptly and headed back in my direction. "Uh-oh," Gary muttered. "Something's up."

My mother approached the counter and waved her cell phone in the air. "I just got a text from Garrett," she announced. "He's tied up and can't get over to the theater."

"That's too bad," I said. "But he showed you around the place, right, Mother? I'm sure you'll be fine."

"Of course I'll be fine," she said. "It's just . . . I was so hoping for a little support on the first day . . ."

Her voice trailed off and she looked at me with wide, beseeching eyes. I sighed. "Would you like me to go with you?"

Her face brightened immediately. "Would you, Crishell darling? That would be wonderful!"

"No problem." I shot an apologetic look Gary's way. "Do you mind holding down the fort? Robbie should be here soon."

Gary waved his hand. "No worries. Have fun."

I stuck my tongue out at him, grabbed my purse and followed my mother out the door.

• • •

"This is what you call a theater?"

Raymond Terrill walked across the stage of the Fox Hollow Players Theater, hands stuffed in his pockets. His expression resembled that of someone who'd just eaten a sour lemon. Terrill reached the edge of the stage, looked around, then threw up both hands. "The acoustics are going to be deplorable in here," he said. "The room is way too dry, and it's so small." He shook his head. "I'm not sure this theater is the best way to showcase this production."

I bit down hard on my lower lip. I'd only just met the man, and he'd done nothing but irritate me since we'd started the tour. I opened my mouth to say something, caught my mother's eye, then closed it again. I glanced over at Tim and Taylor. Just looking at their body language was evidence enough that neither of them cared very much for Terrill. Tim's gaze was focused on the floor and Taylor had folded her arms tightly across her chest and her jaw was thrust forward aggressively.

I took a deep breath and pasted on my best smile. "The Players just took over this building, actually. Before this year they held their productions in a renovated barn."

Terrill rolled his eyes. "A barn! Mercy me! Don't tell me the livestock were in attendance."

I counted to ten mentally, then forced another smile to my lips. "No, the barn had been divested of its livestock years ago. Garrett rented this building because he thought it would be a much better atmosphere, more professional."

Terrill shook his head. "Well, sure it is, if you're comparing it to a barn."

My mother stepped forward. "I don't think Garrett can get another venue at this late date," she said. "The production is behind schedule as it is, and I know he doesn't want to cancel."

I had an idea. "There's a large gazebo out back that would be perfect as a stage," I suggested. "We have a similar one in the town square and our local dance instructor used it to put on a production of *Annie* when my pet shop had its grand opening. There's lots of lawn out there, and I know we can get plenty of folding chairs. We could borrow the speakers from the town's gazebo, too. I know they're top-notch."

Terrill put a finger to his lips. "An outdoor production? Well . . . I have done those before, with some success." He glanced around, his mouth twisted in a grimace. "It might be better than this."

"Why don't we go out back and take a look," I suggested.

"I suppose it can't hurt," Terrill said grudgingly.

We all trooped outside for a look around the theater's massive backyard. By some miracle, Terrill actually seemed happy with the gazebo and the wide expanse of lawn around it. The thick blanket of trees and the rock wall acted like a natural sound barrier and to me it seemed the perfect place to stage a play, better than the actual building. Everyone else seemed to agree as well.

"Now we just have to hope Mother Nature doesn't pull a fast one on the nights of the play," joked Tim.

"Oh, I'll keep a close eye on the weather reports, you can be sure of that," said Terrill. He clapped Tim on the back. "Well, to quote the Bard, All the world's a stage, And all the men and women merely players; we all have our entrances and our exits."

"And one man in his time plays many parts, his acts being seven ages," finished my mother.

"*As You Like It*," whispered Taylor to me. "Act two, scene seven, spoken by the melancholy Jacques."

I looked at her admiringly. "You really know your Shakespeare," I said. "I was practically weaned on the stuff, and even I didn't remember what play that quote was from."

Taylor gave a short laugh. "I wasn't weaned on it like you were, but I always liked studying the Bard. I'd love to do one of his plays on a London stage one day, like your mother."

"What's your favorite part?"

"You think I'll say Juliet, but you're wrong," Taylor said. "To be truthful, I'd love to sink my teeth into Lady Macbeth. She was such a strong character! Take her line right after her husband's dagger soliloquy." Taylor struck a pose. "'Why did you bring these daggers from the place? They must lie there. Go carry them and smear the sleepy grooms with blood.' Talk about a crafty person. Lady Macbeth rivals any serial killer I can think of."

I had to admit I was impressed. "You sound like you could really get into that role."

She gave a vigorous nod. "I really could. I'm tired of playing innocent ingenues . . ."

She paused as a figure came around the corner of the building. It was Josh. His face lit up with a smile as he looked in our direction, and I felt my heart skip a beat. I started to take a couple of steps toward him—and then I stopped abruptly.

Taylor had fairly flown across the lawn toward him, her arms outstretched. As I watched she threw herself at him and he caught her in his arms in a big bear hug. He picked her up and swung her off the ground, pausing to plant a light kiss on the top of her head.

It was all too apparent they knew each other—and very well, at that.

Three

Taylor broke out of the hug. Josh's arm went around her shoulders and hers around his waist. Then, both grinning like Cheshire cats, they walked over to where I stood, still in shock. Josh's gaze met mine, and I saw myriad emotions reflected there. I wasn't certain, though, if it were embarrassment, or uncertainty, or quite possibly a mix of both.

Taylor must have noticed the expression on my face because she said, "It's not what it looks like, Shell." She pulled her arm back and gave Josh a playful punch on his shoulder. "Josh and I are cousins."

"That we are," Josh said. "Taylor's father is my mother's brother." He smiled down at Taylor. "Michelle told me that you were coming to town."

"Yeah, I texted her. We're gonna catch up later, at the tavern where she works. Why don't you join us?"

Josh looked over at me. "What do you think, Shell?"

I passed a hand across my eyes. Now I did recall Michelle, Josh's younger sister, mentioning to me that they had relatives in California. I looked straight at Taylor. "You must be from San Diego."

She nodded. "Originally. Now I have a tiny, postage stamp-sized apartment in Glendale. It's not much, but it's all a struggling actress can afford, and I have to be near where the action is."

"I lived in Glendale when I was starting out myself," I admitted. "Michelle did tell me about having relatives in California, but she never mentioned that one was a cousin who was an actress." I looked pointedly at Josh. "For that matter, no one did."

Taylor waved her hand. "That's not surprising. Not too many of my relatives know what I do for a living." She shot Josh a fond look. "Only some of my very favorite ones know."

I goggled at her. "What?"

"You see, I started out majoring in English literature. I was going to teach the Bard, until I tried out for the school production of *Othello* one semester and decided I'd rather play it than teach it. I was bitten by the acting bug after my first performance onstage." Her pert nose wrinkled. "Needless to say, my father was less than thrilled with my decision. He feels teaching is a much more stable profession than acting." Her lips twisted into a bitter grimace. "He

21

makes no secret of the fact that I'm a disappointment to him."

Josh gave Taylor's arm a squeeze. "I wouldn't say that," he said.

"I would." Taylor reached up to touch Josh's cheek. "You're being very kind, cuz. I think my relationship with my father is the reason I yearn to play a murderess." She turned her head to smile at me. "You have to excuse our enthusiastic greeting, Shell. I haven't seen my cousins in years. Not since I embarked on my acting career and my father practically disowned me."

"Uncle Bud didn't disown you," Josh growled.

Taylor shook her head. "Oh, of course he'd never admit that, to you or any other member of the family. It would destroy the illusion of his perfect family." Her fingers formed air quotes around *illusion* and *perfect family*.

Terrill, Tim and my mother came around the corner just then. Terrill snapped his fingers in the air imperiously. "Taylor, shake a leg. We want to get over to the inn and check in."

"Yes, your Majesty," Taylor muttered under her breath. She threw me an apologetic look. "Sorry—it's not the first time I've worked with Terrill. Each and every time I swear it will be the last but—" Her shoulders lifted in a careless shrug. "I guess I'm just a glutton for punishment." She gave Josh's hand another squeeze. "Tonight? Around eight? I'll text you the details." And with a brisk wave, she hurried off to join the others.

That left me and Josh staring at each other awkwardly. "It never occurred to me to mention I had a cousin who was an actress," he blurted out. "Honest, Shell, it just never crossed my mind."

I nodded. "I believe you. After all, why would it occur to you. Hollywood is filled with thousands of actresses. Besides, if it weren't for my mother getting her to pinch-hit here, our paths might never have crossed."

Josh looked relieved. "So you're not mad?"

I shook my head. "No. I was never mad, not really. Just surprised. Very surprised."

"Yeah, well, like Taylor said, we haven't seen each other in years. We've got a lot of catching up to do."

"So maybe it's better if I don't horn in on your family reunion tonight," I said.

Josh frowned. "You wouldn't be horning in, not at all. I know Michelle and Sue would love it for you to come—and so would I."

I smiled. "We'll see. After all, let's not forget my mother's back in town.

She might have other plans for me tonight."

"Oh, yeah. I forgot about Clarissa," Josh said with a grimace. My mother had flirted shamelessly with Josh when they'd first met, which hadn't endeared her to him at all. As a matter of fact, I was convinced he was frightened of her. "Try to come, if you can," he coaxed. "We'll probably get to the Captain's Club around eight. Michelle's shift ends then, and . . ." He paused, reached into his pocket, pulled out his cell phone. He made a face when he looked at the screen. "I've got to get going. Riser needs my help on a report for the captain."

"I'm sure she does," I murmured. Amy Riser had recently been hired from another district as Josh's new partner. Besides being very strict and by the book, I was certain the attractive detective had designs on Josh, all reasons for my not liking the girl very much. "See you later," I added.

Josh's face lit up like a Christmas tree. "I sure hope so," he said.

• • •

When I returned to Urban Tails Gary was nowhere to be seen. Robbie, my assistant manager, was behind the counter, attired in his usual garb of black T-shirt and jeans. He glanced up with a smile as I approached. "Hey, Ms. McMillan. Mr. Presser went over to see Ms. Niven at the dance studio. He said to tell you he'd be back in about an hour."

"Thanks." I was rather anxious to speak with Olivia myself, and get the scoop on this "charming little bungalow" the realtor friend of hers had found for my mother.

"June from the *Gazette* called," Robbie added. "She said that your ad about the princess will start running tomorrow." He raised an eyebrow inquisitively.

"Ah, yes, the princess. You haven't met her yet, have you?" The shop was empty right now, so I crooked my finger at him. "Come with me. I need to check on her anyway."

Robbie followed me into the back storeroom. Princess Fuzzypants lay supine on the bed I'd made for her in the corner. Purrday lay nearby, his good eye trained on her. Kahlua was, predictably, nowhere to be seen.

"Golly, a new cat! She's beautiful," exclaimed Robbie. He went over and knelt next to her. He reached out his hand to pet her, which elicited a low growl from Purrday.

I leaned over and rubbed the Persian's head. "It's okay, Purrday. Robbie won't hurt her," I crooned.

Purrday gave what sounded like a harrumph and then backed up a bit so Robbie could lean in. "Her fur is so soft," Robbie marveled. "Where did you get her?"

I explained about Purrday's finding the cat earlier in the day. "She's got to be someone's pet," I finished. "She looks too well cared for. So I put an ad in the paper—you know, before Purrday gets too attached."

Robbie stifled a chuckle as Purrday resumed his guardian position. "I think that might have already happened," the youth observed. "Tell you what, I'll ask around and get some of my friends to do the same. If she's a lost pet, we'll find out."

"That would be great, thanks, Robbie."

We both went back into the main shop. The door opened and Melanie Foster hurried in, eyes wide. "Shell! I just heard. Is it true? Your mother got Raymond Terrill?"

I nodded. "Yep. Quite a coup, according to her."

"According to him, too, I bet," Melanie said. "I've heard he's got a large ego."

"He's not alone in that respect," I said. "I know lots of directors with that attribute."

"I guess," Melanie sighed. "Oh, well, I've got to get back to the deli. Keep me posted."

Melanie left, and a young girl came in, looking for collars for her dog. Robbie took her down aisle three, and I stepped behind the counter. No sooner had I done so than the door blew open and my mother swept in. She marched right up to the counter and leaned her elbow on it. "So? What do you think of my find?"

"If you're speaking about Tim Scott, he's an excellent choice for assistant director."

"Of course I don't mean Scott," my mother huffed. "He was thrilled to get any kind of work. I mean Raymond Terrill."

"Oh. Well, then, yes, Mother, that's quite an accomplishment," I said. "It does beg the question, though—why? It seems beneath him, somehow."

"Beneath him? Of course it's beneath him. He's an award-winning director." My mother twined her fingers in the Gucci scarf wrapped around her neck. "Suffice it to say he's doing me a favor, although he did mention it came at a most opportune time."

I frowned. "An opportune time? I wonder what he meant by that?"

"Nothing, I'm sure. He was probably just being polite. You read too much into things people say, Crishell," my mother chided. "I suppose it comes from hanging out with that yummy detective, though."

"Speaking of that—Josh invited me to join him and his family at the Captain's Club tonight. They're having a sort of family reunion." I paused, unsure of whether or not I should say more, but my mother's next words proved that concern unnecessary.

"Oh, you mean Taylor. Yes, she told me she and Josh are related," she added when I shot her a surprised look. "She invited me to this gathering tonight too, but I declined." My mother put her fingers to her lips and yawned. "I'm afraid I'm a bit worn out. I'm going to go back to my new bungalow and take a bubble bath, then turn in early with a good book."

I knew Josh would be relieved my mother had declined to join the party. "Speaking of this bungalow—just where is it, exactly?"

"On River Street. As a matter of fact, it's close to the theater. I could walk if I had to. I believe you can see the top of the gazebo from my bedroom window." She glanced around. "Where is your partner, by the way?"

"On his break. And Gary's not my partner, Mother. He just helps me out."

"Hm. Max told me that he contacted him about several acting jobs, but he turned them all down. He said that he'd gotten used to the small-town life." She gave me a pointed look. "He can't stay unemployed forever—although I imagine living with you rent-free saves him a great deal of money."

"Gary earns his free rent. He's considering a career change right now."

"Career change, eh? I do hope he's considering a culinary school. His cooking is fabulous, that I will say. Much better than his acting." She stifled another yawn. "I've got to get some rest. I'll see you tomorrow, Crishell."

My mother swept out and my cell buzzed with an incoming text. It was from Michelle: *Hey, heard U met Taylor. Hope U can come tonite.*

I texted back: *Wouldn't miss it.*

A few seconds later, an answer:

Fab! Taylor said U can bring Gary, if U want.

As if on cue, the man himself strolled through the front door. "You just missed Mother," I informed him. "She sends her love."

He snorted. "Yeah, I'll bet."

I held up the phone. "Family reunion tonight at the Captain's Club. Taylor specifically asked you come."

Gary frowned. "Family reunion?"

"Oh, yeah—I found out earlier that Taylor Tyson is Josh's cousin."

Gary's eyes widened. "Really? That's a surprise."

"You're telling me? Apparently Tyson is Josh's mother's surname. Taylor is her brother's daughter."

"Well, unfortunately I won't be able to attend," Gary said. "I promised Olivia I'd go to the Orson Welles retrospective with her tonight. It's a double feature—they're showing *Lady from Shanghai* and *Citizen Kane*."

"Darn! I love *Citizen Kane*."

"Well, blow off the detective and his family. You're welcome to join us."

I arched a brow. "You never heard the saying Two's company, three's a crowd?"

He laughed. "In your case, Shell, we'll make an exception."

I shook my head. "No, thanks. Besides, I wouldn't mind getting to know Taylor better. She seems like a sweet girl."

"I'm sure she is. Give her my regrets. I'll take a rain check."

• • •

Gary left at four. He wanted to go home and freshen up before picking up Olivia. They were going to go to a Thai restaurant in the next town for an early dinner before the movie. Robbie had a class. He was studying animal science at UConn, so he left right after Gary. There was a steady stream of customers right afterward, keeping me hopping right up until closing time. On Tuesdays I closed early, so by five thirty I shepherded the last customer out the door and locked it, then flipped the *Open* sign to *Closed*.

Before I could leave, however, I had to make sure my star boarder was well taken care of. Princess Fuzzypants seemed comfortable with her surroundings. I checked her food and water bowls to make sure they were filled, and then summoned my own cats. Purrday was reluctant to leave his new friend, but I coaxed him with the promise of fresh sardines and some extra kibble in his bowl. Kahlua had been hiding behind some empty boxes all afternoon; I decided that until the princess's owner claimed her, the Siamese would be more comfortable staying at the house.

26

Once the children were fed, I took a cue from my mother and went upstairs for a long, luxurious bubble bath. Then I dressed in black jeans, a cream and white wrap blouse and black espadrilles, and since it was such a clear night, decided to walk the short distance to the Captain's Club. The building that housed it stood on the corner's edge and was totally black, save for the battered stone front flanking heavy oaken doors with lights on either side. A wooden plaque right above the doors read in large block letters CAPTAIN'S CLUB, and the title was repeated in gold raised lettering on the large picture window that took up almost all of the building's right side. I entered and went over to the hostess station, where I was informed that the Bloodgood party had not arrived yet. It was only a few minutes after eight, so I decided to wait at the bar. I slid onto an empty stool at the end and a tall male with a military cut and horn-rimmed glasses took my order for a wine spritzer. He placed the glass before me and I'd only taken a sip when I heard a voice cry out, "Shell? What are you doing here?"

I glanced up and saw Wilma Harper heading toward me. An attractive woman in her early forties, Wilma was a hygienist at Dr. Peterman's office and one of the Fox Hollow Players. She dropped onto the stool next to me and clasped her hands in front of her. "Melanie told me that Raymond Terrill is going to be the new director? Is that true?"

I nodded. "Yes. My mother managed to convince him to come here, and since he's between jobs right now, he agreed."

Wilma looked as if all the air had gone out of her. She sighed and sagged forward on the stool. "Oh, no, that's terrible," she moaned.

"Why, what do you mean?" I asked. "I heard Garrett Knute was thrilled when he found out."

"Hmpf," sniffed Wilma. "Obviously Garrett does not keep up with the latest entertainment news. Practically every play Terrill has worked on recently has met with some sort of disaster." She lowered her voice and leaned closer to me. "He directed a production of *King Lear* two years ago in Chicago. The theater burned down the night before the first production. And then he did *Othello* in Kansas a few months after that, and an extra lost her life in a hit-and-run second week. The car had been totaled, but the driver miraculously had walked away. There were a few other incidents, too, which I can't recall at the moment." She rolled her eyes. "I heard that he lost a lot of contracts, because he's now considered a jinx!"

27

I waved my hand. "Oh, Wilma. It doesn't take much to get a story started in the entertainment industry, trust me. I'm sure that Raymond Terrill isn't a jinx. Trust me, if that were true my mother would have nothing to do with him."

"Maybe so," Wilma said, wringing her hands in front of her. "But some of the actors are a little skittish. Myself included."

Josh and his sister Sue came through the front door just then. Josh's gaze strayed to the bar area, and his face lit up when he saw me. He smiled and made a come hither motion with his hand. I waved back, then laid my hand on Wilma's arm. "My friends are here. I have to go, but you have nothing to worry about, Wilma. Trust me. I for one don't believe in jinxes. Nothing is going to happen," I said confidently.

Wilma still looked doubtful. "I hope you're right," she said.

Four

"Raymond Terrill a jinx? That's a good one."

It was Wednesday morning, and Gary and I were alone in Urban Tails. Despite my bravado of the previous evening, Wilma's revelation about Terrill had made an impression on me—so much so that I'd spent much of the morning doing research on the internet. "I'm not so sure," I said. I handed Gary my tablet and pointed to the screen. "That's the article on the theater fire in Chicago that Wilma mentioned. The exact cause was never determined. Even the fire marshal was baffled. No one was hurt, but there was a lot of smoke and water damage. And here—" I took the tablet back, typed in another address and handed it back to Gary. "That's the article from the *Kansas City Star* on the auto accident that took that extra's life. The car that plowed into her hit a telephone pole and was totaled, and the driver managed to walk away. There were some other, smaller incidents too. There was a theft of a diamond bracelet from a wealthy patron at a performance of *As You Like It* that Terrill directed in San Francisco two years ago, and one of the production assistants broke their leg when a sandbag fell on them while he was directing *All That Jazz* in Biloxi."

Gary looked up from the tablet. "That is a lot of coincidences," he admitted. "Still, I've never believed in jinxes."

"Neither have I—but I have to admit, all this gives me pause."

"What does Clarissa have to say about it? Have you discussed any of this with her?"

"I tried to, but she brushed it off. She said that Raymond Terrill is a fine director, and the press always looks to attach stigmas to those types. And, of course, she stressed that she doesn't believe in jinxes."

"I can't dispute that," Gary admitted. "But I have to admit, I'm glad that neither you nor I are connected to Terrill's performance here in Fox Hollow." He paused and studied me closely. "We're not, are we, Shell?"

"Well . . . I did sort of promise my mother that I would help Taylor and Noelle run their lines. After all, they are stepping in with only a week to prepare." I gestured toward the large sign in Urban Tails's front window that read *Fox Hollow Players' Annual Fall Production: Our Town*. "I also said we'd be glad to sell tickets."

"That doesn't sound too threatening," Gary remarked with a chuckle. "I must say I am surprised, though, that your mother didn't try to get us to take a more active part."

"To be honest, I was too. I think that between securing Terrill's services, overseeing the business end of the production, plus helping Sue get started with upscale antique shopping, she's got her hands full."

"Lucky for us." Gary propped his chin in his palm. "So, you told me all about Wilma relaying how Terrill's a jinx, but you haven't said one word about how the dinner with Josh's family went last night."

I frowned. "It was very nice."

Gary arched a brow. "That's it? It was very nice?"

"Yes. The food was excellent. Josh, Sue and Taylor all had filet mignon, Michelle had pasta with clam sauce, and I had the stuffed Cornish hen. Taylor dominated the conversation, telling us all about her life in Los Angeles and her recent acting jobs. She's got a lot of determination and she really wants to make it as an actress. She mentioned she's not too fond of her agent. I thought about referring her to Max."

"Well, Max is a go-getter. No one knows that better than us." He looked at me searchingly. "So everything's okay between you and Josh?"

"Yes. I admit, when Taylor gave him that hearty welcome it threw me for a loop, but—it's all good. And to be honest, I like Taylor. She seems like a genuine sort of person." I grinned at him impishly. "You should have come along. I think she was a little disappointed that you couldn't come."

He waved his hand carelessly, but I could tell he was pleased. "Well, maybe next time."

My cell buzzed and I glanced at the screen. The caller ID read *Fox Hollow Inn.* I frowned, but I answered the call. "Urban Tails."

"Shell? It's Tim."

"Hey, Tim. How's it going?"

"About as I expected," Tim said with a sigh. "Terrill's being his usual pain-in-the-butt self. Today it's the Wi-Fi connection. The inn doesn't have it, and the one at the theater isn't working. Clarissa had someone come out, and they said it would take a few days to fix." He paused. "I hate to ask, but . . . do you have working Wi-Fi at your store?"

"I do," I said.

"Wonderful," he breathed. "Terrill's pretty crazed about not being able to get online. He's insistent about having some sort of work space. Apparently he's got some notes and files for other projects that he simply has to keep his hand in while he's, quote, here in small-town America, unquote. Any chance you could find a spot for him at your shop so things can return to a semblance of normal?"

I thought for a moment. The back storeroom was very large. I could move the princess's litter box and blanket over to my desk and let Terrill use the whole back corner. There was a small, beat-up table back there that could serve as a desk. "Sure," I said. "Tell him to come on down."

The relief was evident in Tim's voice as he replied, "Thanks, Shell. You're a real lifesaver. I owe you one."

I hung up and turned around to find Gary looking at me, eyebrows raised, arms crossed over his chest. "Let me guess. We're going to be entertaining Terrill this morning?"

"Apparently he's in need of our Wi-Fi. But don't worry—I'm going to stick him in the back corner of the storeroom. He won't bother us a bit."

Gary arched a brow. "Famous last words."

• • •

Terrill stood in the doorway of the storeroom, hands on hips, a deep scowl on his face. He stared at the far corner, where I'd set up the table and folding chair, and shook his head. "This won't work," he declared. "I need an actual desk with room to, you know, spread out." His head swiveled in the direction of my office space.

"I'm sorry, Mr. Terrill," I said in as firm a tone as I could muster. "But I need my desk. I know the table doesn't look like much, but it's big enough for a laptop."

He looked down his nose at me. "Well, maybe so . . . if a laptop were all I had. But I have quite a few boxes of files and notes with me. I need to have them spread out around me, so I can have them for easy reference."

I bit down hard on my lower lip, unsure of just what to say. I knew darn well what I wanted to say, but if I did that, my mother would never forgive me. I was weighing the pros and cons of that when Gary, who'd been standing close enough to overhear our conversation, butted in.

"What about that old writing desk back at your house?" he asked.

31

I stared at him. Truth be told, I had no idea what he was talking about. I had a desk in the room I'd set up as a den on the second floor, but that was the only one in my house as far as I knew. "Why—I don't know," I stammered.

Terrill's eyes narrowed. He jabbed a finger in the air at Gary. "Is there a desk I can use or not?"

Gary turned to me. "You know that old shed in the backyard? I went through it the other day. There are some pretty nice pieces in there, and one of them is an antique writing desk." He glanced over at Terrill. "If you don't mind being amidst a bit of clutter, that might suit your purposes."

I frowned. Having Terrill invade my shop was one thing; having him invade my personal space was quite another. And hadn't Gary been the one to mention keeping distance from Terrill was a good idea? Before I could remind him of that, though, Terrill clapped his hands imperiously. "Let's see it," he said shortly. "I've wasted too much valuable time already."

"Sure thing." Gary pulled his keys from his pocket and looked at me. "Robbie can mind the store for a bit. Let's go."

Fifteen minutes later we were all standing in the doorway of the shed in my backyard. My aunt must have used it for pieces that she'd tired of but didn't want to get rid of. The desk Gary had mentioned was in the far corner of the shed, covered by a padded mover's blanket. Gary walked over and whipped it off. The desk was old but appeared to be in decent shape. It had apparently been varnished at one time, but most of it had worn off. The writing surface was medium-sized, and there were two rows of tiny drawers on the back unit and two small doors in the center of the desk. Across from it was a leather chair that also appeared to be in good shape. There was also plenty of vacant floor space. Terrill walked over to the desk and stood for a few moments, studying it, two fingers pressed against his lips.

"Well, what do you think?" Gary ran a finger along the desk's scarred surface. "Not much to look at, to be sure, but . . . it's larger than that table."

"That it is. And there certainly is more than enough room." Terrill turned to me. "This will work," he announced, then paused. "Will your Wi-Fi connection work out here?"

"It should." I pulled my tablet out of my purse and booted it up. It got a signal without a hitch. "Yes, I get on fine. No problem."

"Excellent." Terrill let his fingers rove over the desk's surface. "The desk is smaller than I'm used to, but Gary's right. It's bigger than the table, and there's space to spread out my papers. It'll have to do. I'll have one of the theater staff bring my boxes of files up here later today." He paused. "Do you have a key for this shed?"

I hesitated. Truthfully, I wasn't sure. Thankfully, Gary answered. "Yes. I'll have one made for you. If you're worried about someone stealing your laptop, though, Fox Hollow is very safe. As a matter of fact, most of the residents never even bother locking their doors."

Terrill's shaggy brows flew skyward and his lips turned down. His glance was clearly disapproving as he replied, "Trusting souls, aren't they? Me, not so much, I'm afraid. I have a lot of sensitive material, things I'm sure any gossip rag or reporter would give their eyeteeth to peruse." He glanced at the gold watch on his wrist. "I have to run over to the theater now, but I'll be back around lunchtime for that key."

"Why . . . sure," I said to the man's retreating back. I was still pretty much in shock. After Terrill swept out, I grabbed Gary's arm. "Are you crazy?" I hissed. "What happened to wanting to keep your distance?"

"This is a good distance from the house, and even farther from the store," Gary replied. "I don't know about you, but I wasn't exactly crazy about Terrill invading our work space."

"Oh, but you're happy with him invading our home?"

"No, but the man would obviously be a nag until he got some sort of space. Besides, he's not *in* the house . . . he's outside it," he said with a triumphant grin.

"I guess you're right," I said grudgingly.

"Of course I am. Oh, and by the way, I liked the way you referred to it as *our* home. Makes me feel like part of the family."

I felt my cheeks get hot. "Well, you kind of are," I said. "After all, you've been living here for a few months now."

"Or freeloading, as your mother would put it."

I held up both hands. "Hey, I told her that you earn your keep."

"I know, but I'm not sure she believed you. Anyway, giving Terrill that space might earn me some desperately needed brownie points with Clarissa."

"True, although you might not need them. If you recall, she did rave about your cooking."

"Ah, yes. I believe she mentioned introducing me to Gordon Ramsay at some point. I won't hold my breath for that, though."

33

I chuckled. That was a good idea, especially since my mother had never met Gordon Ramsay. "How's the apartment hunting coming?" I asked. "Or have you given up?"

"I haven't given up. Olivia's friend showed me a few places, but—" He wrinkled his nose. "When I move, I want it to be a step up, not a step down." He reached out and touched the tip of my nose. "I appreciate your taking me in, Shell, don't think I don't. I have no intention of freeloading off you forever, no matter what Clarissa thinks. Just as soon as I decide what it is I want to do with the rest of my life, I promise, I'll be gone."

I felt an odd sense of sadness at those words. "I thought you were thinking of becoming a PI?" I asked him. "Did you change your mind?"

"I'm still considering it, but to be truthful, Shell, if anyone should be a PI, it's you. You've got a real flair for deduction."

I brushed his compliment aside. "Thanks, but I've got all I can handle here. Besides, I don't think Josh would like the idea of me being an investigator."

"True—because you'd probably outshine him."

"I doubt that." I paused. "Do you think you'd want to go back to LA? Resume your acting career? Mother said that you've been offered some jobs."

He shrugged. "I haven't entirely dismissed the notion. Max texts and emails me every day, urging me to return, but so far he hasn't come up with anything that would be worthwhile. They're all the same types of roles, either spies or second bananas, meager supporting roles." He waggled his finger at me. "Now, you, on the other hand . . . I know you could have your pick, if you wanted. That movie that Patrick got tagged to direct? He wanted Max to ask you if you'd consider playing the lead."

"*What!*" I shouted the word so loud that Gary stepped back and put his hands over his ears. "Is he nuts?"

"No, but I might be going deaf," Gary said. "Look, it's nothing personal. Whatever happened romantically between the two of you, Shell, I know Pat has the utmost respect for your acting ability."

"I'm sure he does," I said stiffly. "Pat's a wonderful director, but working with him, after what happened . . . I can't. At least not right now."

Gary nodded. "I know. Max knows that too, that's why he never contacted you, even after Clarissa urged him to."

"What?" I shouted again. "She did *what?*"

Gary reached up, swatted at his ear. "Will you stop doing that? I wasn't kidding about going deaf."

"My mother actually wanted Max to get me to do a movie with Patrick? After all I'd been through with him?" I gave my head a brisk shake. "Obviously my mother didn't believe me when I told her Hell would have to freeze over before I'd ever do another project with Patrick."

Gary nodded. "You know your mother. She was more concerned about your career than your love life. According to Max, she couldn't understand why you wouldn't be able to separate the two."

I sighed. I didn't know why I was so surprised. It sounded exactly like something my mother would do. Dr. Peters, the shrink I'd gone to for a short time, had told me a never-fail method for putting things behind me. I took a deep breath, then closed my eyes. I envisioned an imaginary balloon with Patrick's image emblazoned on it. I flicked at the balloon with the tip of my finger and pictured it spiraling up, up into the clouds and far away. When it was almost out of sight, the balloon went *pop* and exploded.

"What are you grinning at?" Gary asked.

I opened my eyes and looked at him. "I'll tell you someday," I said. "For right now, suffice it to say I was just visualizing an end to a problem."

Gary shot me a knowing smile. "Oh, you used Dr. Peters's balloon trick," he remarked. "Yeah, it's worked for me too."

• • •

True to his word, Terrill came back a few minutes after twelve for the key to the shed. Gary had gone to lunch with Olivia, but he'd left me the key. As I started to pass him the envelope, Princess Fuzzypants hopped up on the counter and cocked her head at him. "Merow," she said.

Terrill's sour expression softened. "Well, well," he murmured. "And who is this pretty lady?" He looked at me. "Is this your cat?"

I shook my head. "That's Princess Fuzzypants. And no, she's a stray that my Persian, Purrday, found ensnared in a vine out back. I'm certain she's someone's pet who's lost. I took out an ad to find her owner."

Terrill reached out to pet the princess, and her pink tongue darted out to lick his fingers. "If no one turns up to claim her, perhaps I'll adopt her," he said. "I used to have a Maine coon cat just like her when I was younger." He

35

looked at the cat. "What say, Princess? Want to come and live in Sunny California?"

The cat blinked her large gold eyes. "Merow."

Terrill laughed. "I'll take that as a yes."

I looked at him. "Are you serious? Would you like to adopt her?"

His gaze was thoughtful as he looked at me. "Is she available for adoption?"

"Good question. If no one shows up to claim her . . . then yes, she would be available."

"I see. Well, I would love to, but unfortunately with my career demands, it wouldn't be practical," Terrill responded. "I'd hardly have any time to devote to her."

"Cats are pretty independent creatures," I said. "They don't need as much attention as a dog."

"That's true," he said. He shot a wistful look at the cat. "I'll give it some thought. Who knows, if her owner doesn't show up, I just might whisk her away."

The princess hopped down from the counter. Terrill picked up the envelope containing the shed key and with a curt nod, exited the store. I leaned against the counter and propped my chin in my hands. Purrday jumped up on the counter and butted his head against my cheek.

"And the shocks just keep on coming," I said. "Terrill a cat lover, who knew?"

I heard a sharp gasp just to the left of my counter. "You're kidding! You can't possibly mean Raymond Terrill?" cried a voice.

I looked up and found myself staring into a pair of wide hazel eyes flecked with gold. The woman standing in front of my counter looked familiar somehow. She was tall and slim, with copper-colored hair that fell past her slim shoulders. She reached up and tucked a stray strand of hair behind one ear and cleared her throat. "I'm sorry," she said. "It's just that the phrase 'cat lover' doesn't match the Raymond Terrill I know. Unless you're not speaking about the director, but another Raymond Terrill?"

"No, it's the director," I admitted. "And it surprised me too." I held out my hand. "I'm Shell McMillan. I own this shop."

"I know who you are." She grasped my hand. For such a slender woman, her grip was surprisingly strong. "I'm a fan of your mother's, and I was also a big fan of *Spy Anyone*. If I couldn't watch it, I always recorded it on my DVR. I'm Noelle Boyd, by the way."

"Oh, yes. You're filling in for Greta. The part of Rebecca Gibbs, right?"

"Right. I'm also understudying Taylor in the Emily Webb role." She loosened her grip on my hand and glanced around the shop. "Your mother mentioned that you run this pet shop now. How on earth did you ever give up acting?"

"It wasn't as hard as you might think," I said. "To be honest, I much prefer the simpler life."

"I guess so," Noelle said thoughtfully as she looked around my shop. She turned back to me and said, "Now me, I can't imagine myself doing anything but acting. I've been eating, breathing and sleeping theater since I was nine and cast as the lead in our school production of *Sleeping Beauty*. I've never imagined myself doing anything else."

"That's great," I said. There was an awkward few moments of silence and then I remarked, "So, I take it you've worked with Raymond Terrill before?"

A slight shadow crossed her face, but it was gone in an instant. "Oh, yes," she replied. She tossed her head so that her auburn hair fell casually over one shoulder. "He cast me in one of his plays after seeing a TV commercial I did." Her lips curved upward. "It wasn't even my best work. It was a cereal commercial. I played a flake."

"Oh, I think I've seen that one," I cried. "Fruity Flakes, right?"

"That's the one. You know it has a large cult following on YouTube. That's where Ray saw it. He liked my performance, he said, and he cast me in his production of *As You Like It* as Rosalind." She shoved her hands deep into the pockets of the heather blue cashmere sweater she wore. "The reviews for my performance were stellar, and I owe it all to him. He has a temper and can be difficult, but he also has a definite talent for getting his actors to dig deep, to pluck every genuine emotion out of them." A shadow fell across her pretty face. "Some find that intimidating, draining too, but . . . it invigorated me. Made me hungry to see what else was buried deep inside me, what new challenges I could rise to."

"That's very interesting," I said. "My mother also likes him. She says he's a very talented director." I hesitated and then added, "I understand there was some drama connected with that play."

Noelle looked puzzled. "Drama?"

37

"Yes. I read that the play closed early because one of the theater patrons was robbed during intermission of a valuable bracelet."

Noelle's brows drew together. "Oh, that," she said. "That woman made a real stink. She went to the ladies' room at intermission, and then when she returned to her seat noticed the bracelet was missing. Some of us were in the restroom at the same time and she practically accused all of us of the theft at one point or another. The detective assigned to the case even got a bit testy with her. I think she was pressing hard to have Taylor arrested for it."

"Taylor?" I said. "Do you mean Taylor Tyson? She was in that play too?"

Noelle nodded. "Yep. She only had a small part, but she was very good. She had the bad luck to have bumped into that woman in the ladies' room. The woman swore she lifted the bracelet off her wrist. Of course Taylor denied it." Noelle shook her head. "I still think the old bat swiped her own bracelet to get the insurance money. Supposedly it was never recovered."

"That's a shame," I said. "I imagine Taylor was pretty upset about it too."

Noelle shrugged. "I suppose. I didn't keep up much with her after the play closed. To be honest, all that real-life drama left a bad taste in my mouth. I dropped out to study acting for a while. I just recently started auditioning again. That's why I was so pleased when Ray called me and told me this part was available. It will be the perfect vehicle for me to get my feet wet again." She glanced at the watch on her wrist. "I thought I might catch Ray here. I stopped by the theater and one of the staff there said he'd come over here."

"Actually you just missed him. He came by to pick up a key to the shed at my place." As Noelle's brow lifted inquiringly, I added quickly, "It's rather a long story."

Noelle let out a tinkling laugh. "Let me guess. He needs some sort of quiet place to go over all his notes and papers, right?" She waved her hand carelessly in the air. "It's one of his quirks. I see that hasn't changed."

I looked at her. "You sound as if you know him very well."

Her fingers twined in the thin gold chain around her neck. "You could say that," she said softly. She glanced around, then leaned in closer to me. "I confess, for a while we were more than just friends. Then my life went in a different direction. But there will always be a soft spot in my heart for Ray."

I wondered if Terrill held as soft a spot in his heart for her. I debated asking Noelle her opinion on him being a jinx but thought better of it. She glanced at her watch again and took a step back from the counter. "I suppose

I'd best get back to the theater. We're supposed to have a read-through at two. Ray just hates it when the actors are late." She paused. "It was nice to meet you, Shell."

"You too."

Noelle shot me a wide smile, then glided out. No sooner had she gone than my phone buzzed. It was a text from my mother: *Chloe held up at her job. Can U come to theater to help with read-thrus?*

I sighed. Chloe Baxter was one of the original Fox Hollow Players, and she was also Gretchen Walker's assistant at the animal hospital. I figured that whatever prevented her from attending the read-through had to be pretty important, so how could I refuse? I texted my mother back:

No problem. C U at 2.

. . .

Gary came back a little after one, and I explained to him where I was going. "Have fun," he said. "And take care the acting bug doesn't bite you again."

"No worries on that score," I assured him. I left the shop in his and Robbie's capable hands and decided to walk the short distance to the theater. I let myself in the stage door and followed the hall to the side stage entrance. As I walked down the narrow hall, I could hear angry voices. At first I thought they were coming from the stage, but then I realized they were coming from behind a closed door off to my left.

"Raymond, please listen to me. I told you I didn't want to get involved."

I paused. That sounded like Taylor. Curious, I drew closer.

"Now you listen to me." The second voice was masculine, and I recognized it immediately. Terrill. "You'll do as I say, or else I'll expose that dirty little secret of yours. I'm sure you wouldn't want any of your family finding out about it, now would you?"

"You—you wouldn't do that." There was a pause, and then, "If you say one word, I'll—I'll—"

Terrill's laughter was harsh. "Please don't threaten to kill me. I've met my quota of that for the month." Then his voice dropped down so low I couldn't catch anything else. My thoughts were whirling though. I recalled what Noelle had told me about the play in San Francisco. Had Taylor really been involved in the theft of that bracelet? Was that the secret Terrill was threatening to expose?

I was just about to continue down the hallway when the door suddenly flew open. Raymond Terrill, his face looking like a thundercloud, stood framed in the doorway. He raised his arm and pointed at me in dramatic fashion.

"What are you doing, spying on me?" he shouted.

Five

For a moment I was so startled by Terrill's accusation that I couldn't speak. "I beg your pardon," I said at last, drawing myself up to my full height. "I was most certainly not spying on you." I refrained from mentioning that if he'd wanted privacy, he should have, at the very least, lowered his voice.

Terrill's gaze narrowed. "Then what are you doing back here?" he demanded. "You're not part of the troupe."

I met his gaze unflinchingly. "That's true, I'm not. I came here because my mother asked me to help out with read-throughs," I said coldly.

Terrill stared at me, apparently confused. "Your mother?"

"Yes. Clarissa McMillan. Ask her if you don't believe me."

"Ask me what?"

We both turned as my mother stepped forward. She slid her arm around my shoulders. "I asked Crishell to pinch-hit for one of the actresses who's held up at work. Is that a problem, Ray?"

Terrill passed a hand over his eyes. He stared at me as if seeing me for the first time. "Crishell—Shell. Of course." He took a step toward me and held out his hand. "I do apologize," he said. "I didn't recognize you at first. There's no excuse for my behavior other than stress, I suppose. I'm working on some other projects that are not going as I planned. I didn't mean to take it out on you."

I wasn't sure I believed him entirely, but I had no desire to make a scene, especially not in front of my mother. I took his proffered hand. "Apology accepted," I murmured.

Terrill looked relieved. "Good."

Tim Scott bustled up to us, a concerned look on his face. "Everything okay here?" he asked.

"Yes, no thanks to you," Terrill snapped. "These read-throughs should have started long ago."

"I know, Mr. Terrill, but the actress who usually does them couldn't make it . . ."

"I realize that. However, Tim, as second in command, it is your job to find a solution, not Clarissa's. It's not the first time you've dropped the ball on a project, though, is it," the director said with a curl of his lip.

I saw the tips of Tim's ears flame, and he cast his gaze downward as he mumbled, "No, sir."

Terrill waved his hand. "Try to improve, Scott. Right now let's get on with the read-through, shall we?"

He turned and swept down the corridor. My mother went over to Tim, said something to him in a low tone. He shook his head and walked back into the auditorium. My mother came back over to me, slid her arm around my shoulders. "Are you all right?" she asked.

I nodded. "I'm fine. He just startled me," I admitted. "Noelle mentioned he had a temper but I didn't expect such a violent reaction."

"Ray can be as dramatic as a diva sometimes," my mother said. "What was he so upset about?"

"He thought Shell heard us arguing."

My mother and I both turned to see Taylor standing in the doorway. She tucked a strand of hair behind one ear and continued, "We were having a minor disagreement, and he got a little loud. I think he was embarrassed."

I raised a brow at her calling what I'd overheard a minor disagreement, but before I could challenge her my mother threw back her head and let out a loud laugh. "Embarrassed? Ray Terrill? I doubt that."

Taylor shifted her weight from one foot to the other. I noticed that her gaze didn't meet mine as she answered, "Raymond likes his privacy, and I just think he got upset at the thought of it being invaded. It was my fault, as well," she added. "I should have just dropped the subject."

"If it makes you feel better, it wasn't just us he got testy with," I said. "He nearly took Tim Scott's head off, too."

"Poor Tim," Taylor murmured. "Ray's had it in for him for a while. I can imagine he was none too pleased to find him here."

That remark surprised me. Before I could question Taylor further on that, my mother waved her hand. "Well, it's forgotten now, so let's get on with the read-through, shall we? Are you hungry, Shell? I think there still might be some leftovers from that delicious lunch."

"No, thanks, Mother."

She shrugged and linked her arm through Taylor's. I followed them down the hall to the rehearsal room, thinking that the incident was far from over. After what Noelle had told me about the incident in San Francisco, I couldn't help but be concerned. I fully intended to have a chat with Taylor at the first possible opportunity.

• • •

About an hour into the read-through, Terrill got a call and told us to take a break. As he stalked off, cell phone glued to one ear, I decided it was the perfect time to seek out Taylor. I went into the actors' lounge, but she was nowhere to be found. I went back outside and decided to check out the main lobby. No sign of Taylor anywhere, but my mother was there with Kenny Parsons, one of the handymen, pointing out where she wanted one of the lobby cards hung. As Kenny moved off, she turned and saw me. "Crishell! So, how do you think the play is going?"

"The read-through's going well," I said. "All the actors are very good. Taylor in particular."

"Yes, she is very talented," my mother said. "I've seen her in a few plays and she's got a real star quality, don't you think?" She reached out and patted me on the shoulder. "I'm sorry Ray spoke to you that way," she said softly.

I shrugged. "No harm done. Truthfully, I was more surprised than angry, especially after I'd seen another side of him earlier at the pet shop."

My mother's eyebrows winged skyward. "Oh? And what side might that be?"

"His softer side, apparently. He was quite taken with a stray cat I'd found the other day. He even mentioned he might want to adopt it."

The corners of my mother's lips drooped downward. "Somehow I find it hard to picture Ray Terrill as a cat lover."

I chuckled. "Funny, Noelle Boyd said the same thing. She showed up right after he left."

"Oh?" My mother quirked a brow. "Well, Noelle should know. She and Ray used to be close . . . quite close."

"So she said." I paused. "I didn't realize Terrill had a history with Tim as well."

"Oh, that." My mother waved her hand in a dismissive gesture. "From what I understand it was a long time ago, during some play in San Francisco. I honestly thought that they'd kissed and made up by now."

"Apparently not." I let out a breath, wondering if it was the same play where the incident with the bracelet had occurred. "Mother, I'd like to talk to you about Patrick." Her eyes widened and I rushed on, "I know that he wanted me to be in that new movie he's directing, and I also know that you pushed

Max to try to get me to take the part. Did Patrick ask you to do that?"

My mother's hand fluttered over her heart. "Crishell, really! What put that idea in your head—oh, wait. Let me guess. Gary?"

"Gary said that Max told him you were pushing him to persuade me to take the role."

"Max said that? What till I get ahold of him," my mother huffed. She eyed me. "Even you have to admit, though, starring in that movie would have been a wonderful career opportunity for you."

"Yes, it would, if I were still interested in pursuing an acting career. I resent the fact that you sided with Patrick and went behind my back to try and get Max to influence me, Mother."

"Now hold on." My mother's hand shot up, traffic-cop style. "I admit when Patrick first approached me, I considered it. And I did mention it to Max, but then I told him to forget it."

I goggled at her. "You did?"

"Yes, I did. In the first place, it wouldn't have gone anywhere. You're very strong-willed, Crishell. It's a quality you get from both your father and myself. When has anyone ever really been able to stop you from doing anything you wanted to do—case in point, move out here to the boonies to run Tillie's shop. Max couldn't talk you out of that, so why would he be able to talk you into doing a movie abroad?"

I tried to smother a grin but couldn't. What she said was all too true.

Her tone took on a softer quality as she added, "Secondly, it would have been awkward for you to work with Patrick now. I know how much his infidelity hurt you, Crishell. It's not like I can't relate to it."

I knew she was referring to the fact that my father had run off shortly after their divorce and married Darlene, her best friend. "Daddy hurt me too," I said quietly.

"That's what I mean. How much hurt can one woman take?" she said softly, and I knew she wasn't only talking about me. She brushed at her eyes with her fingertips. "Look, I won't lie. I'm not thrilled about this new lifestyle you've chosen. I'm hoping one day you'll wake up and realize Hollywood is where you belong, not selling pet collars and dog food. But until then, if ever, you are my daughter and I intend to support your decisions—however misguided they might be."

I looked at her, the corners of my lips twitching. "Thank you?"

She let out a laugh. "You're welcome." Her fingers closed around my hand. "I have to add, I am pleased about the upswing in your love life."

"My love life?"

She shot me one of her Clarissa McMillan patented exasperated looks. "Don't play coy. I'm referring to that yummy detective who's always making goo-goo eyes at you, and vice versa. I can understand why you'd want to stay here and pursue that, but trust me, darling, if his feelings for you are genuine, I can tell he's the type who wouldn't stand in your way, career-wise."

"You and I both know long-distance relationships never work out, Mother. And Josh's career is here."

"Maybe it is now . . . but they need good homicide detectives out in LA too, you know, and they probably need them more out there than here in Frog Hollow."

"Fox Hollow."

My mother's shoulders lifted in a dramatic shrug. "Whatever." She gave me a long, searching look. "You've got a good man there, Crishell. Don't blow it for yourself."

I drew myself up straight. "What makes you think that, Mother? FYI, I didn't blow my last relationship. Patrick did that."

"So he did," my mother murmured. She waved a hand. "Just forget I said anything, will you?"

With pleasure, I thought. My mother did seem genuinely upset, though, so much so that all of a sudden I heard myself say, "Would you like to come over for dinner tonight, Mother? If you don't have other plans, that is. I think Gary wanted to try a new recipe tonight. He mentioned making Lamb L'Arabique." I wasn't lying. Gary had mentioned wanting to make that dish—only he wasn't planning on doing it tonight.

She staggered backward. "You're kidding! That's one of my favorites! What time?"

"It's Robbie's night to close the shop, so seven should be good." It would also give me enough time to text Gary and inform him of the change in menu and our extra guest. I glanced at my watch. "I guess we should be getting back to finish the read-through."

As we started back down the long hallway, my mother remarked, "You know, it doesn't surprise me that Taylor and Ray were having an argument. There's a lot of unresolved feelings there."

I looked at her. "Unresolved feelings?"

"Yes." She glanced around and then said in a low tone, "I heard that during that play in San Fran, they had a brief 'thing' going. Supposedly Ray dumped her, and not too gently, either. Rumor is Taylor never really got over him."

• • •

When we returned to the rehearsal hall, however, Terrill announced that he had to cancel the rest of the read-through. He blamed an "important meeting" that he'd forgotten about. "What a crock," I heard one of the actors mutter. "What important meeting could he possibly have here in Fox Hollow? He doesn't know anyone here. He's probably just fed up with coaching a small-town troupe he feels is beneath him."

I couldn't fault that train of thought, but whatever Terrill's reasons for canceling were, I was grateful for the extra time. I started after Taylor, but got waylaid by a few of the actors looking for tips on their performances. I answered them as quickly as I could and then took off for the dressing room area. No sign of Taylor. In the lobby I bumped into Kenny Parsons, who'd just finished hanging the lobby cards. "H-H-Hi, Shell," he said.

"Hi, Kenny." Kenny had done some minor repair work at Urban Tails, and I knew he was self-conscious about the way he stuttered. "Have you seen Taylor Tyson, by any chance?"

He shook his head. "Nope, sorry." He paused and pulled a pack of gum out of his pocket. The wrapper was very colorful—pink and purple stripes, with yellow dots in between. The words *Super Juicy Gum* were printed across it in bright green neon. He picked out a stick, unwrapped it and popped it into his mouth. He paused and then held the packet of gum out toward me. "Want s-some?"

I shook my head. "No, thanks." I looked at the package. "I've never seen that brand. Is it any good?"

Kenny nodded. "They don't make it anymore. I like it though, so I order it on Amazon. It tastes like real f-fruit." He hesitated then added, "That's something', h-h-huh, your mom g-g-getting a big director like Raymond Terrill f-f-for this little play."

"Yes, it's something, all right," I said. I saw my mother heading for the side

46

exit and quickly excused myself to Kenny. "Mother," I called after her. She paused and turned as I hurried up to her. "Have you seen Taylor?"

"I think she left already. She promised to run some lines with a few of the girls at the hotel."

"Oh. I guess I'll catch up with her tomorrow, then."

My mother eyed Kenny, who was busy wiping something off the wall. "Nice man," she murmured. "Too bad about his stuttering problem. He said he's had it since he was ten. He was going to counseling and it was improving, but then he was in some sort of accident and it came back ten times worse. He chews that gum as a sort of therapy. Too bad it doesn't seem to help much."

"Really? I've never heard of chewing gum being used as therapy for stuttering."

"It's quite common. Chewing widens the mouth and relaxes the muscles in that area. Chewing while speaking is generally bad etiquette, but for the stutterer it can be used as a therapy."

I shook my head. "You amaze me, Mother. How do you know so much about that?"

"Years ago when I first started out, I had a slight stutter myself. Chewing helped me overcome it." She adjusted the pink and cream Hermès scarf around her neck. "I should get going. I know Sue wanted me to stop by the shop and look at some articles she took on consignment. Then I want to take a nap before dinner."

"Fine, Mother. Remember it's at seven . . ."

"Sharp, yes, I know. I'll see you then, dear." She swiped her tongue across her lower lip. "Tell Gary I can't wait to sample his lamb dish."

I hoped Gary would be as thrilled to make it as my mother seemed to be to sample it. We'd walked outside while we were talking, and now my mother blew me an air kiss and turned in the direction of her bungalow. I went back to the pet shop, where I found Gary hunched over the computer in the storeroom. He glanced up as I entered, made a frowny face at me and shook his fist in the air.

"Thanks for the abrupt change of menu," he growled. "I had to call the butcher over in Meadham to get the cut of lamb I wanted. And I've got to pick it up in—oh, gosh—twenty minutes!"

"Sorry. I know you mentioned you wanted to try making it, and it was the only thing I could think of to thank my mother for her support this afternoon." I gave Gary the CliffsNotes version of the afternoon's events. When I finished, he let out a low whistle.

"Okay, I get it. I did want to try out that recipe, anyway. Does Clarissa know she's my guinea pig?"

"No, and your secret will die with me."

He chuckled, then sobered. "I'm glad she didn't coerce Max into trying to convince you to do that movie."

"No, apparently it was just Max and Patrick." I gave my head a brisk shake. "The male ego is a wonderous thing."

"Sure is. Good thing I don't have one."

"Oh, get out of here." I picked up a pencil and threw it at him. He grinned and disappeared out the back door. I went back out front and stopped in surprise. Raymond Terrill was leaning against my counter. He appeared to be deep in conversation with, of all people, Melanie Foster. Both wore frowns, Terrill a particularly fierce one. Melanie seemed to be ill at ease. As I approached they broke apart quickly, but not before I thought I saw Melanie slide something into Terrill's outstretched hand. "I don't mean to interrupt," I said.

"You aren't interrupting, Shell," Terrill said with an urbane smile. He inclined his head toward Melanie. "I was just complimenting this young lady—Ms. Foster, correct?" As Melanie nodded, he continued, "I met her earlier when lunch was delivered. I was just complimenting her on the food selections for the crew."

My glance strayed from Terrill to Melanie. She'd regained her composure, but I couldn't help but think their conversation had been about a topic other than food. Before I could say anything, Terrill abruptly turned his back on Melanie and made a low bow to me. "I just wanted to apologize to you again for my behavior, Shell. I do hope all is forgiven?"

I nodded. Out of the corner of my eye I saw Melanie duck down the nearest aisle. "Of course. I understand."

"Excellent." He reached into his pocket and pulled out the key to the shed he'd picked up earlier. "I was just on my way out to your house. My boxes are being delivered."

"Boxes?"

"Yes, the files I mentioned earlier. I'll probably be out at your shed quite late in the evenings, working, which leads me to my next question . . . I forgot to ask if the shed has an electric hookup?"

"There is an overhead light that works."

His brows drew together. "I was rather hoping that there might be a lamp I could use."

"Actually, I do believe there are two lamps in the shed . . . but wait!" I snapped my fingers. "I recall there was a banker's lamp that went with the desk. It should be there. I think it runs on batteries, too, if I'm not mistaken. I'm not sure if it's C or D batteries, but . . ."

"Perfect. I'll check it out." He reached out and grasped my hand. "Thank you, Shell. I mean it. I'll make all this up to you."

With another smile, he released my hand and swept out of the shop. Melanie Foster came over, set a package of dog treats on the counter. "He's still a control freak, I see," she remarked. "Always has to be his way or the highway." She shot me a curious look. "Did I hear right? He's borrowing your shed?"

"Yep. I offered him part of the storeroom but he said it wasn't big enough. Apparently he needs a lot of room for all his papers."

Melanie rolled her eyes. "Like I said, control freak." She hung her head. "I'm sorry, Shell. I really didn't mean to eavesdrop."

"No worries," I said, ringing up the sale. "There's a lot of that going around today."

I remembered what my mother had mentioned, that Terrill and Taylor had a brief "thing" and Taylor had never gotten over it. It made me wonder, however, just what Taylor's motive might be for accepting a role in a play directed by a man she might still have strong feelings for. Was she planning some sort of revenge? From the little I knew of Taylor it didn't seem possible, but then again, I'd also learned there was something to that phrase about a woman scorned.

I was also curious about the argument I'd overheard between them after what Noelle had told me about the diamond bracelet. Was that the "dirty little secret" Terrill had threatened to reveal? And I recalled Taylor's remarks the other night about her "perfect family." Josh and his sisters seemed very fond of her and I hated to think of her in a bad light, and yet . . . I squared my shoulders, filled with resolve. Tomorrow I'd track Taylor down and find a way to get to the bottom of everything.

Six

Tim Scott came into the shop just as I was getting ready to leave, a little before five. "I'm glad I caught you," he said. "Can we talk? Privately?"

I was about to say that I had to get home to help Gary get things ready for dinner, but Tim looked so woebegone and sounded so intense I didn't have the heart. "Sure," I said. I motioned toward the storeroom. "We can talk in there."

We went inside the storeroom and I closed the door. I motioned Tim to sit in one of the leather chairs by my desk. When we were both seated I asked, "So? What's on your mind?"

Tim let out a large sigh. "What else? Raymond Terrill. I'll be lucky if the guy doesn't fire me."

I leaned forward. "First of all, Tim, Terrill can't fire you because he didn't hire you. My mother did on behalf of Garrett Knute and the Fox Hollow Players. But what happened that has you so upset?"

Tim leaned back in the chair and stretched his long legs out in front of him. "I just had a humdinger of an argument with him over the way he's been treating Taylor. He's been snapping at her all day, barking commands like a king to his slave, and I just got sick of it."

I nodded. "I overheard them arguing earlier, when I came to help out with the read-throughs. As I understand it, there's some history there?"

Tim frowned. "History?"

"My mother said something about their having a fling in San Francisco?"

"Oh, that." Tim lifted his hand, studied the tips of his fingers for a few moments before he continued. "Yeah, that's true. They did have something going then, but it's long over." He shook his head. "Terrill never did take rejection well."

"Terrill? I thought he was the one who broke up with Taylor?"

Tim's lips formed an O of surprise. "Who told you that? Doesn't matter," he added quickly, waving his hand. "It's not true. What happened was, they got friendly during rehearsals and went out a few times. Terrill thought it meant more than it did, made a move, and was put in his place. He never got over it."

I looked at him. "You seem to have a pretty good handle on this story, for someone who wasn't there firsthand—or were you?"

He hesitated and then said, "Guilty. I was the assistant director on that play, and Terrill got pissed at me because I took Taylor's side. He started finding fault with everything I did. Whenever something went south, I got blamed. I'm convinced he set me up, but I could never prove it." Tim swiped at his forehead. "I thought time and distance might have mellowed his attitude toward me, but no dice."

I tapped my finger against the side of my desk. "I get the feeling there's a bit more to the story than you're telling."

He flushed. "Can't fool you, can I, Shell? Okay, Taylor and I got involved while we were doing that play. Our relationship started after she dumped Terrill, but he didn't see it quite that way." He leaned forward, the expression on his face earnest. "I know what a pain in the butt the guy can be. He's territorial and a control freak, and he doesn't like it when he's not the one that ends a relationship. I'm pretty sure that's why he's got it in for Taylor."

"Noelle Boyd also mentioned something about Taylor being accused of stealing a diamond bracelet?"

Tim's eyebrows rocketed skyward. "Leave it to Noelle to keep spreading that story around," he growled. "Taylor was never accused of theft, but she was in the restroom with that woman just before she noticed her bracelet was missing. She made a big stink, and told the police to search Taylor because she'd bumped into her." He gave his head an emphatic shake. "There was nothing to the accusation, of course. The bracelet wasn't on Taylor, and it wasn't anywhere in the theater. The thief must have made off with it during the intermission before Mrs. Bagley noticed it was gone."

He reached out and grasped my hand. "Noelle was—still is, probably—a bit jealous of Taylor. Noelle and Terrill also had a fling, and in that instance, Terrill did the dumping."

"For Taylor?"

Tim nodded. "As a matter of fact, Terrill is probably the reason for the downswing in Noelle's career."

"How so? Did he blackball her?"

"I'm not sure of the details, but I do know that after that play ended, Noelle's work became very sporadic. She dropped out of sight for months, and when she resurfaced, she only got very small roles. She just doesn't seem to have been able to get it together."

"She said the bracelet incident left a bad taste in her mouth. She also mentioned taking a sabbatical to study acting."

Tim rubbed absently at his chin. "That's true. Supposedly she went to New York to study with Claude DeBennedetto."

I raised an eyebrow. Claude DeBennedetto was a world-famous acting coach. He just didn't take on anyone. "Really?"

"It didn't ring true to me, so I called DeBennedetto's school. Noelle was registered there." His shoulders lifted in a shrug. "According to Noelle, he's been a big influence on her. You'd never know it by her acting, though. And you'd also think that with DeBennedetto as a reference, she'd get more jobs than just small-town theater and understudying the lead role."

I agreed with Tim, even though I didn't voice that thought aloud. "So you think there's more to this than she's let on?"

"In a word, yes. But to be perfectly honest, Shell, I don't really care about Noelle. The person I'm concerned about is Taylor. She was really mad at Terrill today when we quit. I've never seen her so angry."

I recalled the snatch of argument I'd overheard. "Yes, I heard her arguing with Terrill earlier," I repeated. "But she seemed okay afterward, unless something else happened between them?"

"He pulled her aside a few times. Once his face started to turn purple."

"He's definitely got a temper." I paused and then asked, "I suppose you've heard all the rumors about Terrill being some sort of jinx?"

Tim let out a dry chuckle. "Everyone has. I'm sure that adds to his touchy attitude. In my opinion, Terrill brings his bad luck on himself." He raised his hand and ran it through his hair, mussing up the sides. "I can tell you this though. If he doesn't stop treating Taylor like garbage, I won't be held responsible for what I might do to him."

I looked at Tim. "It sounds to me as if you still have feelings for Taylor."

He shot me a wistful smile. "Call it a case of unrequited love."

• • •

It was a quarter to six when I finally got out of there, and I decided to take a different route home. This one took me right past my friend Olivia Niven's dance studio, and as I passed I saw lights on in the main floor. I hesitated, then decided what the heck? I was going to be late anyway. I went up to the studio and peered in the window. Olivia was seated at her desk, going over some papers. She looked up, saw me, waved, and hurried over to let me in.

"Hey, pal," she greeted me. "Long time no see. How've you been?"

We hugged, and then I said, "Busy. Mother's back in town."

"I heard. And according to Gary, she's brought reinforcements."

"Yes. Lots of drama there. One bright spot, though, at least now she's got her own place, thanks to you."

"Oh, not me." Olivia brushed the comment aside. "Thank Joannie Adams. She's on a mission to make real estate salesperson of the month. I think she was disappointed she couldn't talk your mother into an actual sale. They count for more than rentals, but, believe me, she was happy to get that." Olivia looked at me. "You're not upset, are you, Shell? After Clarissa signed on with Sue, she was determined to get her own place. She asked me for a recommendation and I gave her Joannie's name."

"I'm not upset, just . . . surprised you never mentioned anything."

"I wanted to, several times, but both our schedules have been so crazy lately . . . I'm sorry," Olivia said, hanging her head. "I should have let you know."

I reached out and patted Olivia's hand. "It's not anyone's fault. It seems as if we hardly see each other lately. We're either both busy, or you're out with Gary," I added with a twinkle in my eye.

Olivia blushed. "We're taking that slow . . . almost as slow as Gary's apartment hunting. If you don't watch out, Shell, you and Gary are both going to grow old in Tillie's house."

I laughed. "Heaven forbid. Anyway, one day you and I are going to have to have lunch and catch up."

"I'd like that," Olivia said.

I looked at my friend. I could tell something was bothering her. "Olivia, is everything okay?"

Olivia tugged at a dark curl. "Yes. It's just that . . . oh, I don't know."

"Is it Gary?"

Her cheeks reddened a bit. "Yes," she said finally. "I really like him, Shell, but . . . sometimes I get the feeling that his mind is somewhere else."

"Mind? I wasn't aware Gary had one."

Olivia wagged her finger at me. "Don't joke. I'm serious. Sometimes I get the distinct impression that he'd rather be elsewhere than out with me."

I frowned. "Just where do you think he wants to be?"

Olivia looked straight at me. "With you," she said.

I couldn't help it. I burst out laughing. "S-sorry," I finally managed. "That couldn't be further from the truth, Olivia. Gary and I are like brother and sister. Trust me, he's not romantically interested in me, or vice versa."

Olivia still seemed doubtful. "Are you sure? Lots of times when we're together, he starts in with 'Shell said this' or 'Shell did that.' Sometimes I feel like we're three on a date."

"If you want, I'll pass some subtle hints. Men, right?" I reached over and squeezed her hand. "Believe me, he's not staying in Fox Hollow because of me. He's just living with me because it's rent-free, and Gary is basically cheap."

Olivia laughed. "He'd say frugal."

"He sure would. Say, what are you doing tonight? Around seven?"

"As luck would have it, I have no classes scheduled tonight. Why? What did you have in mind?"

I explained about Gary's cooking a special dinner for my mother. "It's always good to have lots of distractions around Mother, so . . . how would you like to join us?" I finished. "You and Gary can have a sort of impromptu date. If you think you can put up with Clarissa, that is."

Olivia's laugh tinkled out. "What a lovely left-handed invitation. Lucky for you I'm not proud—and I never refuse a good home-cooked meal. I'll be there. I can even bring dessert—I stopped by Mueller's Bakery today and overindulged on one of their chocolate concoctions."

"Chocolate sounds perfect."

Olivia walked me to the door. As we stood on the stoop chatting, I suddenly cocked my head. "Did you hear that?" I asked.

Olivia nodded. "It sounded like a cat." She pointed to the bushes underneath the dance studio window. "It's coming from over there."

I walked over and cautiously peered behind the shrub. Princess Fuzzypants squatted there. She blinked her big gold eyes at me. "Merow."

"Oh, for goodness sakes." I reached down and gathered the cat into my arms. Olivia walked over and reached out a hand to pet her.

"What a beauty," she exclaimed. "Is this the stray Gary told me about?"

"In the flesh." I dropped a kiss on the cat's forehead. The princess snuggled closer to me and started to purr. "She must have snuck out the back door when Tim and I left."

"She's gorgeous. Someone must really be missing her."

"I would, if she were mine," I said. "I even checked for Maine coon breeders, thinking perhaps she might have wandered off from one of them, but the closest one is fifty miles away."

"It could have happened like that," Olivia remarked. "I remember reading about a cat who traveled from California all the way back to its home in Pennsylvania."

"Possible, but not probable." I looked at the cat. "I might as well bring you home with me tonight," I said. "No sense going back to the shop now. Purrday will be thrilled to see you." I sighed. "I wish I could say as much for Kahlua." I looked at Olivia. "Come prepared. There might be kitty fireworks tonight."

I left the dance studio, the princess tucked firmly in my arms, and turned down the street that led to my house. As I approached, I saw lights on in the shed and figured Terrill must be in there. As if he'd read my mind, the shed door flew open and the man himself appeared. He saw me with the cat in my arms and hurried down the short path to meet me. "Well, well. I see you're bringing the cat home? Does that mean no one's claimed her?"

"The ad has only run for one day," I said. "She got out, and I decided I might as well bring her home tonight." I shifted the princess in my arms. "I'm not sure how my Siamese will like her, though. Kahlua takes her time adjusting. It was weeks before she accepted Purrday."

"You can leave her with me, if you want," Terrill said. The suggestion was so unexpected that I gasped. Terrill let out a short laugh. "No worries, Shell. I know how to take care of a cat, trust me. Besides, I keep the shed door locked while I work. She can't get out. She'll be safe, trust me."

"I believe you," I said. "I'm sorry, I just have trouble adjusting to the idea of you being a cat person."

To my surprise, he grinned. "I know. It's totally the opposite of my image, but, what can I say. This little lady has bewitched me."

Terrill held out his arms, and I placed the princess in them. She snuggled against his broad chest and started to purr like a race car. "Okay," I said. "She can stay with you here. I'll bring up some food and water and a spare litter box."

I left Terrill snuggling up to the cat and went back to my house. As I entered through the kitchen door Gary called out, "Clarissa called. She's going to be a little delayed. She quote unquote needs time to regroup."

"Good," I said. "More time for us to get everything ready." I walked over to the oven, sniffed at the air. "Man! That smells good!"

"And tastes even better, I hope," Gary remarked. "There's two bottles of Chardonnay in the fridge. Want to break one open? I need a drink."

"Sure. Oh, and by the way, I talked Olivia into joining us. I hope that's all right."

He looked up and smiled. "Hey, that's terrific. I've sort of been neglecting her lately."

I wanted to answer *You sure have* but figured now wasn't the right time. Gary was mixing together some sort of rice thing in a large casserole dish. I poured a glass of wine and set it down next to him. As I picked up my own glass he remarked, "I heard some women talking when I was in the butcher shop."

"Wow, fascinating," I said. "What about?"

"Believe it or not, about the Fox Hollow production—and Raymond Terrill. One of the women was all excited because she recognized him coming out of the McCloud Building in Fox Hollow. She was tempted to ask for his autograph, she told her companion, but nixed the idea because he looked so preoccupied."

I tapped one nail against the stem of my glass. "The McCloud Building, huh? He did end the read-through early. Said he had an important meeting." I eased my hip against the counter. "What's in the McCloud Building, anyway?"

Gary's lips scrunched up as he thought. "Some lawyers and investment counselors, I believe. Oh, and if I'm not mistaken, a detective agency. I know that because I considered going in and picking their brains on how to become a private investigator."

"I doubt Terrill would be visiting a detective agency," I said. "And he surely has his own lawyer and investment counselor back in California. So what was he doing there?"

"Maybe he was just using it as a meeting place. The building has a large lobby and there are plenty of small nooks where one could have a private meeting and be virtually unseen." Gary picked up a towel and bent to check his creation in the oven, then turned and gave me a critical once-over. "Wearing that to dinner?" he asked.

I set my wineglass on the counter. "With my mother coming? Heck no."

• • •

I scrounged up some food and bowls for the princess and dropped them off at the shed, then hurried back. I took a quick shower and had just changed

56

into a pair of palazzo pants and a cream lace top and freshened my lipstick when the doorbell rang. Olivia and my mother arrived at the same time. I poured them both a glass of wine, and we made small talk until Gary announced dinner was served. Then we all trooped into the dining area to sample Gary's Lamb L'Arabique, a casserole of lamb shanks and vegetables, including lentils and chickpeas, seasoned with Middle Eastern spices. My mother proclaimed it one of the best dishes she'd ever eaten (high praise indeed!) and after dinner we adjourned to the living room, where we sipped espresso and indulged in the chocolate blackout cake Olivia had brought. It was a little after eleven when my guests finally said good night. I was pleased to see Gary linger a bit longer with Olivia at the back door. I went upstairs and changed into my jammies, then returned to the kitchen, where Gary was loading the dishwasher. He glanced over his shoulder at me, then inclined his head toward the window.

"Looks like our star boarder is having a late night," he remarked.

I stood behind him to peer over his shoulder out the window. Sure enough, lights still burned in the shed. "No wonder. You should have seen all the boxes he had brought in there," I remarked. "It's a wonder they all fit."

Gary chuckled as he rinsed off a dish. "The guy must have more projects going on than we give him credit for," he remarked.

"Maybe. When I dropped off the food and litter box I saw the princess hop up on one of his boxes and start to paw at it."

"Uh-oh. Did he explode?"

"Oddly, no. I saw a vein pop in his neck, but he didn't say a word. Just went over, got the princess and started cooing at her." I shook my head. "I wonder if he was serious about adopting her. They might be a good match. I've never seen anyone take to a cat that quickly, and vice versa."

"Apparently he gets along better with animals than humans. And it wouldn't surprise me if Tim takes a swing at the guy. I like Tim, but he does have a hair-trigger temper."

"Let's hope it doesn't come to that." I sighed. "I wonder what catastrophe will befall the production tomorrow."

• • •

I woke up around two in the morning. Purrday was snoring loudly at the foot of my bed. Kahlua was ensconced on top of my dresser, also snoring. Thirsty, I fumbled for my robe and slippers and went downstairs. As I moved toward the refrigerator I glanced out the back window. The shed was dark. Apparently sometime between eleven and two Terrill had decided to go back to the inn. I wondered idly if he'd taken the princess with him or left her in the shed.

That question was answered as I heard a loud scratching at my back door, followed by a series of plaintive meows. I hurried over to the door and flung it open. The princess squatted on the stoop. "Princess Fuzzypants," I cried. I frowned. Well, my question had been answered. Apparently Terrill had decided to leave her, but he mustn't have closed the door all the way and she'd gotten out. Which was odd, considering how insistent he'd been about getting a key. Why hadn't he locked the shed door?

I looked at the cat. "Is everything all right, Princess?" I whispered.

The cat turned around twice, let out a loud meow, and started up the trail that led to the shed. I hesitated and grabbed a flashlight from a drawer. The cat paused, her tail swishing, and let out a much louder meow. "All right, all right," I said. "I'm coming." I hurried into the dark night after the princess. When I reached the shed, I saw immediately how the cat had gotten out: the door was ajar. "Great," I muttered. "Just wait until I see Terrill tomorrow—I mean, later today." I pushed the door open and the princess shot inside like a rocket. I went to flip the switch for the overhead light, but nothing happened. "The bulb blew, I guess," I muttered. I thought perhaps that might be why Terrill had finally decided to call it a night. I switched on my flashlight and played the beam around—and gasped as I saw, sticking out from underneath the desk, a man's shoe.

I fought against the sinking feeling in my stomach and moved closer. I swung the flashlight beam slightly to the right. The shoe was attached to a leg, and next to it was a shoe and another leg. I drew closer, playing the flashlight beam upward, up across the broad chest that Princess Fuzzypants had rested against only mere hours ago, right up onto the familiar face with its slack jaw and sightless eyes.

Well, one thing was certain. Raymond Terrill wouldn't be arguing with anyone anymore—because he was stone-cold dead.

Seven

I started toward the body when I heard a slight noise behind me.
"Shell?"

I jumped and spun around, sending the beam of the flashlight full into Gary's eyes. He jumped back with a cry. "Hey, put that down. I thought I heard a cat crying, and I looked out the window and saw you and the princess coming up here. Is something wrong?"

"You could say that." I turned back and played the flashlight beam once again over the corpse in the corner. "We have to go back to the house and call 911," I said as I knelt beside the body. "Raymond Terrill is dead."

"What?" Gary shouted. He pulled the plaid bathrobe he had on tighter around him and stepped forward to get a better look. "Oh my gosh," he cried. "How did this happen?"

I leaned over Terrill's inert form. I could see what looked like blood on the collar of his shirt. A closer look revealed a ragged open wound just below his right ear. "Looks like a bullet to the side of the head," I remarked. I touched two fingers to the base of his throat. "I don't think he's been dead all that long, either."

"Good Lord," Gary exclaimed. "Then the killer might still be around here!"

I hadn't thought of that and scrambled quickly to my feet. "Let's go," I said. "We can call the police and then come back."

• • •

Ten minutes later a paramedic truck pulled up in front of my house. Thankfully, they didn't have their lights blazing, or they might have woken up the sleepy little neighborhood. I went down to the curb to meet them. I recognized one of them, LuLu Beekman. She often stopped into Urban Tails to get seed for her canary. "The body's in the shed, back there," I informed her with a sweep of my hand.

A police cruiser pulled up behind the paramedic truck. I was hoping it would have been Josh, but Amy Riser and a young uniformed officer got out. They both walked right over to me. "Shell." Amy touched two fingers to her forehead in greeting and whipped a notebook and pen out of her jacket pocket. "What happened here?"

"The deceased is Raymond Terrill," I said.

Both Riser's eyebrows rose. "The director? What was he doing in your shed?" She flipped some pages in her notebook, then stood, pen poised, waiting for me to continue.

"He needed an office and the inn doesn't have Wi-Fi, so I offered him the use of the shed," I explained. "He was in there earlier tonight, and Gary and I saw the lights still on at eleven after our dinner guests left. I got up at two and noticed the lights were off, and then the princess started making a commotion. I followed her to the shed and found his body."

Amy looked up from her scribbling. "The princess?"

"Princess Fuzzypants. She's a Maine coon cat, a stray I found the other day. I was keeping her at the shop on account of my Siamese, who isn't too accepting of other cats. She got out, so I was bringing her here. Terrill saw her and offered to watch her."

"So the cat was in the shed when Terrill was killed?" Riser shook her head. "Figures an animal would be the only eyewitness."

I shot her an annoyed look. "I wouldn't be so quick to knock that fact," I remarked. "Or are you forgetting about Honey Belle and Adrian Arnold?" Honey Belle was a parrot who'd witnessed her owner's murder a few weeks earlier. Her ability to mimic a phrase the killer had uttered had eventually led to his capture.

"That was different. Unlike parrots, cats can't talk." Riser scribbled something else down, then raised her gaze to meet mine. "Did you touch anything?"

"I pushed the door open, but other than that, I don't think so. But earlier both Gary and I were in the shed, making it useable for Terrill, so our fingerprints are probably all over everything."

"Hm." Riser made another note, then tucked the notebook back into her jacket pocket. "Okay, Officer Quinn and I will be right back. I'll need to speak to you and Gary when I'm done."

"Sure." As Amy started to move away, I reached out impulsively and grabbed her arm. "He was shot," I blurted out.

Amy's gaze narrowed. "How do you know that?"

"I did touch the body—a little. I just wanted to make sure he was dead," I added defensively. "I saw a hole by his right ear, like a bullet had entered the side of his head."

Amy gave me a brief nod, then motioned to Officer Quinn. They tramped up the walkway to the shed. I was just about to go into the house and get Gary when I saw a dark-colored car I didn't recognize pull in behind the cruiser. Josh got out of the driver's side. He saw me and reached my side in two long strides. "Hey," he said.

"Hey yourself," I said. I glanced at the sedan. "New car?"

"Nope. Taylor needed a car tonight, so I told her she could have mine. This is one of the station cars. I heard the call over the police radio. What happened?"

"Raymond Terrill's dead. I found his body in my shed."

Josh's eyebrows lifted. "What was Terrill doing in your shed?"

"Working on papers he'd brought with him. The inn didn't have Wi-Fi and I do here, and he needed office space. Gary and I set up a desk for him to use in the shed."

"Okay." His hand started to move toward my shoulder, then abruptly dropped to his side. "I'm going to go to the shed. Wait here."

I wrapped my arms around my body as Josh hurried up the walkway. My robe wasn't all that heavy, and there was a slight chill in the air. Gary emerged from the house just then. He had a fleece hoodie in his hand, which he held out to me. "Here," he said. "You look like you could use this."

"Thanks." I slid my arms gratefully into the hoodie and zipped it up. "We got the big guns tonight. Both Josh and Amy are here."

"Smiley Riser?" Gary had nicknamed the woman that because she rarely smiled. He held her in the same deep affection I did. He'd changed from his pajamas into jeans, a plaid shirt and a barn jacket. He shoved his hands deep into the pockets of the jacket. "I imagine this'll be good. Which one of us do you think Riser will finger as the killer?"

"They're going to have a lot of questions, and I admit I do as well," I said. "The major question being, who would want to kill Terrill?"

"Good point," Gary said. "I mean, the guy was a bit of a diva, but that's no reason to kill someone."

"It had to be someone who knew that he was using my shed as an office, and that he'd be here tonight," I mused.

"Well, that can't be a very long list—or can it?"

"Mother knew," I said. "And so did Tim and Noelle and—and the rest of the Fox Hollow Players."

"Well, you can probably eliminate the latter," Gary suggested. "They don't know Terrill, so why would any of them want to kill him?"

"Someone did," I said. "He talked about coming here tonight at the read-through, and he wasn't exactly speaking softly." I paused. "Tim came to see me at the shop today. He said that he overheard Terrill berating Taylor, and if he didn't stop it that Tim wouldn't be held responsible for what he might do to him."

Gary's jaw dropped. "Oh, Shell, be serious. Tim's not a killer. Sure, maybe he said something like that in the heat of the moment, but he'd never act on it."

I shoved my hands into the hoodie's pockets. "Oh, I don't know, Gary. Maizie Madison never seemed the killer type either, remember?"

"Yeah, but we're talking about Tim here. Tim, who we've known for years. Tim, who worked beside us every day."

"I didn't accuse Tim of murder. I just pointed out that he knew Terrill would be here last night, and he wasn't too happy with him."

"Insulting his girlfriend isn't a motive for murder," Gary shot back.

"That's true." I scratched at my head. "Hey, I like Tim too. I really can't see him as a killer either, but even you have to admit there aren't a lot of options here."

Gary was silent for a few moments and then he said, "I know you probably don't want to consider her, but what about Taylor?"

I nibbled at my lower lip. Truth was, I had considered Taylor. Not only had I overheard her arguing with Terrill earlier, but there was also the fact she'd borrowed Josh's car—why? Had she driven here, killed Terrill, and then left? Far-fetched maybe, but . . .

I shrugged. "You're right. I don't want to consider her, but I'm going to have to. I mean, when you get right down to it, by her own admission she doesn't have much to do with this branch of the family. What do Josh and his sisters know about her, really? Sue and Michelle didn't even know she'd appeared on our show. Plus, she really seemed into those villainous Shakespearean roles." I sighed. "Still, I don't get that sort of vibe from her."

"But you get it from Tim?"

I sighed. "No, not really." Suddenly another thought occurred to me, and my eyes popped wide. "There was no gunshot."

Gary looked at me. "Huh?"

"I don't remember hearing a gunshot, do you? And I think a gunshot would probably have not only woken me up, but half the neighborhood too."

"Speak for yourself. When I fall asleep, I'm pretty much dead to the world."

"That's true, you do sleep like a stone." I chewed at my lower lip. "If neither of us heard anything, then that would mean the killer used a silencer. Which indicates planning to me." I looked at Gary. "I'd sure like to know what that mysterious meeting he had was all about."

Gary placed his hands on my shoulders. "Listen, Shell. I think this is one time you should let the police handle this. Let them investigate and track down the killer. There are a lot of unknowns here, and it's starting to sound pretty dangerous."

I didn't answer, mainly because I agreed with him. There were a lot of questions and no answers. Gary suddenly squeezed my arm and inclined his head. I saw Josh leave the shed and head straight toward us. He nodded briefly at Gary and then looked at me.

"It's late. The coroner's wagon will be here shortly, but you two don't have to stick around outside. Go on back to bed. I'll be in touch with both of you later today."

He gave me another long, searching look, and then turned and walked back toward the shed. I sighed. I knew that look. It was Josh's "you're not going to get yourself involved in my investigation, are you, Shell?" look.

The only problem was, Raymond Terrill had been murdered on my property. Whether Josh liked it or not, I was involved.

Eight

Gary and I waited until the coroner's wagon came and Terrill's body was loaded into it, and then we both decided to try and get some much-needed shut-eye. Fortunately Robbie was opening Urban Tails tomorrow, so neither of us were expected at the store until noon. I didn't think I would be able to sleep after the evening's events, but I dropped off like a stone the moment my head touched the pillow. I slept soundly until I felt something rough and wet rubbing against my chin. I opened my eyes and looked straight into Purrday's good blue one.

"Merow," he said. Translation: *Get up, you lazy human slug. I'm hungry.*

Kahlua jumped up beside Purrday and added her throaty Siamese meow to the mix. I pushed them both away, laughing. "Okay, okay, I get the hint." I glanced at the clock on my nightstand and saw that it was almost eight thirty. "Yowza," I said. I'd slept for nearly five hours. I'd needed the rest, though, after the events of the evening before. I pushed back my comforter and swung my feet off the bed. I slid into my slippers, grabbed my robe, and followed the cats downstairs, where the delicious aroma of frying bacon beckoned me to the kitchen. Gary had just removed a pan from the stove. He glanced up as I entered and pointed to the Keurig.

"Good timing. I just brewed a cup of your favorite blend," he said. "If you didn't come down by the time my frittata was done, I was coming up to get you."

I got my coffee, added cream and sugar, and then slid onto one of the chairs at the dining table, which was all set for breakfast. "You seem pretty perky," I observed. "How long have you been up?"

"About forty minutes. I had a good night's sleep, though. Dropped off like a stone."

Kahlua suddenly started to growl. I turned my head and saw what had caused the reaction. Princess Fuzzypants was just getting out of the spare cat bed I'd set up for her the night before. She stretched her forepaws, then ambled over to the bowls of food and water that I noticed Gary had filled. The princess hunkered down in front of Kahlua's bowl, eliciting another yowl from the Siamese.

"Be nice," I told the cat. "She's a guest. A guest who might have witnessed

64

a murder. Tell you what, I'll get you a brand-new bowl from the shop later. A pretty pink one."

Kahlua cocked her head as if considering my offer. Then she blinked her big baby blues at me, stretched across the counter and closed her eyes. I smiled. "That's my girl."

I reached for one of the slices of buttered toast that was on a platter in the middle of the table and eyed Gary, who'd already wolfed down two slices and reached for a third. "I see murder doesn't affect your rem cycle," I remarked. "I slept pretty good, all things considered."

Gary paused mid-bite. "What do you mean?"

"I had a weird dream. Terrill and the princess were pawing through all those boxes in the shed. The princess fell through one, and when I went to get her Terrill grabbed my wrist, told me that I was better off keeping out of things if I didn't want to get hurt."

"That was weird." Gary got up and went over to the oven. He pulled out a pan, and a few minutes later set a platter with a large, yummy frittata in front of me. He cut generous slices for both of us, then pulled out the chair next to me. "Do you think it meant anything?"

"Probably not. I told you I saw the princess pawing at the boxes earlier in the evening and it didn't faze Terrill in the least. I don't believe in precognitive dreams anyway."

Gary cut off a large piece of frittata and popped it in his mouth. I wasted no time doing the same. "God, this is good," I mumbled between mouthfuls. "If I were you, I wouldn't rule out culinary school." For a while there was silence as we downed the frittata and coffee. When my plate was finally cleaned, I pushed it aside, picked up our mugs, and went over to the Keurig for a refill. As I handed Gary his mug he remarked, "I know the answer, but I'm going to ask the question anyway: Are you going to sit back and let Josh and the police handle the investigation into Terrill's death?"

I took a long sip of coffee before I answered. "I'd like to stay out of it, I really would, but I don't see how I can, Gary. After all, Terrill was killed on my property. I'm involved whether I want to be or not."

Gary leaned back and laced his hands behind his neck. "That was what I was afraid you'd say. Well, then, it seems as if the investigative duo of McMillan and Presser is back in business."

"Why don't you sound all that disappointed?" I chuckled. "Admit it, Gary.

You love investigative work."

"Love is such a strong word. Let's just say I find it to my liking."

I saw my cell phone on the kitchen counter start to vibrate. I rose, walked over and snatched it up. I saw Olivia's number on the caller ID, mouthed "Olivia" to Gary, and then hit the answer button. "Hey. What's up?"

"I should be asking you that," Olivia declared. "Terrill was found dead at your house?"

"Yes, but how—oh, wait. Don't tell me. It's the lead story in the *Fox Hollow Gazette*?"

"Bingo."

I looked over at Gary. "Did you get the paper yet?"

He jumped up and headed for the door. "Forgot all about it. Don't tell me—we're front-page news?"

"What do you think?" I made a huffy sound. "I'm surprised Watson didn't come banging on our door looking for a quote; then again, that's not the way that guy operates."

"Don't worry, I'm sure he'll grill us at some point." Gary hurried outside and I resumed my phone conversation. "Gary's getting the paper. So, what does Watson have to say about it?"

"Well, let's see." I could hear paper rustling in the background. "He's got a pretty nice photograph of Terrill on the front page, although I don't think it's a recent one. He hasn't got a goatee and his hair looks to be pitch-black. The headline reads *Noted Director Found Dead at Former Actress's Home*."

I let out a groan. "Oh, swell. Talk about a lurid headline. Watson should write for those Hollywood gossip rags. That's exactly the kind of headline the *Tattler* would run. And just for the record, Terrill was killed in the shed."

"He doesn't mention where the body was found. The article says 'Shell McMillan, proprietor of Urban Tails Pet Shop and former star of *Spy Anyone*, found Terrill dead on her property in the wee hours of the morning. The Fox Hollow police are conducting an investigation.'"

"That's it?"

"Yep. The rest of the article is just a lot of filler about Terrill's career as a Shakespearean director, and how he was here at the 'invitation of Garrett Knute and Ms. Clarissa McMillan to direct the annual Fox Hollow Players' production of *Our Town*.'"

"It's interesting he doesn't include more details about the murder. I guess his famous sources were asleep at the switch, thank goodness," I said.

Gary came back and laid the paper down in front of me, then held up one hand, imitating answering a phone call. He mouthed "Clarissa" at me. "Oh, gee, I'd better call Mother before she reads this in the paper," I said.

"You've got time. Your mother doesn't get up before noon, right?"

"She tends to get up earlier when she's working on a project. I bet she's had at least three cups of coffee by now." No sooner were the words out of my mouth than a furious pounding sounded on my back door. "Too late," I sighed. "I'll give you a call later." I tossed the phone on the table and went to the back door. My mother came bustling through, fire in her eye, a copy of the paper clutched in her hand.

"Is this true? Raymond was killed here last night?" she cried before I could utter a word. "And you didn't bother to call me?"

Gary turned away from the Keurig and approached my mother, steaming cup of java in hand. "Here, Clarissa. Drink this."

My mother shot daggers at him. "I don't need coffee," she snapped. "I need answers."

"You'll like this," he assured her as he pressed the mug into her hand. "I put a double shot of whiskey in it."

Her eyes lit up. "Oh, well, in that case . . ."

My mother downed the coffee in two gulps and held the mug out for a refill. As Gary prepared another cup, I guided her over to a chair. She sat down, crossed her legs, and glared at me. "I'm waiting," she said as Gary handed her the mug.

"We didn't find his body until very late, Clarissa," Gary answered. "And we only just got up about an hour ago. We were about to notify you when you showed up."

My mother made a strangled sound deep in her throat. "I don't care how late it was, one of you should have contacted me," she grumbled. "I'd just unfolded the paper to that glaring headline when that awful detective showed up on my doorstep this morning. I got a double whammy."

"I can't do much about the glaring headline, Mother. That's all on Quentin Watson, and I assure you he didn't speak to either Gary or me. And Josh is not an awful detective. He's just doing his job."

"Heavens, I'm not talking about Josh. I would have loved to have him interrogate me." Her lips scrunched up into a moue of distaste. "I refer to that horrid woman who interrogated me during the last murder investigation, Detective Rosen."

"Riser," I corrected. "Amy Riser."

"Whatever. She asked me all sorts of questions about Raymond, most of which I couldn't answer."

I pulled out the chair next to my mother and plopped into it. "What did she want to know?"

My mother waved a bejeweled hand in the air. "Oh, she asked me about Raymond's associates, and I told her that I wasn't all that friendly with him, I'd just worked with him a time or two. I said that he'd agreed to come here and help out with the Fox Hollow production as a favor to me, but he seemed glad to do it because it came at an opportune time. Then she wanted to know what he meant by that, and I informed her I had no idea, I wasn't a mind reader."

I smothered a smile at that remark. I figured it probably hadn't gone over well with Riser. "What else?"

"She inquired if Raymond had any enemies. I asked her if she thought the sky was blue. Of course the man had enemies. He'd made a ton of them over the years. I told her that I thought he was a toad, as well. But had any of them followed him here to Fox Hollow to kill him? I told her that was her job to find out, and none of my concern." My mother passed a hand across her eyes. "I've got a bigger problem now. Who am I going to get to direct this production? There's really no time for me to go back to Hollywood. Besides, I had a devil of a time getting Raymond, and the show goes on in two weeks." She let out a long, drawn-out sigh. "I know Tim Scott would love to take over as the director, but his experience is only in the assistant capacity. He's never had to man the helm of a production before. Frankly, I don't think Garrett would want to take a chance on him."

Gary set down his cup and eased a hip against the kitchen island. "This is just an idea, Clarissa, but . . . what about you?"

Her head snapped up, and she put one hand over her heart. "Me?"

Gary folded his arms across his chest. "Why not? You're an experienced actress who's worked with many fine directors. And if I'm not mistaken, you've often given them advice, have you not?"

My mother tapped one lacquered nail against the tablecloth. "That's true. On my last tour I was very helpful to our director."

I put my hand over my mouth to stifle a laugh. I remembered that tour. The director had been a young newbie, no match for her. I was certain he'd breathed a sigh of relief when the tour ended.

She pushed back her chair and stood up. "I think you've got something there, Gary," she said. "As a matter of fact, I think I'll go over and see Garrett Knute right now." She gave a low chuckle. "I don't see how he can refuse at this late date. Besides, I'll have Tim Scott to assist me." She touched my cheek. "I'll call you later, darling."

My mother sashayed out, hips swinging. Apparently all was forgiven. The minute the door closed behind her I turned to Gary. "Those actors are never going to forgive you for this," I said.

He laughed. "Don't be surprised if Clarissa ends up being quite good at this. After all, she's a champ at bossing you around, right?"

"True." I paused. "I didn't know Tim had designs on becoming a director, did you?"

Gary shrugged. "He did mention it a time or two during our last season." He gave me a sharp look. "You're not thinking Tim would murder Terrill just to get a stab at directing this small-town production, are you?"

"No. But he was pretty upset over the way Terrill was treating Taylor."

"I'm sure there are far better suspects than Tim. We just have to figure out who they are."

Gary went upstairs to shower and I sat back down at the table to enjoy another cup of coffee. Purrday hopped up on the chair beside me, while Princess Fuzzypants hovered around my ankles. Kahlua perched herself on the kitchen island. I looked at my furry friends.

"So," I said to them, "Raymond Terrill is dead. I found his body early this morning."

Both Purrday and Kahlua made mewling noises deep in their throats. Expressions of sympathy?

Princess Fuzzypants butted my ankle. "The princess, here, most likely witnessed the murder," I said. I reached down to pet the cat. "I know Amy Riser scoffed at me, but I know what animals are capable of. Honey Belle gave me a good clue that led to me figuring out who murdered Adrian Arnold. Maybe you can do the same?" I said hopefully to the cat.

The princess let out a soft merow and snuggled down at my feet.

"Anyway, I have to agree with my mother for once. I'm sure Terrill had a lot of enemies, but I'm also sure none of them traveled from California here to Fox Hollow to kill him. No, the killer has to be someone in this vicinity. Now, who are the suspects?"

Purrday, Kahlua and the princess all looked at me expectantly.

"That's a good question. I guess everyone who came with him to help out with *Our Town* could be considered a suspect."

Purrday cocked his head and let out a soft meow. "No, I don't think the list would include my mother. She didn't seem to have any issues with him."

The cats looked at each other, then let out loud meows of assent.

"Okay, so then who? Well, there's Noelle Boyd. She seemed all sweetness and light toward him, but Tim said that Terrill was the reason behind the decline in Noelle's career. Then there's Tim himself. I hate to think of him as a killer, but as I mentioned to Gary, he did tell me yesterday that if Terrill didn't stop harassing Taylor he couldn't be held responsible for what he might do. Which," I said on a sigh, "brings me to Taylor. I hate to think of her in that light either, but she did tell me she yearned to play a murderess, like Lady Macbeth." All the cats' ears perked up at that remark. "In spite of that, she doesn't seem the type," I continued. "Still, I did overhear a humdinger of an argument between them. And she did threaten him, though I doubt it was serious—at the time, anyway."

Both Purrday and the princess let out enthusiastic meows.

"Of course it could be someone else, someone we don't know. After all, Terrill did have that mysterious meeting yesterday," I said. "I need to find out more about that. Also why Terrill told my mother doing this production came at an opportune time. Why? Had he been planning a trip here to meet someone anyway? What sort of business would bring a famous director here to Fox Hollow?" I sighed. "These are the sorts of questions I wish I could ask Josh—but instead of answers, all I'd get is a lecture on not interfering in police business."

I rubbed my hand absently across my forehead. Some people would say I was nuts, discussing a murder with cats. Something, some thought, was niggling at my subconscious, struggling to break free. What was it? I glanced at the cats again. All three stared at me for about a minute, then all three heads simultaneously swiveled toward the back door. After a second I heard a knock.

"How do you guys do that?" I said, rising. I knew cats had good hearing but this was pretty amazing. "Too bad you can't tell me who it is," I remarked. An involuntary groan escaped my lips. "Lord, I hope it's not Amy Riser."

"Shell? You in there?" came a familiar voice.

I froze. It was worse than Amy Riser. It was Josh.

Nine

I hesitated, then rolled my head from one shoulder to the other and flung open the door. "Well, hi there," I said.

Josh frowned. His hair was windblown and I could see he needed a shave. He'd probably been up all night. "You seem surprised," he said. "I told you I'd be in touch with you later, remember?"

"That you did. You did that," I babbled.

There was an awkward pause and then Josh said, "If you've got some time now, I have a couple more questions."

"Oh, sure." I stepped aside to let him enter. "Come on in."

He came inside, hands shoved deep into the pockets of his leather bomber jacket. Purrday and Kahlua were sitting by the refrigerator but came over to sniff at Josh's ankles. Josh bent over and smiled at the cats. "Hey there, kids."

Kahlua let out a screechy meow while Purrday dipped his head in acknowledgment.

Another awkward pause and then I moved over to the Keurig. "Want a cup of coffee?"

He ran a hand through his already messy hair. "I'd love one, even though I must have had at least two pots already."

"You've been up all night, haven't you?"

"Pretty much." He went over and flopped into one of the chairs. "Let's just say it was a long night."

I brought a large mug of coffee over to him, waited until he added cream and sugar and took a sip, and then sat down opposite him. "You have questions?"

"I do." He took a long sip of coffee, then closed his eyes. After a moment he opened them, then reached inside his jacket pocket for his small notebook and pen. He flipped to an empty page. "Tell me again how you found Terrill's body."

"Well, as I told you, Terrill was using my shed as his private office. Gary and I had Olivia and my mother over for dinner, and when they left around eleven the light was still on in the shed. I woke up around two and came downstairs to get a glass of milk, and I saw the light was off. I thought Terrill had gone back to the inn, but then the princess started making a racket—"

Josh held up his hand. "Back up a minute. The princess?"

"Yes. Princess Fuzzypants." I inclined my head toward the cat bed in the far corner of the kitchen. As if she knew we were speaking about her, the princess raised her furry head and blinked her big gold eyes. "Merow."

Josh swiveled his head to look at me. "When did you get another cat?"

"I didn't—not exactly. Purrday found her behind the pet shop. I'm thinking she must be someone's pet that got out. I placed an ad in the *Gazette*. Terrill really took a liking to her. As a matter of fact, he offered to watch her. I wasn't entirely certain of the welcome she'd get from Kahlua."

Kahlua, still beside Purrday in front of the refrigerator, lifted her head, looked in the princess's direction and let out a low growl.

"So that cat—Princess Fuzzypants—she was with Terrill?"

I nodded. "Yes. She came to the back door and kept scratching, and when I went to let her in, she led me right to his body. I did tell Detective Riser this," I added. "It must be in her report."

Josh passed a hand over his eyes. "I haven't had a chance to read Amy's report yet," he admitted. "Did you notice anyone lurking around?"

"No, but then again, I wasn't looking. It was dark." I leaned forward, let the tips of my fingers graze Josh's wrist. "When I bent down to check the body, it didn't seem as if Terrill had been dead very long. Gary and I figured we'd better not stick around, just in case."

"Gary was there as well?"

"He woke up and saw me from the window."

"Swell," Josh muttered under his breath. "You said you woke up around two? Anything wake you up?"

"I was thirsty."

"So, no strange sounds?"

"If you're trying to ascertain whether or not I heard a gunshot, the answer is no," I said.

"Why would you think I'd want to know if you heard a gunshot?"

"Because I told Detective Riser that I noticed what appeared to be a bullet hole on the right side of Terrill's head. That should also be in her report, which you said you didn't read," I answered.

Josh muttered something under his breath, scribbled in his notebook. "Okay, so you touched the body. Did you touch anything else?"

"No, but Gary and I set up the work space for Terrill earlier, so you're bound to find our fingerprints all over everything," I said.

Josh reached for his mug, took another long sip of coffee. He set the mug down, then traced his finger around the inside of the mug handle. "You didn't see or hear anyone. Did you happen to notice any strange cars on the street?"

I shook my head. "No, but like I said, I really wasn't looking." I leaned back a bit in my chair. "Since you seemed interested in whether or not I heard a gunshot, I'm assuming that's what killed Terrill?"

"Appears that way. I'm waiting on the official report from the coroner."

"The fact that he was shot, plus the fact I didn't hear anything, could mean the killer had a silencer on the gun. Which would indicate premeditation."

Josh's lips twitched slightly. "Good deduction, Nancy Drew," he remarked. "I take it Terrill wasn't a popular guy."

"He was definitely not a popular guy, at least not in the theater world."

"Not too popular out here in Fox Hollow, either, from what I understand. Rumor has it some of his coworkers had issues—axes to grind, so to speak."

I folded my arms across my chest. "Now you sound like Quentin Watson," I said, trying to make my tone light. "You'd have to talk to his coworkers on that subject. Tim Scott, Noelle Boyd . . . my mother."

Josh's nose wrinkled as I mentioned my mother. "That's where I'm going next, to track them down. I'm sure they know the news by now, thanks to the *Gazette*. I know Amy spoke with your mother earlier, but . . ."

"She didn't get very satisfactory answers. I know . . . my mother was here a little bit ago. She was furious that neither Gary nor I called her immediately upon finding the body."

"I can imagine." Josh pushed back his chair and stood up. "Okay, thanks. If I need anything else I'll be back."

"Did you want to speak with Gary? He's upstairs getting ready for work."

"I don't want to disturb him. I'll stop by the pet shop later."

I walked him to the door, where he paused and gave me a long, deep look. "Shell, I know how you love a good mystery, but—"

I held up a hand. "I know you don't want me to get involved, but Terrill was killed in my shed, Josh. Which kind of makes it my business."

"It should definitely make you concerned, but murder is not your business—it's mine. Please, Shell. I need you to stay safe. Please refrain from sticking your nose in and let me do my job."

It was only after the door had closed behind Josh that I realized neither of us had stated the obvious: that his cousin Taylor was also one of the coworkers with an axe to grind against Terrill.

• • •

Gary came downstairs, dressed in jeans and a plaid shirt. "I know we're on the noon-to-close schedule, but I don't want Robbie there alone," he said. "I'm sure everyone's read the *Gazette* by now, and they'll be swarming in, plying him with questions."

"Good idea," I said. "Tell you what, you and Robbie can both leave at three and I'll close."

Gary eyed me. "Are you sure?"

I nodded. "I'm sure. I might be a little late coming in, though."

"Okay, if you're sure." He inclined his head toward the door, where Purrday and Kahlua squatted, waiting. "Shall I take the children with me?"

I glanced over at the cat bed in the far corner. Princess Fuzzypants was curled up in a ball, snoring lightly. "Yes, take them. I think the princess deserves a relaxing day here. After all, she probably witnessed a murder last night."

After Gary and the cats took off, I went upstairs, showered, dried my hair and pulled it back into a ponytail. I pulled on dark denim jeans and a light blue top and went downstairs. The princess had arisen from her bed and now twined around my ankles. I bent down to give her a scratch behind her fuzzy ears. "If only you could talk," I murmured. "What would you tell me, Princess?"

The cat blinked her big eyes. "Merow."

I refilled her food and water bowl, gave her head another pat, and left. I got into my convertible and headed not for the pet shop but for Olivia's dance studio. Olivia lived in the apartment above the studio. I found a parking space right out in front and eased my car into it. I hurried to the side entrance, and Olivia flung the door open before I had a chance to ring the bell.

"Come in, come in," she cried, grabbing my arm. "Rita and Ron have both called already, wanting to know if you mentioned any details to me." Rita and Ron were Rita Sakowski and Ron Webb. Rita owned Sweet Perks, the town coffee shop slash bakery, and Ron owned Webb's Florist. Both were good friends of mine and Olivia's. "Rita already asked Josh if you were going to help in the investigation."

I rolled my eyes. I knew Rita thought very highly of my investigative skills, particularly since I'd been instrumental in having her cleared of murder charges just a few short weeks ago. "No wonder Josh seemed so reserved," I said with a sigh as I followed Olivia up the stairs and into her kitchen. "He came by to see me this morning. He needed more details about how I found the body, and if I'd heard or seen anyone prior. He also read me the riot act about butting my nose into the investigation. The guy was killed in my shed. I can't help but feel responsible."

"Whoever wanted Terrill dead would have found a way to off him, whether it was in your shed or somewhere else," Olivia pointed out.

"Whoever killed him had to know he was using my shed as an office," I said. "That could be practically anyone in the Fox Hollow Players troupe. It wasn't exactly a secret. And who knows who else Terrill might have told."

"What do you mean by that? Terrill didn't know anyone here in Fox Hollow, did he? How could he? He was never here before." She motioned to a full pot of coffee on her stove. "Want a cup? I just made it."

"Sure." I waited until Olivia had poured coffee for both of us and set the steaming mugs in front of us before I continued. "Terrill's never been here before, or at least not that we know of. He ended the read-throughs early yesterday, because he had an important meeting—at the McCloud Building."

Olivia's eyebrows skyrocketed up. "The McCloud Building, huh? Who do you think he was meeting there? One of those fancy high-priced lawyers? Or maybe he was seeking out a new investment counselor?"

"Gary said there's a detective agency in the McCloud Building."

Olivia nodded. "Skillman Investigations. Randy Skillman owns it now. He inherited it from his daddy, Farley Skillman. But why would Terrill be visiting a detective agency?"

"He probably wasn't, but we still have to consider it. He could have met with just about anyone. Gary said there are lots of private nooks and crannies in the seating area where people could sit and remain virtually unseen."

"That is true. They've got those odd-shaped leather couches and chairs arranged in all sorts of places in there." Olivia tapped at her bottom lip with her forefinger. "You said this guy Terrill had lots of enemies. Do you think someone could have followed him all the way from California out here just for the express purpose of murdering him?"

"It sounds a bit fantastic, I know, but someone obviously wanted him dead. I hate to think it could possibly be someone I know."

Olivia pursed her lips. "Maybe it's not. Was the guy a gambler?"

I raised an eyebrow. "You're thinking a hit man? I suppose that's not impossible. I only had a quick glimpse but that gunshot wound looked pretty clean."

Olivia gasped. "He was shot? Watson escaped reporting on that little tidbit."

"I noticed what appeared to be a bullet hole in his neck, and Josh practically confirmed that earlier. He kept asking me if I heard anything right before I found the body."

"A gunshot!" Olivia's lips formed a perfect O. "Did you?"

I shook my head. "Nothing. Which leads me to believe the murderer used a silencer. Which leads me to believe it was premeditated."

"Wow! Who, I wonder? And why?"

"Those are the million-dollar questions." I took a long swig of coffee, set the mug down. "Something's been nagging at me, some little detail, but I can't put my finger on it."

Olivia regarded me over the rim of her mug. "Something about Terrill?"

I nodded. "Yes, but I just can't place it."

"It'll come to you. That happens to me, and things come back usually right when I'm in the middle of something else."

I picked up a spoon, tapped it idly against the side of the mug. "I have a feeling that Josh thinks Taylor might be involved."

"His cousin? Really?" She angled her head at me. "Judging from the look on your face, you think that too, don't you?"

I set the spoon down and rested my chin in my hand. "I don't want to, but . . . darn it, she could be. I overheard her and Terrill having quite an argument yesterday. He threatened to reveal some secret of hers, and she got pretty upset."

Olivia's eyebrows winged skyward. "Upset enough to kill him?"

"I don't know. But Josh did say she borrowed his car last night. She had errands to run."

"And you think one of her errands was coming here in the dead of night to murder Terrill?" Olivia let out a breath. "I sure hope not. Imagine how Josh would feel if he had to arrest his own cousin?"

"I can't imagine," I murmured. "The captain might make him recuse himself, and then Riser'd be in charge."

"Ugh," said Olivia. "There's a horrid thought."

We were silent for several seconds digesting that, and then Olivia cleared her throat. "What's going to happen to the production of *Our Town* now that Terrill's dead? Are they going to cancel it?"

"Believe it or not, my mother is going to offer her services as director."

"Clarissa? Really?"

I chuckled. "As Gary put it, she's had experience bossing directors—and me—around for years. Frankly, I think she'd be a natural for the job. And she'd have Tim Scott to help her. According to Mother, Tim has directorial aspirations."

"Good. That'll make Chris Contey happy." Chris was the owner of Tasty Bites. "Melanie was saying just the other day how much she enjoyed catering the rehearsals, even though I got the idea she wasn't too fond of Terrill either."

"Yeah, I got that impression too," I said. A little warning bell jangled in my head. I closed my eyes for a moment and replayed the conversation I'd had with Melanie at the shop just after she slipped something into Terrill's hand.

He's still a control freak, I see, Melanie had remarked. *Always has to be his way or the highway.*

My head snapped up and I met Olivia's interested gaze. "She said *still*," I cried.

Olivia looked at me blankly. "Huh?"

I could feel the excitement mount in my tone as I replied, "Melanie. She mentioned that Terrill was still a control freak. *Still.* But how could she have possibly known that, unless . . ."

Olivia let out a startled gasp. "You mean . . ."

We both said it at the same time. "They knew each other!"

Ten

Pieces started clicking together in my head, and for a few moments Olivia and I just stared at each other. I could feel a knot forming in the pit of my stomach. "Melanie and Raymond Terrill knew each other," I said slowly. "That has to be it."

Olivia gave her head a brisk shake. "I don't know about that, Shell. I know Melanie. She's been taking jazz dance classes here for months. She's not a killer."

The wheels were spinning in my head now, and I wasn't about to let my friend deter me. "She told me she's originally from California," I said. "And she mentioned trying her hand at acting. Her path and Terrill's could have crossed. Terrill had a reputation for loving 'em and leaving 'em, and not too gently either. Maybe that happened with her."

Olivia scrunched up her lips. "Oh, I don't know. That's such a stretch, Shell."

"Is it?"

"Weeel . . ." Olivia let out a resigned sigh. "I guess it could be possible they might have had an affair . . . maybe . . . but I'd bet my bank account she didn't have anything to do with Terrill's death."

I glanced at my watch. "Well, I guess there's only one way to find out. Melanie should be at the theater now, setting up lunch. I'll just go there and ask her."

Olivia crossed her arms over her chest. "Wouldn't that qualify as interfering in Josh's investigation?"

I stuck my tongue out at my friend. "Sometimes you can be such a killjoy."

Olivia raised both hands. "Hey, I'm just looking out for you. Why don't you call Josh, tell him this, and let him do the interrogating."

I gathered up my purse and started for the door. "You're right. That's probably what I *should* do."

Olivia clucked her tongue. "But you're not, are you?"

I shot her a wide grin. "Heck, no. I'll fill you in later on what I do—or don't—find out."

• • •

I arrived at the theater a few minutes before twelve and parked my convertible right behind the Tasty Bites truck. I went inside and walked down the long corridor. I passed the room where we'd done the read-through and paused for a moment. Inside I could hear the murmur of voices. Apparently my mother had managed to rally the troops—not that I'd ever had a doubt. I continued on down the hall until I came to the break room and pushed open the door. The first thing I saw was a long white table situated at the far end of the room. It was covered with a white tablecloth, and there were several covered Sterno platters on top of it, along with other platters of what appeared to be thick sandwiches. I saw a woman at the far end of the table arranging two bowls of salad. Her back was to me, but she was Melanie's height and her hair, pulled back in a ponytail, was the same coppery color. I hurried over, but as I approached, she turned her head and I saw that she wasn't Melanie but Robin Pittasi, another girl I'd seen working in the deli. She glanced up, saw me, and a puzzled expression crossed her face. "Shell? What are you doing here? Don't tell me you joined the Players?"

"Hi, Robin," I said. "No, I haven't joined the Players."

She let out a soft snort. "Too bad. They could use an actress of your caliber. Are you looking for your mother? They should all be here in a few minutes for lunch."

"No, actually, I was looking for Melanie. Is she here?"

"Nope." The corners of Robin's lips pulled downward. "She called in sick today. Chris called me in at the last minute to substitute. Today was supposed to be my day off."

"That's too bad," I said. "So she's at home, then?"

"I suppose. She *said* she had a migraine." It was evident from the tone of Robin's voice she didn't believe the excuse. "It's not the first time," she added.

I looked her square in the eyes. "You sound like you don't believe her."

Robin's gaze skittered away and she flushed guiltily. "I wouldn't say that, exactly," she muttered. "It's just the last time she called in sick, I found out she went with a friend to the movie complex over in Kingston to see the new Tom Cruise movie. I got stuck working a double shift that day too," she added in a somewhat defensive tone.

"So you think she did something similar today?"

Robin let out a long sigh. "No, today I think she's really sick. I drove past her house on the way here. Her car was in the driveway, and I saw her through the window. She was in her bathrobe and she was holding an ice pack to her head."

I nibbled at my bottom lip as I thought. If Melanie truly had a migraine, I figured my chances of getting to talk to her were pretty slim. It was probably best for me to wait until later on, or tomorrow. I let my gaze rove over the table. "Well, you did a marvelous job of setting up," I praised her. "Everything looks wonderful."

Robin's expression brightened a bit. "Thanks. I actually enjoy catering. I don't get a chance to do it very often, though. To be honest, I wouldn't have minded doing it today, except I had plans."

I made a sympathetic sound. "Oh, that sucks."

"Yeah. My boyfriend is taking me to New York this weekend. We're gonna see the sights, you know, Empire State Building, Statue of Liberty. Do the whole tourist thing. He got front-row seats to *Phantom*, too, for Saturday night. I wanted to go to McKinnon's and get something really fab to wear. They're having a big sale today." She pulled at her messy ponytail. "By the time I finish up here and get over there, though, all the good stuff will be picked over."

An idea percolated in my brain, and I leaned forward. "What if I spell you here?" I asked.

She looked at me. "What, you mean—you'd serve lunch?"

"Sure, why not. I used to help out sometimes at the commissary at the studio where we filmed our TV show," I said. "I'm closing the pet shop tonight, so I can stick around. That way you'll still have time to find something fabulous at McKinnon's."

Robin wasted no time untying her apron and handing it to me. "You've got a deal. Thanks. Once they've finished with lunch, just gather up all the trays and carry them out to the van. Greg will be by around one thirty to pick everything up." She grasped my hand. "Thanks, Shell."

"Don't mention it."

Robin hurried off. I tossed my bag under the table and tied the apron around my waist. If I couldn't talk to Melanie, then maybe someone else could provide some sort of a clue about her past, and I had a good idea where to start. I took the lids off of the Sterno trays and had just unwrapped the last sandwich tray when the door to the break room pushed open and the acting troupe flowed in. Naturally the first person through the door would be my mother. Her jaw dropped as she saw me standing behind the table.

"Crishell?" she cried. "What on earth are you doing here? Where's Melanie?"

"Melanie's sick today," I said. "I volunteered to help out."

Tim came up behind my mother. He tossed me a wink behind her back. "Hey, it's good to see you, Shell. Boy, seeing you behind that table brings back memories." He turned to my mother. "Shell used to help out in the commissary quite a bit, back when we were doing the show. To tell you the truth, I always figured her for a closet chef."

"That would be Gary, not me. I just always liked to help dish out the food so I could talk to everyone—catch up on the latest gossip."

Tim let out a laugh. "That's true. There's no place like a commissary for that. It's better than reading the *Enquirer* or *Tattler*—and more accurate, too."

I looked at my mother, who had a horrified expression on her face. "Can I recommend the chicken marsala?" I asked sweetly. "I've had it before and it's very good."

"I have no doubt," my mother grumbled. She picked up a plate and made her way over to the silver chafing dish. "I have to say, the lamb Gary prepared last night was top-notch. He really outdid himself."

"I'll tell him you said so."

As my mother busied herself with heaping chicken marsala on her plate, I turned my attention to Tim. "So, how did everyone take the news about Terrill?"

Tim's expression sobered. "Pretty much as you'd expect. Shock and disbelief. I mean, the guy was a real jerk, make no mistake about it, but for someone to actually kill him?" He shook his head. "Our rehearsal started late, thanks to the police. This female detective questioned everyone."

"Amy Riser." I nodded. "She's very thorough."

"She asked me about my relationship with Terrill. I didn't lie. I told her the truth." He let out a chuckle. "When she asked me who I thought might have wanted Terrill dead, I told her that little notebook she had wasn't big enough."

"That might be true back in LA, but I doubt anyone would have followed him here for the express purpose of murdering him."

Tim jabbed his finger in the air. "You know, that detective said the same thing. And I'll tell you the same thing I told her. Don't bet on it." He picked up a plate from the stack and sighed. "So far the only negative result I can see from his death is the fact your mother's appointed herself the new director."

I stifled a grin. "My mother is a force of nature, isn't she?"

"You can say that again. I have to admit, though, she's a good director. Almost as good a director as she is an actress."

"Don't say that too loud," I cautioned. "She'll get a swelled head. By the way, she mentioned that you could be a big help to her, that you also wanted to be a director."

"I've been toying with the notion for a while," he admitted. "I'll be honest. This experience could make me or break me."

I smiled at him. "Let's hope it's the former."

Tim moved off and I was busy for the next fifteen minutes, handing out plates and chatting with the cast members. Finally, I spotted Taylor at the end of the line. She looked tired, and her eyes appeared dull and vacant. She looked surprised when I handed her a plate.

"Shell? You're catering the food now? What happened to Melanie?"

"I'm just helping out today," I said. "Melanie called out sick, and her replacement had other plans." I gave her a sympathetic look. "How are you doing?"

She closed her eyes for a second and I saw some of the tension leave her shoulders. She opened her eyes again and looked straight at me. "It was . . . a shock," she said slowly. "Truly the last thing I expected to hear today, I can tell you that." She rubbed at her eyes. "I had a late night myself. I went over to Closter to visit an old friend of mine. Josh loaned me his car. I drove in from her house a little after one and barely got any sleep; and then, to hear that news . . ." She shot me a wry smile. "How are you holding up? After all, he was killed on your property."

"It was no picnic finding him like that," I admitted. "Someone must have really hated him."

"Raymond had that effect on people."

Taylor and I both turned to see Noelle Boyd standing there. She picked up a plate and shook her head. "You either loved Raymond or hated him—sometimes both." She shot Taylor a searching look. "Right, Taylor."

Taylor's back stiffened. "And just what is that supposed to mean?"

Noelle shrugged. "Nothing. I'm just stating a fact."

"I hate to sound cliché, but people who live in glass houses and all that," Taylor said with a curl of her lip. She looked at me. "Nice to see you, Shell," she murmured, and then moved on down the line.

Noelle watched her go and shook her head. "Touchy, touchy. She doesn't fool me. Raymond's death has affected her."

I looked at Noelle. "How about you? It must have affected you as well. You were close to him, you said."

Noelle shrugged. "*Were* being the operative word. As I told that lovely female detective who woke me up this morning, I had nothing but the utmost respect for Raymond Terrill." She pulled the suede jacket she wore more tightly around her. "Of course I'm upset. Who isn't? It's horrible to think of someone dying that way."

A tall man who I'd seen around town sauntered over to us. "Noelle, Clarissa wants me to run those lines with you right after lunch."

Noelle rolled her eyes. "Sure, Mark." As Mark drifted away, she shook her head. "No offense, but your mother is pretty picky. She makes Raymond look like a saint."

Noelle moved off in a huff. Most of the actors had finished eating and were starting to head back to the theater. My mother had already disappeared, and Tim and Taylor too. I was just about to start cleaning up the plates when out of the corner of my eye I saw Wilma Harper hurry in.

"Thank goodness. I thought I missed lunch. I had phone calls to return, and the time got away from me." She stared at me as if seeing me for the first time. "Shell? What are you doing here?"

"Melanie called in sick, so I'm helping out," I said.

Wilma frowned. "What happened to Robin?"

"She had some errands she had to run."

Wilma's frown deepened. "I bet. That girl's always looking for time off. I've a mind to speak to Chris about her." She shook her head, then turned her attention to the food. "I know I'm so late . . . anything good left?"

"As a matter of fact, yes." I handed Wilma a plate. "The chicken marsala's really good, and there's enough left for a plate."

No answer. I reached out and touched her wrist. "Wilma? Did you hear me?"

Wilma looked up with a start. "What? Oh, no . . . sorry, Shell. I was thinking about something." She picked up a plate, passed it to me. "Sign me up."

I dished out the remainder of the chicken marsala and handed the plate to Wilma. As she took it I remarked, "You seem a bit preoccupied, Wilma. Is everything okay?"

Wilma gave a quick glance around and then leaned closer to me. In a low tone she said, "Since you asked . . . I could use some advice."

I raised an eyebrow. "What sort of advice?"

"Well . . . I know you're friendly with Josh Bloodgood. I heard he's in charge of this investigation. I'm just wondering . . . if I should tell him something or not."

"Is it related to the murder?"

Wilma wrinkled her nose. "It could be." She set her plate down and pulled at the hem of her cream-colored cardigan sweater. "It happened yesterday afternoon. I left rehearsal early, but then I forgot my phone and had to come back. I saw them in the parking lot."

"Them?"

"Raymond Terrill and Melanie."

"Melanie!" I'd been expecting her to say Taylor or Noelle. "Are you sure?"

Wilma nodded. "They were talking—no, that's not right. They were arguing. I could hear the tone of their voices, even though I couldn't make out the words. Terrill was waving his arms around, and Melanie's face was beet red. They didn't see me, so I started to backtrack to get to the side entrance. As I skirted around, Melanie raised her voice and I heard what she said to Terrill." Wilma paused. "Shell, I think that they knew each other. That they had some kind of past."

I felt my pulse quicken. "Why do you say that?"

Wilma let out a breath. "Because of what I heard Melanie say. That she should have gone through with it when she had the chance. They'd both be better off for it." She spread her hands. "I have no idea what it was, but from the expression on Melanie's face . . . I think it was bad, Shell. Very bad."

Eleven

I t was almost two o'clock when I got to the pet shop. Robbie was behind the counter, ringing up some hamster food for a teenaged girl. He glanced up as I walked by. "Hey, Ms. McMillan," he said.

"Hey, Robbie. Sorry I'm so late."

"No problem." He slid the container of hamster food into a plastic bag, handed it to the girl, and then leaned both elbows on the counter. "I've been asking around, and so have my friends. No one so far is missing a red Maine coon cat."

I'd forgotten he'd offered to do that. "Thanks anyway, Robbie. I appreciate your effort."

"No sweat. After all, you're the boss. Besides," he added with a wide grin, "Mr. Presser said you were closing tonight."

"That is true." I glanced around the shop. "Where is Gary?"

"In the back." Robbie jerked his thumb in the direction of the storeroom. He hesitated a moment and then blurted, "That was something, huh? I mean, that director getting killed on your property and all."

"Yes, it was . . . something."

"Everyone's been talking about it," he went on. "Speculating on what happened. Do the police have any leads on who did it?"

"Not so far, but then again, they've only just started investigating."

He rubbed at his chin. "I heard he wasn't very well liked. Still, it's odd, right? I mean, he was a virtual stranger here. Whoever wanted to kill him had to have known him, right?" He gave a small shudder. "If not, then there's a killer loose in town." He shot me an earnest look. "Say, if you're scared to stay at your house, you know, in case whoever did it comes back, my aunt Frieda has some rooms for rent. I mentioned it to Mr. Presser too."

I reached out and touched Robbie's hand. "Thanks for the thought, but I think we'll be okay."

"Okay . . . but if you change your mind, let me know. Oh, yeah, I almost forgot!" He reached underneath the counter and pulled out a sheet of paper. "Gretchen was here earlier. She wrote this note for you."

I took the slip of paper. Gretchen's handwriting was the type I found typical of most medical students—cramped and hard to read—so it took me a few moments to decipher the message:

> *Shell:*
>
> *I got my regular microchip machine back so anytime you want to bring the princess in I can do another scan. I've checked with several animal rescue groups in the immediate vicinity, and no one has reported a missing cat, let alone a Maine coon. I've got a few more resources to check, though. I'll keep you posted.*
>
> *Gretchen*

I had to admit, I felt elated at the fact that Gretchen had failed to get a bead on Princess Fuzzypants' owner. My ad had run for two days, and so far no responses. I hated to admit it, but I was getting just as attached to that cat as Purrday. I was going to have to take the cat in for a microchip scan, though, just to be sure. I thanked Robbie for the note, shoved it into my tote bag, and headed for the storeroom. I found Gary hunched over the computer. Purrday was seated in the chair next to him, watching. Kahlua lounged on the windowsill. Gary glanced up and wiggled an eyebrow. "Hey, Shell. Nice of you to show up. How'd the sleuthing go?"

I stopped next to him, tossed my tote bag on the floor. "What makes you think I was sleuthing?"

He laughed. "Well, we all know that in spite of any good intentions you might have to stay out of Josh's investigation, you can't help yourself. Besides, Olivia called and told me you went down to the theater, and why." He held up his hand as I opened my mouth to speak. "Don't get mad at her. I had to pry it out of her, honest."

"I'm not mad." I went over and flopped down in the beat-up chair beside Gary. "I could use a sounding board, if you're interested."

He leaned back in the chair, which was a bad move, considering its rickety springs. He righted the chair and leaned forward instead, propping his elbows on the desk. "I'm all ears. Shoot. What did Melanie have to say?"

"Nothing, because she wasn't there. She called in sick—a migraine."

"Sick, huh. Sounds pretty convenient."

I nodded. "Doesn't it, though. Robin, who was called in to sub for her, seemed to think she might be faking."

"What do you think?"

I shrugged. "I don't know. I drove by her house on the way home. It was dark, which isn't unusual for people with migraines. I rang the bell. No one answered, but as I was walking away, I was sure I saw a curtain in one of the upstairs windows part just a little." I sighed. "Or I could have imagined it. It all happened so fast." I ran my hand through my blonde curls. "I keep going back to yesterday, to when I saw Melanie and Terrill talking here. Terrill looked annoyed. And for a split second, I could have sworn Melanie looked frightened."

"Well, Terrill could be a pretty frightening guy," Gary admitted. "Olivia said that you thought she and Terrill might have known each other before?"

I explained about Melanie's remark about Terrill still being a control freak. "I no longer think that *might* have been the case, I'm *certain* of it, after what Wilma told me she overheard."

"Which was?"

"That she should have gone through with it when she had the chance."

Gary wrinkled his nose. "That's a pretty vague statement. What is 'it,' exactly?"

"I have no idea, but Wilma thought it might be something pretty bad."

"Bad? Bad like what? Another murder?"

I threw up my hands. "I don't know, Gary. I wish I did. That's why I wanted to see Melanie. I was hoping she'd be able to clarify everything."

"If Melanie lied about not knowing Terrill, what makes you think she'd come clean about this?"

"She didn't lie . . . not exactly. She just never mentioned she'd met him before. The clues were all there, though. She's originally from California. She said she tried her hand at acting, but she got discouraged and quit. Maybe Terrill was the one who discouraged her."

"So she killed him years later?" Gary shook his head. "Even you have to admit that makes no sense."

"I'm not saying Melanie killed Terrill—at least, not yet." I tugged at a curl. "There are a lot of unknowns, though." My jaw dropped as a sudden thought occurred to me. "Holy cats!" I said. "Do you think that maybe Melanie was Terrill's mysterious meeting at the McCloud Building?"

Gary frowned. "I guess it's possible. There's only one way to know for sure, though."

"I do intend to ask Melanie about it," I said. "Tomorrow, first thing."

Gary stretched his legs out in front of him. "I don't know. Something's not hitting me right about that whole thing. Do you seriously think Melanie had something to do with Terrill's death?"

"Maybe not," I said slowly. "But I think she's hiding something. It just seems like an awfully big coincidence, don't you agree?"

Gary pushed his chair back and stood up. "I agree that there's something off about that whole thing. What I think you should do is tell Josh. He's a good detective. Let him figure it out."

"I would, but . . ."

"But?" Gary prompted as my voice trailed off.

I let out a huge sigh. "But, I'm trying to stay out of his way in the investigation. I really am," I added defensively as Gary raised both eyebrows. "If I tell him this, he'll want to know how I found out and . . ."

"And accuse you of playing junior sleuth, which you are," Gary finished.

I glared at him. "You needn't sound so righteous," I sniffed. "You like to investigate even more than I do."

"That's true." He sat back down again. "I guess that's why there's something else that bothers me about the Melanie-Terrill thing."

"And what's that?"

"You said that Terrill mentioned he'd met Melanie when she delivered the lunch that day. But obviously, if what Wilma overheard was true, that wasn't the case. So . . . why did he lie about not knowing her too?"

I paused, digesting that. "Maybe . . . maybe they had a thing."

"A thing?"

"You know what I mean." I picked up a pencil, scissored it between my fingers. "Maybe it happened back when Melanie was trying to break into acting. Maybe they were attracted to each other and had a wild affair. Maybe afterward they were both ashamed at what they'd done and agreed to pretend it never happened."

"That's a lot of maybes," Gary remarked.

I tried to get a mental picture in my head of Melanie and Terrill together, and couldn't. "You're right. Melanie's not Terrill's type."

"Oh? And what is Terrill's type? Or should I say, what was his type?"

"He seemed to like them thin and glamorous. Like Taylor, or Noelle Boyd. Melanie's an attractive woman, but she's on the plain side, and a little overweight. Not glamorous at all."

"Not now she's not," amended Gary. "But back when she was a starlet in Hollywood, it might have been a different story."

I reached over, pulled the laptop in front of me. "Well, there's one way to find out."

I called up Google and typed in *Melanie Foster–images*. Dozens of Melanie Fosters appeared. I scrolled through them all but could find none that looked like the Melanie Foster I knew.

"She could have used a stage name," suggested Gary.

"Which she probably did." I pushed the laptop off to the side. "There's no getting around it. I'm going to have to ask Melanie some tough questions."

"Without letting your detective boyfriend find out."

I squirmed in my chair. "I hate keeping secrets from Josh."

"Then don't. Tell him all this. Let him do the detecting. Not that you're not good at it, Shell, because you are. But whoever did the deed knows where we live. And if you get too close for comfort . . ."

"I get it. I could be putting both of us in danger." I clasped my hands in front of me. "I guess I'm homing in on Melanie because I'm trying not to home in on someone else."

"And who might that be?"

"Taylor," I confessed. "Last night when Josh came I noticed he was driving a different car. He said Taylor borrowed his because she had some errands to run. I thought it odd at the time—I mean, what sort of errands could she have had, unless maybe one of them was . . ."

"Dropping by the shed to kill Terrill?"

"She knew he'd be there. Everyone did. He wasn't making a secret of it. But today she told me she'd been visiting a friend in Closter. She said she stayed late and drove back after one, so I guess she's in the clear."

Gary was silent for several seconds, then he cleared his throat. "Josh has a dark SUV, doesn't he?" he asked.

I nodded. "Yes. Why?"

Gary ignored my question, countered with another of his own. "A Chevy Terrain, I do believe. Black or navy, with ski racks?"

"Black and the racks are removable. Why are you asking?"

Gary looked decidedly uncomfortable. He ran his hand through his thick crop of hair, messing up the sides. "I have a confession to make," he said at last.

I felt the hairs on the back of my neck start to tingle. "What sort of confession?"

"I didn't mention anything at the time, because truthfully I wasn't sure of what I saw. I'm still not one hundred percent, but the more I think about it . . ."

I got up out of my chair and clenched my fists at my sides. "Will you please just spit it out?"

"Okay, fine. Last night, before I followed you out to the shed, I happened to glance out the front window. I saw a dark SUV with ski racks take off like a shot from down the block. I didn't say anything because quite frankly, I'd forgotten all about it—until now, when you mentioned Taylor borrowing Josh's car."

I stared at him. "You saw a dark SUV? Are you certain?"

"Like I said, I sort of pushed it out of my mind. It was dark, and it all happened so fast. To be honest, I can't absolutely swear about the ski racks, but it was a dark SUV, all right. And my first impression was that it was a Chevy Terrain."

An uncomfortable silence settled over us, broken finally by me clearing my throat. "Even if you did, it might not mean anything."

"True," he said after a moment. "Maybe whoever it was forgot something and was in a hurry to go get it. At two in the morning."

"It happens."

"Uh-huh. This happened on the night someone was murdered in your shed. Right around the time of the murder."

I passed a hand across my eyes. "You should tell Josh," I said finally. "Even if there's nothing to it—and there probably isn't—you should tell him."

Gary nodded. "Okay. I will." He looked at his watch. "I told Olivia I'd be by at three. She has some boxes she needs help moving, and then we're going to catch dinner and an early movie. Are you okay to stay tonight? If not, I can cancel and take your shift."

I was tempted to take him up on his offer for a minute, but then I waved my hand. The last thing I wanted to do was be the reason Gary broke a date with Olivia. "No, no, you go on. Tell Olivia I'll talk to her tomorrow."

"Okay, then." He gave me a long, searching look and left. I sat at the desk, my chin propped in my hand. Purrday jumped up on the desk, came over to give me a headbutt.

I reached out to stroke his soft fur. "Maybe Gary was wrong," I said to the cat. Purrday let out a low growl. "Yeah, yeah, I know. Gary's good with noticing things. And he knows his cars. Although, there are a lot of people in Fox Hollow with dark-colored SUVs."

Purrday cocked his head, almost as if he knew that the only one I'd ever seen with ski racks was Josh's.

And Josh had loaned his SUV to Taylor, who claimed she'd been with a friend in Closter all evening. But if what Gary had seen was correct . . . she hadn't been.

"Tell me I'm wrong," I said to Purrday. "Tell me Gary was mistaken. That the SUV he saw was a different color than Josh's."

Purrday rubbed against my arm and made a little growling sound deep in his throat. Deep down I knew he was right.

The SUV Gary had seen was more than likely Josh's, which meant I now had two good suspects . . . and God help me, I really didn't want the killer to be either one of them.

Twelve

Customers were in and out for the remainder of the afternoon, and I'd been so busy that I had little time to reflect on the recent developments. Things finally slowed down around five thirty.

I'd just finished ringing up one of Kathleen Power's handmade dog sweaters for Nina Frankel's poodle when the shop bell jangled and Quentin Watson sauntered in. I gritted my teeth and squared my shoulders, fully prepared to do battle. As Nina moved off with her purchase, Watson strode up to the counter. He rested his forearms on it and flashed me a disarming smile.

"Good afternoon, Shell. How's business?"

I bared my teeth in a semblance of a smile. "Booming, thanks. How's the newspaper business? Or should I say gossip rag?"

Both of Watson's bushy eyebrows rose, and he clucked his tongue. "Whatever do you mean, Shell? What I reported wasn't gossip, it was fact. Or wasn't Raymond Terrill murdered on your property?"

"He was," I said. "It would have been nice, though, if you had called me for a quote or to confirm the facts before you splashed it all over the front page."

Watson looked amused. "Would you have spoken to me if I'd called?"

I let out a huge sigh. "Probably not," I said finally. "But you could have at least tried."

"Point taken." Quentin ran his finger along the edge of the counter. "My sources tell me the man was shot, presumably at close range."

"I saw what appeared to be a bullet hole below his ear," I admitted.

"That most likely means he knew his assailant, if he let the person get that close," mused Watson. "Has Josh mentioned to you whether or not they're closing in on anyone?"

"Josh doesn't discuss police business with me," I said shortly.

"Oh, I thought perhaps in this particular case he might—since his cousin is one of the suspects."

My head jerked up. "Taylor's a suspect? Where did you hear that?"

Quentin shook his finger again. "Now, now. You know I can't tell you that. But I have heard from several witnesses that Taylor and Terrill had a few arguments—loud ones—both at the theater and at the inn."

"Terrill was a volatile kind of guy," I responded. "My mother can attest to that."

"Yes, I spoke briefly with Clarissa." Watson's brow furrowed at the memory. "She rather reluctantly confirmed the fact that Terrill and Taylor were ex-lovers, and from all accounts their breakup didn't end well."

"I can't speak for that," I said, "but Taylor wasn't the only person that Terrill had a relationship with."

"That's true. Terrill was quite the ladies' man in his day."

"I heard he and Noelle Boyd also had a thing."

Watson's lips twisted in a grimace. "Ah, yes. Ms. Boyd. She was quite forthcoming about her relationship with Terrill—a little too much so, perhaps. And very willing to point a finger at Ms. Tyson, I might add."

"That doesn't surprise me," I said dryly. "I got the feeling there's a bit of professional jealousy there."

Watson tapped at his chin. "Ms. Boyd seems to be an enigma, that's for sure. And then there's Tim Scott, who I believe both you and Gary know quite well. He had issues with the deceased too."

"Yes, Tim and Noelle and Taylor all had issues with Terrill," I said. "I'm sure a lot of other people did as well."

"True, but how many of them are here in Fox Hollow?"

I leaned across the counter. "I don't know, but someone killed the man. He had an important meeting yesterday at the McCloud Building with someone. Maybe that led to his death."

Watson's eyes narrowed. "A meeting, you say?"

I shot him a shocked look. "You mean your gaggle of informants didn't keep you apprised of it? Yes, he had a meeting with someone there yesterday. He canceled a read-through of the play to go to it. I know, because I was there."

Watson fiddled in his jacket pocket, whipped out a pen and notebook. "No one even mentioned him going to the McCloud Building to me," he muttered. "Damn."

I felt an odd sense of triumph at Watson's obvious discomfiture. "Regardless, the killer had to be someone he knew—someone he trusted."

Watson looked up from his notebook. "Why do you say that?"

I paused. I'd been about to say because he'd been shot at close range, but I stopped because I wasn't sure if the police had released the cause of death. I shrugged. "Just an educated guess," I said. "After all, he was killed in the shed, and it's not very big. Plus, he'd told me he was locking the door, so I just assume he must have let whoever killed him in."

"That makes sense." Watson snapped his notebook shut and jammed it back into his jacket pocket. "Well, thanks for the info, Shell. I'll be seeing you."

"Not so fast," I said. "Since I'm the one who gave you the lead on the McCloud Building, I'd appreciate it if you'd let me know what, if anything, you find out."

"A little tit for tat, eh? Well, all right. Why not."

He shot me a toothy smile and headed for the door. He jerked it open and almost collided with Sue Bloodgood. He pushed past her, and Sue shook her head and made her way over to my counter. "What's his problem?" she asked.

"Life in general, I think," I said with a light laugh. "He was here pumping me for more information on Terrill's murder."

"Oh, that!" Sue rolled her eyes. "Who hasn't he pumped? He was over at the theater on the heels of the police, trying to question anybody he could corral." Her lips curved upward in a smile. "He tried to strong-arm your mother, and she let him have it, in spades. She gave me a blow-by-blow reenactment."

"Now *that* I would have liked to have seen." I gave Sue a quick once-over. "Is everything all right? You look a bit frazzled."

Sue put a hand self-consciously to her cheek. "Do I? Well, business has been booming lately. Your mother has been a big help, Shell. She put me in touch with a few people who had good high-end items for consignment, and two of them sold."

"Really? That's wonderful."

"It is, but . . . I didn't realize how much work it is to source out high-end antiquities. You really have to know what you're looking at. That's why I'm so grateful that your mother decided she wanted to invest in my store." She let out a chuckle. "I have to admit, she shocked me a bit when she offered. I honestly didn't figure that she'd want to stick around Fox Hollow."

"Mother can be full of surprises. I'm glad it's working out, though."

"Yeah, me too." She paused again. "Have you spoken to Josh lately?"

"I saw him this morning," I said. "He had some more questions about finding Terrill's body, and then, of course, I got the obligatory warning not to mess in his investigation."

95

Sue reached out to squeeze my hand. "You know that he's only trying to keep you out of danger, right?"

"I know, but he forgets Terrill was killed on my property. If that doesn't involve me, then I don't know what does."

"True. That must have been awful, stumbling across him like that."

"Oh, I don't know," I answered with a wry smile. "You know, once you've seen one dead body, you've seen 'em all."

Sue laughed. "Very funny. Still, it's got to be upsetting."

"I wouldn't recommend it."

Sue eased one hip against my counter. "I was talking to Taylor earlier. She was upset."

"Over Terrill's death?"

"That, and she said Riser was grilling her pretty hard. Wanted to know her whereabouts on the night Terrill was killed, practically minute by minute."

I felt my heart start to hammer hard in my chest, but I strove to make my tone of voice as casual as possible. "Really? I wonder why?"

"Probably because everyone and their brother told the police about the arguments that Taylor and Terrill had." Sue paused. "She told me they dated for a while."

"Yes, I'd heard that."

"Taylor was the one who broke the relationship off, and Terrill hated that. She said he was a big control freak, and he flipped when he didn't control a situation. He held the breakup against her."

"If he made her so miserable, why did she consent to work with him?"

"Exactly what Riser asked her. She said that regardless of their personal interaction, Terrill was an excellent director and she always learned a lot from working with him. She felt that she, at least, could put personal feelings aside and not let it interfere with business. She also told Riser that Terrill wasn't as successful as she in that department."

"So, are the police looking at Taylor as a suspect in his death?"

"I think they were, but fortunately she was visiting a friend in Closter at the time Terrill was killed."

I took a deep breath and exhaled slowly as I recalled what Gary had said to me earlier. "She can prove that?"

Sue frowned. "I guess so. She gave them her friend's name—Jordan something, Rich or Richmond, something like that—and she told them she borrowed

Josh's SUV to go visit her. She even has a receipt where she stopped for gas."

"That's good. And this friend can verify she was with her when Terrill was killed?"

"I would think so."

"That's good to hear," I said. Maybe Gary had been mistaken. He'd admitted he wasn't entirely certain, and it was dark. Maybe the SUV was a different color or make than Josh's. Maybe he'd been mistaken about the racks. But even as the thought passed through my mind, I knew deep down it wasn't very likely. If there was one thing Gary was an expert on, other than women, it was car makes and models.

"Anyway," Sue's voice broke into my thoughts, "I was on my break and I just figured I'd come over and say hello. What with my expanding business and all, we haven't seen too much of each other lately, save for the other night."

"Yeah, that was fun. We should all do it again soon, before Taylor leaves town."

"Well, *Our Town* will be running for a month so we should have plenty of time to plan a get-together." Sue glanced at her watch. "I'd better get back. See ya."

Sue left, and I pulled out my iPhone, called up a search engine, and typed in *Jordan Rich, Closter, Connecticut* and hit Enter. No Jordans with the last name of Rich came up, but I got three Jordan Richmonds, two Jordan Richters, and one Jordan Richman. I checked their ages, and was able to eliminate two out of the three Richmonds and one Richter. I was about to choose one of the remaining Jordans to call when my phone rang. It was Tim Scott.

"Hey, Shell. How's it goin'?"

"I should be asking you that, Tim," I answered.

I could hear the agitation in his voice. "That Detective Riser is like a little pit bull. I told her that I was asleep alone in my room at the time Terrill was killed but she keeps questioning me on it like she expects to trip me up or something. And I can't even talk about how she's been dogging Taylor. Thank goodness she's got an alibi."

"Yes, visiting her friend Jordan something, right?"

"Yeah, Jordan Richter. They went to college together. Listen, Shell, I need a favor."

I gleefully crossed all the other Jordans off my list. "Sure, Tim. What do you need?"

"Well, Terrill mentioned he had a notebook with some notes on a production of *Our Town* he did a few years ago, and we thought maybe it might be of some help. Only problem is . . . they're probably in one of his boxes in your shed."

I couldn't help but shiver. I hadn't been inside the shed since I found the body. "You want me to look for them?"

"If it wouldn't be too much trouble. It would really be a big help to us. Not that Clarissa isn't a good director, but . . ."

"But she's not a pro. I know. Sure, I'll take a look when I get home. I close at seven tonight, so I'll go right up to the shed."

"Thanks, Shell. Talk to you soon."

I disconnected from Tim, and then dialed Jordan Richter's number. I got a pleasant, well-modulated voicemail. I really didn't know what to say on a message, so I decided to call back later.

. . .

I closed up at seven and went directly home. Gary was still out with Olivia, so I fed the cats, changed into jeans and a flannel shirt, and then decided to take my trek to the shed. Princess Fuzzypants squatted by the door and looked at me with wide gold eyes.

"You want to come with me, don't you?" I asked the cat.

"Merow."

"Well, why not. Maybe you'll give me some sort of clue as to what happened to Terrill that night."

Together we walked to the shed. I noticed that someone had come by earlier in the day and taken down the crime scene tape. Good thing, because I'd planned on entering anyway. I switched on the light and stared at the mountain of boxes in the corner beside the desk.

"Oy," I said, putting my hands to the sides of my face. "Where to start?"

Even Princess Fuzzypants looked confused. I looked at the cat. "You could take a nap while I go through the boxes," I suggested.

She looked at me and her whiskers twitched as if she were considering the idea, then her gold eyes narrowed and she jumped on top of the desk. I noticed several papers scattered across its top—things Terrill might have been working on, perhaps? I looked at the cat. Was she trying to tell me something?

I bent over the desk and sifted through the papers. Most of them were scrawled, barely legible notes on the current production. On one paper he'd written down very uncomplimentary things about Wilma's performance, and a few other actors. He had scrawled: *Improvement needed* next to Taylor's name. Beside Noelle's was one word: *Hopeless*. As I lifted up the pile of papers to move them to the other end of the desk, a business card fluttered to the floor. I picked it up. *Horace Wagenstein, Attorney at Law. Wagenstein, Brooks and McSnell. McCloud Building, Fourth Floor, Fox Hollow, Ct.*

I tapped the card against my chin. McCloud Building. Was Wagenstein the mysterious meeting he'd had that day? Why would he be seeing a lawyer?

I slid the card into the pocket of my plaid tunic and decided to turn my attention to the boxes. Finish one task before starting another was something my father had taught me from a very young age. I walked over to the stack of boxes and opened the flaps of the top box. Princess Fuzzypants jumped up on the stack beside that one, craning her neck trying to get a look inside. The smell of smoke had settled inside the carton. The princess sniffed, then let out a loud merow.

"Yeah, I'm not too thrilled with the smell either," I told the cat.

The papers were all loose inside the carton. I pulled out a handful and took them over to the space I'd cleared on the desk and spread them out. The cat hopped onto the desk and watched me, sniffing at everything and occasionally batting at a paper with one paw.

As I sifted through the pile, I couldn't help but wonder how one man could generate so much paper. Especially in today's age. One would think he'd have kept his notes on a laptop, or a tablet. It would have been far more efficient. Then again, my mother had said that Terrill was old-fashioned in many ways. This, apparently, was one of them.

The princess, bored, started sniffing around the second box. She put one huge paw on the top of the carton, and the top caved in. She jumped back, causing the box to topple over. It landed on its side, sending the contents scattering across the shed floor.

"Great," I muttered. I bent to start picking up the scattered contents and noticed that the princess had a piece of paper stuck to one of her paws. I went over to the cat, knelt down, and gently pried the sheet free of her nails. I held it up for a closer look. The paper was rose-tinted, and across the top of the page the words *Fox Hollow Players* was printed in gold embossed lettering. I noticed something else too: the note wasn't written in Terrill's small, angular penmanship. This writing was large and flowing. The message was crisp and to the point:

You are a horrible person, and I wish you were dead.

The note was signed simply "T."
T. for Taylor?

Thirteen

For a second all I could do was stare at the note. Was that Taylor's handwriting? I'd never seen it, so I couldn't be sure. The only two people with the initial *T* were Taylor and Tim, and I was fairly certain this wasn't Tim's handwriting. If I recalled correctly, his handwriting was small and his letters tilted slightly to the left. Besides, Tim wasn't the type to put something like this in a note. If he wanted to call Terrill a horrible person, he'd do it to his face.

I set the note on the desk and then knelt down and started to gather up the scattered contents of the box, glancing at each one as I worked. A great many were in Terrill's handwriting, notes on the actors and the production, the tone of which was generally unflattering. I noted that he had quite a bit to say about Taylor and Noelle's performances, not much of which was complimentary about either woman. His notes on the regular troupe weren't much better, and the few things he'd jotted down about the theater itself would have made Garrett Knute's blood boil, I was sure. I finally came across one on Tim Scott:

> *Tim should learn to mind his own business and concentrate*
> *on learning more about directing and less on being a cheerleader*
> *for TT. He obviously hasn't learned how to recognize real talent.*

Ouch, I thought as I shoved that note into my pocket. I knew Tim wouldn't have taken kindly to that, if he'd ever read Terrill's note. Then again, if he had, maybe he would have left Terrill a note like the one I'd just found. While the note wasn't exactly a threat, it wasn't a love letter either. And Josh deserved to know about it, regardless of who might have written it.

Suiting action to my thoughts, I whipped out my cell phone. The princess, who'd settled her queenly form across the edge of the desk, looked at me as I pressed Josh's speed dial number. "Merow," she said.

"I know," I said to the cat. "But how can I not tell him?"

Josh's phone kicked over to voicemail. I explained that I was sorting through Terrill's boxes in my shed at Tim Scott's request, and I'd come across something that might or might not be related to Terrill's death. I didn't mention anything about Taylor, just asked him to return my call as soon as possible.

I finished sorting through the loose papers. Nothing else of interest came to light. I shoved them all back into the box, pushed it over to the side, and returned to the box I'd first started rummaging through. I pulled out another handful of loose papers and thumbed quickly through them. Nothing stood out, so I dived in for more. In the middle of the stack I came across a cream-colored envelope, with *Ray* written across the front in the same flowing handwriting as the note on the Fox Hollow Players stationery. I eased one hip against the edge of the desk, took a deep breath, and opened the envelope. Inside was a single sheet of paper, which I unfolded. It was dated three years ago, and the message was short and concise:

> Ray:
> I'm sorry that you feel differently, but I can't pretend to love you when I don't. Our relationship was good while it lasted. Please don't spoil my memories of you with your cruelty. I would hate to remember you as a horrible person.

The note was signed simply "T."

I looked at the date again. It coincided with the time frame during which Taylor and Terrill were reputed to be having an affair. I felt the knot in my stomach tighten.

I dived into the box again, and this time I pulled out a small black notebook. One glance at the inside page, entitled "Notes on *Our Town*," assured me this was the book Tim had requested I find. I'd just replaced everything in the box when I heard a *tap tap tap* on the shed door. I whirled around and saw Josh framed in the doorway, and let out a gasp of surprise.

"Hey, I didn't mean to startle you," Josh said. "I just went off-duty a little bit ago, and I only just checked my messages. I came right over."

He stepped inside, and I got a better look at him. He was wearing cotton duck khakis and a leather jacket over a "Fox Hollow PD" T-shirt. The ends of his hair looked slightly damp, as if he'd just gotten out of the shower. That thought prompted my imagination to wander to places it probably shouldn't, and I quickly averted my gaze. "Thanks for getting here so quick," I said. "You needn't have rushed though. I mean, it's not an emergency or anything."

He walked over to the desk. Princess Fuzzypants struggled to a sitting position, let out a soft meow. Josh paused to stroke her head, and the princess let out a rumbling purr. He gave the princess's head a final pat, then turned to me. I saw his "cop face" firmly in place, and his tone shifted to authoritative as he asked me, "What did you find?"

"Tim Scott asked me to do him a favor and look through Terrill's boxes for this." I held up the notebook. "It's notes on an old production of *Our Town* Tim thought my mother might find useful. Anyway, the princess knocked over one of the boxes and when I was scooping up the papers, I found this."

I slid the first note across the desk to him. He picked it up and looked at it, and I saw the muscles in his jaw tighten. He swallowed. "Where exactly was this?" he asked, without looking up.

I pointed to the box. "In this one. Actually, the princess found it. The edge of the note was stuck to her paw." I paused. "Then, in another box, I found this. It's dated three years ago."

I handed him the second note. Josh read it, then looked up. His eyes held a faraway look. He gestured toward the boxes. "What is all this?"

"Terrill's notes. Apparently he took them with him when he traveled."

Josh nodded and then turned his attention back to the note. He stared at it as if transfixed.

I moved closer, laid my hand on his arm. "That's Taylor's handwriting, isn't it?" I asked softly. "On both notes?"

He waited a few seconds, and then raised his gaze to meet mine. "Yes," he said. His head dipped again. I really didn't know what to say. Finally he reached inside his pocket for his phone. "I have to call the station," he said in a terse tone. "Someone else will have to deal with this."

He stepped away from the desk. I stood and watched him, feeling helpless. I didn't know Taylor very well, but I liked her. I couldn't imagine her shooting anyone in cold blood, as Terrill had been. But those two notes could put her in a different light, at least as far as the police were concerned. Then there was the question of her borrowing Josh's car the night of the murder. Although, according to Sue, she had an alibi.

Josh slid his phone back into his pocket and turned to me. "Amy's on her way," he said.

I wrinkled my nose. "Why did you feel you had to call Detective Riser in on this, Josh?"

He let out a long sigh. "Because, Shell, I'm not sure I can be objective—not about this case."

"Because of these notes?"

"No—there are other things."

"Such as?"

He shoved his hands deep into his jacket pockets and stared off into space for several seconds. Then he looked at me. "You know Taylor borrowed my SUV the night Terrill was killed."

"Yes, you told me. She was visiting a friend."

"So she says."

I cocked my head at him. "You don't believe her?"

I heard the pain in his voice as he answered. "I want to. I went to the woman's house to verify Taylor's alibi. Her landlady told me that she'd gone off on some sort of retreat—wouldn't be back for two weeks."

I raised an eyebrow. "Maybe the landlady could vouch for Taylor?"

"She was home that night, but she kept dozing off while she was watching TV. She knows that Jordan was home, at least for part of the night. She can't vouch for certain for the time frame between one and one thirty, which is when the coroner placed the time of death." He removed one hand from his jacket pocket, reached out to stroke the princess, who'd shifted her position to rub against him.

"And what did Taylor say?"

"She said she was with this friend till after one, and then she drove home."

"So right now you just have her word? What about her gas receipt? Sue mentioned that Taylor stopped for gas."

"Yes, she did—on the way there, which was hours earlier. She'd have had plenty of time to circle back and do the deed."

I bit down hard on my lip. I could see why Josh was upset. "I know that note looks bad, but—it's all circumstantial evidence, Josh. There's no tangible evidence that Taylor was anywhere near the shed on the night—" I broke off with a little gasp as Gary's words came back to me.

Josh looked at me sharply. "What's the matter, Shell? What are you keeping from me?"

"I-it's really not my place to say," I stammered. "Has Gary called you?"

"Gary?" Josh pulled out his phone and a few seconds later I heard Gary's voice: "Say, Detective Bloodgood—Josh. This is Gary Presser. Give me a call when you have a chance. I may have some news to relate about the night of Terrill's murder."

Josh replaced the phone in his pocket. "You know what Gary wants to tell me?"

"Yes. He remembers seeing a dark SUV peal away from the corner shortly before we found the body."

Josh's eyes narrowed. "A dark SUV? Could he be more specific?"

"I can't speak for him, of course, but . . . he thought it might have been yours."

Josh's face paled. He looked as if all the life had suddenly been sucked out of him. His shoulders sagged, and he leaned heavily against the desk.

"That-that's what I was afraid of," he murmured. "I had a feeling Taylor might be . . . lying."

"Lying about visiting her friend? Or killing Terrill?"

Josh swallowed. "Visiting her friend. Maybe the other too."

"Oh, no," I cried. "I don't know Taylor very well, Josh, but I don't think she's the type who would deliberately kill someone."

Josh moved his foot in a circle and studied the tip of his shoe. "I understand they had a bad breakup," he said at last.

"I heard that too, but I believe any hard feelings were all on Terrill's side. If anyone was being badgered, it was Taylor."

"What makes you think that?"

I tapped at my stomach. "Gut intuition."

Josh looked down at the notes he held in his hand. "Normally I trust that intuition of yours, but I'm not so sure this time. In both these notes she calls him a horrible person. A good DA might be able to convince a jury that they show motive, particularly if there are witnesses who say Taylor went bananas after their breakup."

"Witnesses? Like who?"

"Noelle Boyd, for one. She's already mentioned it in her statement."

"I don't know if I'd take Noelle's word on that. She supposedly had an affair with Terrill as well. And Tim Scott said that Noelle was jealous of Taylor because Terrill threw Noelle over for her. Noelle could be lying to get Taylor in trouble as revenge."

"So you think Noelle killed Terrill?"

"I don't know," I admitted. "I'd pick her over Taylor though." I paused and then added, "You know, Noelle and Taylor aren't the only women Terrill had affairs with."

"I'm sure not, but they're the only two around here."

I remembered the conversation Wilma had overheard. "Maybe not," I said slowly. "There could be—"

I stopped speaking as a loud knock sounded on the door, and Amy Riser pushed her way inside the shed. She nodded at me, and then looked at Josh. "You said some new evidence has surfaced?"

Josh nodded and handed Riser the notes. She read them and then looked from me to Josh and back to me again. "Who found this?"

"I did," I said. "I was looking for a notebook in Terrill's things for Tim Scott, and the notes were in one of the boxes."

Riser shot Josh a sympathetic look. "I'm sorry, Josh," she said softly. "You know what the captain will say when I show him this, right?"

Josh's lips set in a grim line. All the fight seemed to have drained out of him. He cleared his throat and said, "He doesn't have to worry. I plan to recuse myself from this case immediately."

"Oh, no," I cried. Both Josh and Amy Riser turned to look at me. Then, to my surprise, Riser walked over and slid an arm around my shoulders.

"He has to, Shell," she said in a quiet tone. "It's getting a little too close to home for comfort. But don't either of you worry." She removed her arm from my shoulders and took a step backward. "I'll make sure everyone involved in this case is treated fairly. No one will get railroaded into anything on just the basis of a note."

She took both notes, dropped them into plastic bags. "After the fact, but still have to preserve the chain of evidence," she said. She shot Josh a look. "I'll see you back at the station?"

He nodded. "Yep. I might as well get this over with."

Amy left, and Josh lingered behind for a few minutes. He took both my hands in his. "Thanks for your support, Shell. I just have to have faith that everything will work out."

I gave his hands a squeeze. "It will, Josh. You'll see."

He bent over, gave me a quick peck on the cheek, and then was gone. I looked at the princess. "I suppose I should also have told Riser about Gary seeing Josh's car here the night of the murder, but I'm sure Josh will tell her."

I picked up the notebook Tim had wanted and then left the shed, the princess at my heels. I knew Josh. In spite of his recusing himself from the case, I was pretty sure that wouldn't keep him from investigating on his own.

No matter what Taylor might or might not have done, she was family, and Josh was nothing if not loyal to his family. I stopped and looked down at the princess.

"Josh won't back off, and neither will I," I said. My fingers closed over the business card I'd shoved into my pocket. I drew it out, turned it over in my hand.

Horace Wagenstein, Attorney at Law.

"Terrill had this card for a reason," I told the cat. "I'm not quite sure just what that was, but I've got a feeling it had something to do with that mysterious meeting he had at the McCloud Building. And I'm not going to rest until I find out just what that was all about."

Fourteen

Purrday and Kahlua greeted me with loud meows when I walked through the door, and Kahlua raised one paw and pointed (accusingly, I thought) at the empty food bowls. Then I remembered I'd left for the shed in such a hurry, I'd forgotten to check on them.

"Okay, okay, I apologize. I just took it for granted Gary would feed you before he took off. He must have figured I'd do it."

I spooned out food for all of them, tuna for Purrday, salmon for Kahlua and the princess, and then my own stomach rumbled. I'd been so intent on completing my mission at the shed I'd forgotten I hadn't eaten a bite since lunch. I opened the refrigerator, but there were no leftovers. I'd have to fend for myself—no easy feat, because I'd gotten spoiled with Gary doing all the cooking. Still, there were a few things I did know how to make.

I inspected the refrigerator's contents, and after some deliberation pulled out two eggs, a block of cheddar cheese, two green peppers and a small onion. I grabbed a frying pan from the cupboard and coated it with butter, then set it on a low flame. I pulled out a carton of milk and cracked the eggs into a bowl. I added the milk, stirred the mixture briskly. I chopped up the peppers and onion and set them on the side, then poured the egg mixture into the pan. I added the peppers and onion, and while that was cooking I cut off a hunk of the cheddar cheese and chopped that up. When the eggs were almost done, I added the cheese and folded it over. A few seconds later, I slid my omelet onto a plate, poured myself a glass of milk, and sat down at the kitchen table to enjoy.

Gary entered through the back door just as I raised the first bite to my lips. He sniffed at the air, then looked over at me. "Wow. Something sure smells good."

"Omelet," I said, and shoved the forkful into my mouth. I chewed, swallowed and then remarked, "Not half bad if I do say so myself."

Gary walked over to inspect my plate. "It smells good. It even looks passable. Dare I say you've learned something from my presence here all these months?"

I lofted a brow at him. "Don't flatter yourself. I could always make an omelet."

"Yeah, but yours were always a bit runny on the inside. That one looks perfecto."

I stuck my tongue out at him. He laughed and moved over toward the refrigerator. He pulled out the carton of eggs, set it on the counter. "Don't tell me you're hungry," I said. "I thought you ate dinner with Olivia."

"I did, but that was a few hours ago." He rubbed at his stomach. "Besides, I only had a hamburger." He took out three eggs, cracked them deftly into the bowl. "I received a very interesting text from Detective Riser a few minutes ago," he said.

I paused, my glass of milk halfway to my lips. "Oh?"

"She'd like to see me down at the station tomorrow morning, nine a.m. sharp." He angled an eyebrow at me. "Any idea what that could be about?"

"Actually . . . yes."

While Gary prepared his own omelet, I filled him in on recent events. When I finished, he let out a low whistle. "That explains the summons," he said. "I've got to be honest, though. I can't absolutely swear that it was Josh's SUV I saw."

"I know." I paused. "Josh seemed to think it might be, though. It seems he has doubts about his cousin."

"Poor guy. That's a tough situation to be in." Gary slid his finished omelet onto a plate, poured himself a glass of milk, and came over to the table. "Those notes sure don't make it look good for Taylor." He picked up his fork, sliced off a hunk of the omelet, popped it into his mouth, then rolled his eyes and let out a sigh. "Ummm. Delicious." He swallowed and then said, "Do you think it was a coincidence? Your finding that note, I mean?"

I stared at him. "What are you getting at?"

"Well, you wouldn't have been poking around in those boxes if Tim Scott hadn't asked you to. I guess what I'm driving at is, do you think Tim might have set it up so you'd find that note?"

I paused. That idea had never occurred to me at all. "I doubt that. Tim's always been supportive of Taylor. Why would he deliberately try to set her up?"

Gary shrugged. "To take the heat off of himself, maybe?"

"You really think Tim could have killed him?"

"I don't want to think that, but you know as well as do I anyone's capable of murder, if the right buttons are pushed."

I let out a deep sigh. "That is true. To be honest, I can't believe either Taylor or Tim capable of such an act."

Gary reached across the table, picked up the card I'd laid there. "What's this?"

"Oh, yeah. I found that among Terrill's things. I'm wondering if it had to do with that mysterious meeting he had at the McCloud Building yesterday."

Gary frowned. "I wonder why he'd be seeing a lawyer. Was he getting ready to sue someone?"

"Knowing Terrill, it's a distinct possibility," I replied. "I know someone who might be able to help." I got up, walked over to the counter and picked up my cell phone. I punched in Rita Sakowski's number. She answered on the second ring. "Hey, Shell. What's up?"

"I'm sorry to call so late, Rita," I apologized. "I know you get up early."

"No problem, honey. What's up?"

"Have you heard of an attorney by the name of Horace Wagenstein?"

"Wagenstein, Wagenstein." I heard the *click click* of Rita's nails as she tapped them against the edge of her phone. "Oh, yeah. He's come into the shop once or twice."

"You wouldn't happen to know what he specializes in, would you?"

"Well, now, I don't. Like I said, he's only come in once or twice and I never engaged him in conversation. His assistant, Juliet Broome, though, is another story. Nice girl. She can be a bit of a gossip, though, if you get her going. Not that there's anything wrong with that," Rita added with a laugh. "I've noticed Juliet always gets chatty when she's plied with sweets. Chocolate chip cookies are her favorite." Rita paused. "Are you in need of a lawyer, Shell? If so, I can recommend a good one."

"Ah, I was thinking about consulting one on a work matter, but it's not a life-or-death situation," I said quickly. "It'll keep for now. Thanks anyway, Rita."

"Anytime."

I disconnected and then looked at Gary. "Can you open the pet shop tomorrow?"

He narrowed his gaze at me. "I guess so. Why? What are you planning to do?"

I came back to the table, leaned over and snatched up the business card. "I was just thinking. I never had a new LLC drawn up after Aunt Tillie died. I thought I might approach Mr. Wagenstein on it, see if he can be of service."

"Uh-huh." Gary set down his glass of milk. "You don't fool me, Shell. Wagenstein won't tell you anything, especially if Terrill is, or rather was, his client. There's a little thing called attorney-client privilege."

"I thought that ceased upon death. It's irrelevant, anyway. I have no intention of plying Mr. Wagenstein with questions about Terrill."

Gary's eyes narrowed. "You don't?"

"His secretary, however, might be a different story. Rita said she's especially fond of chocolate chip cookies." I looked straight at Gary. "You make a delicious chocolate chip cookie."

Gary pushed his chair back. "Oho. So you not only want me to get up early and open up on my day off, mind you, now you want me to bake?"

"Please? Pretty please?" As Gary continued to scowl, I sighed. "Okay. I'll give you the whole weekend off."

He grinned. "Now you're talking. Okay, so . . . do you want plain chocolate chip cookies, or with coconut?"

• • •

At exactly nine a.m. Friday I entered the lobby of the McCloud Building, a box of Gary's chocolate chip cookies tucked away in my tote. There was no receptionist on duty at the wide marble desk that took up one-third of the lobby, but the giant directory mounted on the wall showed that the office of Horace Wagenstein, Esquire, was located on the fourth floor. I got in the elevator, pressed the button, and was immediately whisked upward. I exited the elevator and saw a sign on the wall that indicated Wagenstein's office was down the long, carpeted hallway. I followed the black arrow all the way down to the end and saw two glass doors. Etched on them were the words *Horace Wagenstein, Attorney-at-Law*. I pushed open the doors and found myself in a tiny reception area. Against one wall were several serviceable chairs and a small table loaded with magazines. At the moment, all the chairs were empty. Off to one side was a wood desk with a computer. A young girl with long blonde hair wearing a crisp white shirt sat behind the desk, talking animatedly on her cell phone. The brass nameplate on the edge of the desk read *Juliet Broome*. As I approached I heard her say, "Yeah, and he didn't go home till one a.m. Can you imagine." She glanced up, saw me, and said hurriedly, "I'll have to call you back." She set down the phone and turned to me with a wide smile. "Can I help you?"

"Yes. I'd like to speak with Mr. Wagenstein, if he's available."

Juliet frowned. "Did you have an appointment?"

I shook my head. "No, I'm a walk-in. I got Mr. Wagenstein's name as a referral."

"Really? Which of our clients referred you?"

I hesitated. "Raymond Terrill."

"Raymond Terrill?" Her expression darkened slightly. "I'm sorry, we have no clients with that name."

"No?" I ducked my head to cover my surprise and pulled the business card from my pocket. "I got this from him. Are you sure? He's a tall man, around six-three, dark hair streaked with silver. He's got a British accent, and he's very aristocratic-looking. He's an actor."

Juliet looked at it then shook her head. "I'm sorry, but I don't remember any client of ours that fits that description. And believe me, I think I'd definitely remember someone like that. Anyway . . ." She picked up a pad and a pen. "Mr. Wagenstein is in court this morning, but if you care to give me the particulars of your matter, I can fill him in when he returns and have him call you to set up a time to meet."

"Ah . . . okay. Well, it's about setting up a new LLC."

Her head snapped up, and her carefully penciled brows drew together. "LLC?"

"Yes. I recently inherited my aunt's pet shop, but I never had a new LLC drawn up specifically naming me as the new owner. I thought Mr. Wagenstein might be able to take care of that for me."

Her eyes widened, and she closed her notepad, pushed it off to one side. "I'm afraid Mr. Wagenstein doesn't handle those types of cases," she said.

I let a small sigh escape my lips. "He doesn't?"

"No." She hesitated, then motioned for me to lean in a bit closer. When I did so, she whispered, "You know, you really don't need a lawyer to set up an LLC. There are forms online. You can prepare the paperwork yourself and file it."

"I know, but I had some other questions I wanted to ask Mr. Wagenstein." I gave Juliet Broome my sunniest smile. "I realize he's a very busy man, but I'm quite willing to pay . . . anything."

Juliet shook her head, more emphatically this time. "I'm sorry. His caseload is very tight right now." She let out a dry chuckle. "Apparently there are lots of very unhappy couples around here."

I frowned. "Did you say unhappy couples?"

Juliet nodded. "Oh, yes. The dissolution of the matrimonial state is his specialty. And he's very good at it."

"Is that all he handles?"

"Well, no. But divorce is his specialty, and believe me, they keep him so busy he has very little time for other cases."

My head was spinning. As far as I knew, Terrill wasn't married. He'd have no reason to consult Wagenstein on that. It could have been on another matter, but Juliet had been quite emphatic that no one matching Terrill's description had visited their offices.

My thoughts drifted back to the argument between Melanie and Terrill I'd witnessed in the pet shop. I'd thought at the time Melanie might have slipped something into Terrill's hand. Wagenstein's card, perhaps? I shifted the large tote on my shoulder and let it hang partially open. The smell of Gary's chocolate chip cookies wafted out. I saw Juliet Broome's nose twitch and her head shot up. She sniffed at the air. "Am I nuts," she said, "or do I smell chocolate chip cookies?"

"You aren't nuts," I reassured her. "I forgot I had these cookies in my bag. My roomie baked a whole batch last night." I tilted the mouth of my bag in her direction. "Would you like some?" Without waiting for her to answer, I pulled out the box, set it on the desk, and flipped the top open. Juliet reached up, grabbed a cookie and took a huge bite. Her eyes rolled heavenward. "Oh, my God! This is heavenly. You said your roommate baked them?"

"Yes. Have some more." I pushed the box toward her. Juliet plucked five cookies out of the box, set them on a napkin near her monitor. She practically beamed at me. "Hey, thanks. These are great."

"I'm glad you like them. And I'm sorry to have troubled you," I said. "I only came here because I heard such nice things about Mr. Wagenstein from Mr. Terrill and from Melanie Foster."

Juliet's face immediately brightened. "Oh, so you know Melanie too? She's a sweetheart. I liked her from the first moment she came in here." She broke off another piece of cookie. "I'm surprised she recommended Mr. Wagenstein to you, though."

"I didn't mention why I wanted to consult a lawyer," I lied. "Only that I was in need of one." I paused. "I have to say, though, I'm a bit surprised. I've known Melanie awhile, and I had no idea she was married."

Juliet barked out a laugh. "Want to know something? Neither did she!"

I stared at her. "What?"

The phone rang just then. Juliet excused herself to answer it while I remained standing at her desk, puzzled over her odd remark. Juliet spoke softly into the receiver for a few moments, and when she hung up, turned back to me. "I'm sorry," she said. "But my boss needs me to look up some information for him pronto. As to your situation, if you really feel you need to consult an attorney, there are several others right here in this building who could help you. I'd be glad to write down a few names for you, if you want."

I shook my head. "That won't be necessary. I think I'll take your advice and look up the paperwork online. If I still have questions, I'll come back for that list."

"Sounds good." Juliet gave the box of cookies a longing glance. "And thanks so much for the cookies. It was a great pick-me-up."

She turned back to her computer, a sure sign our conversation was over. I turned away, both disappointed and puzzled. What had Juliet meant by that remark, *neither did she*? How could Melanie possibly not know she was married? And if Terrill hadn't consulted Wagenstein, why did he have his card in his possession? Had Melanie indeed slipped it to him, and if so, why?

It seemed all my visit had done was produce more questions and virtually no answers.

Back in the hallway I glanced at my watch. It was only a little after nine thirty. I decided to swing by Melanie's house. Chances were good she hadn't left for work yet, and I needed to get some answers *now*. I turned and headed down the hallway toward the bank of elevators. A woman, her back to me, stood there, tapping one foot impatiently. The elevator doors opened and she ducked inside. I hurried forward, but I wasn't fast enough. The doors began to slide shut, but not before I caught a glimpse of the woman's profile. I let out a sharp gasp as recognition surged through me.

Taylor Tyson!

"Taylor, wait! Hold the elevator," I called, but the cage had already begun its rapid descent. I pushed open the door marked *Stairs* and raced down, taking them two at a time. I burst into the downstairs reception area in record time, but there was no sign of Taylor anywhere. Of course, I'd only had a quick glimpse, and I could have been mistaken, but . . . I didn't think so. It had been Taylor, all right. What on earth was she doing here?

Outside on the street I paused and took stock of the situation. I needed to talk to both Taylor and Melanie as soon as possible, that was certain. I got in my car and drove straight to Tasty Bites, where the girl behind the counter, Gladys, informed me that Melanie had taken a few days off. "Personal reasons, she said," Gladys remarked in her nasal twang. Next I drove by Melanie's house. There was no car in the driveway, and the house appeared deserted. On an impulse, I fished around in my tote and came up with an old envelope. I scribbled a hasty note on the back:

> *Melanie,*
> *Please give me a call when you can. It's important.*
> *Shell*

I folded the envelope and slid it under the front door, then got back in my car and drove back to Urban Tails. I didn't see Gary there when I walked in, but Robbie was just ringing up a sale. Once the customer left, he turned to me. "Gee, I'm glad you're back, Shell. The joint's been jumpin'."

I smiled. "That's good."

"You had a few calls." He reached beneath the counter and pulled out a few slips of blue paper. He looked at the first one and pulled a face. "Your mother called . . . twice."

Uh-oh. "Swell. What'd she say?"

"She wants you to call her right away. Something about the police coming to the theater."

Apparently Amy Riser wasn't wasting any time. "Okay. Who else?"

Robbie squinted at the paper in his hand. "A Phyllis McInyre. She said she'd call again. Didn't say what it was about."

The name wasn't familiar at all. I shrugged. "Probably someone who wants to know if we carry a particular brand of pet food." I reached out and plucked the papers from Robbie's hand. "Thanks, Robbie."

Back in my office, I called Melanie's number. No answer. When the answering machine kicked on, I repeated the message I'd left on the envelope. I took a deep breath, steeled myself, and dialed my mother's number. She answered on the first ring.

"Crishell. It's about time you returned my calls," she said.

"Hello to you too, Mother," I said. "What's up?"

My mother's voice dropped to a whisper. "The police have been here. Not your Josh, but that other one. You know . . . the woman."

"Amy Riser."

"Yes, her. She's looking for Taylor. Apparently she's not at her hotel, and no one has seen her. She didn't show up for rehearsal, either." My mother let out a long, exasperated sigh. "Honestly, I don't know how I'm going to get this production ready on time when I get absolutely no cooperation from anyone."

"If I know you, Mother, you'll figure it out," I said soothingly.

"Thanks for that vote of confidence, Crishell, but even Houdini got more cooperation from his assistants than I'm getting." Another long, drawn-out sigh. "Anyway, I wanted to know if you'd spoken to Josh today. I thought he might know where Taylor is."

"I haven't seen Josh today, Mother," I said. I decided not to mention my possible earlier Taylor sighting. After all, I wasn't one hundred percent certain it had been her. "But I'll ask him if and when I see him."

"Thank you. And if by some chance she should come by your shop, please tell her Detective Riser needs to speak with her—and I need her to get her carcass down here asap!" I could visualize her putting a hand to her forehead as she added, "I desperately need to get a cohesive reading just once with all cast members present!"

"Will do. By the way, you haven't seen Melanie today, have you?"

"Who?"

"Melanie Foster. The girl who does the catering. Has she been by the theater at all today, by any chance?"

"Oh, yes, now I know who you mean. Now that you mention it, she's been MIA too. They sent some guy today. Crishell, if anyone ever again asks me to direct one of these plays, please . . . tie me to a chair and gag me. It's just not worth all this aggravation."

"Now, Mother, you know you thrive on this sort of thing," I said. "Just stay calm. Everything will work out fine, you'll see."

"Well . . . maybe," my mother said grudgingly. "The power of positive thinking and all that?"

"Exactly. Now, can I ask you a favor? If Melanie should happen to come to the theater, could you ask her to please get in touch with me?"

"If I see her, I'll deliver the message. Oh, dear. Garrett is signaling to me. Now what? I have to go, dear."

"Okay, Mother. Take care and don't wor—"

I stopped speaking. I was talking to air. I leaned back in my chair and nibbled absently on the end of my pen, pondering what my next move should be.

Princess Fuzzypants leapt into my lap and nuzzled her furry head against my chin. I stroked the cat absently. Suddenly the office door opened, and Robbie stuck his head inside. I took one look at his expression and said, "Robbie, what's wrong?"

Before he could answer, he was shoved roughly aside and a woman stepped inside. She wore a pair of dirty jeans and a flannel shirt, and her hair was a mass of frizzy brown curls. The hiking boots she wore had seen better days, too. She fixed piercing blue eyes on me and said in a rough voice, "I'm Phyllis McIntyre. I called earlier. Are you the woman who placed the ad?"

For a moment I was puzzled. "Ad?" I asked.

"Yes, the ad." The woman's gaze fell upon Princess Fuzzypants, who'd been startled when the commotion started. She let out a squeal and pointed to the cat.

"It's true. You've got my cat! My goodness, I never thought I'd see her again."

Fifteen

I was so startled by Phyllis McIntyre's claim that for a few seconds I couldn't speak. Then I found my voice. "Princess Fuzzypants is *your* cat?" I squeaked out.

The blue gaze hardened. "Princess Fuzzypants? Is that what you've been calling her? Lord, that's a mouthful." She made a tsking sound deep in her throat and took a step forward. "Her name is Iris. Here, Iris, good girl. Come to Mommy!"

The cat stared at Phyllis, then her lips peeled back, exposing her sharp teeth. She let out a loud hiss, jumped from my lap and scurried under the desk.

The woman's head jerked up and she pointed an accusing finger at me. "What have you done to Iris? You've turned her against me." Her hand dropped to her side and her lips scrunched up. She looked as if she might cry. "How can I get my cat back, now that you've turned her against me? Why did you put the ad in the paper if you didn't want me to find her?"

I felt a little dizzy, but I tried to keep my expression neutral. I rose from my chair and faced the woman. "Ms. McIntyre," I said. "Are you certain that is your cat? She didn't seem to know you."

Phyllis's sad expression morphed into a sneer. "That's because you've turned her against me."

"Hey, Ms. McMillan would never do anything like that!"

We both turned. I'd forgotten all about Robbie, who was still standing in the doorway. He came forward and faced the woman, hands on his hips, his eyes blazing. "Ms. McMillan is one of the kindest people I know. When Purrday found the princess, she was in a bad way. Ms. McMillan took care of her. You've got a lot of nerve, coming in here and making accusations like that!"

I walked over to Robbie and laid my hand on his arm. "It's okay, Robbie. Why don't you go back out front now. I can handle this."

He looked uncertainly from me to Phyllis then back to me. "Are you sure?"

I nodded, and he left, rather reluctantly. Once the door closed behind him I turned to face her. "Can we talk about this calmly?"

Phyllis shrugged, feet planted apart. "I guess so," she mumbled. "What did that guy mean—when you found her, she was in a bad way?"

"She'd gotten tangled up in some vines. Her paw was sore for a few days, but she's fine now." I hesitated and then said, "She had no collar on her, no identification."

"Iris never liked to wear a collar," she mumbled.

"My cats aren't fond of them either. Is Iris microchipped?"

Phyllis looked puzzled. "Microchipped?"

"Lots of people do it nowadays. A vet inserts a chip about the size of a grain of rice under their skin. That way, if they get lost and are taken to a clinic or an animal shelter, the pet will be scanned for a microchip to reveal their unique ID number. The number is then called into the pet recovery service, and the owner located. My vet checked manually but couldn't detect a microchip. We were going to recheck when her scanner was fixed."

An odd look came over Phyllis McIntyre's face. She shook her head emphatically. "Waste of time. Iris isn't chipped."

The princess emerged from underneath the desk and hopped up onto the chair I'd vacated. Phyllis McIntyre immediately hurried over to the cat. "Here, Iris. It's time we headed home," she said, and reached for the cat. The princess hissed and shrank back in the chair. Undaunted, Phyllis again stretched out her hands. Quick as a flash, the princess's paw snaked out and Phyllis drew back with a little scream. "Oh my gosh," she cried. "That mangy cat scratched me! I'm gonna bleed to death!"

I hurried over and grabbed Phyllis's wrist. There was indeed a long scratch, and a thin stream of red trickled out, but it certainly wasn't gushing blood. "I think you'll be fine," I said. I opened the desk drawer and pulled out alcohol and a Band-Aid. I splashed the alcohol on the wound, and Phyllis grimaced.

"That stings," she muttered.

I put a Band-Aid over the scratch and then looked at her sternly. "The princess certainly doesn't act as if she's your cat," I said. "And you don't act like a cat owner either. No matter how many times my cats have scratched me, I've never referred to them as mangy. Why don't you just admit the truth," I added in a kinder tone. "This isn't your cat, is it?"

Phyllis sighed and pushed her hand through her short crop of hair. "Okay. She's not my cat. I don't own any pets and if truth be told, I really don't want to."

Gee, why was I not surprised by that admission. I folded my arms across my chest and asked sternly, "Then why did you want to claim the princess?"

Phyllis's lips twisted into a grimace. "Because I read that Maine coons are valuable cats, and I thought maybe I could sell her," she admitted. "I heard that pedigreed ones can sell for as much as two thousand dollars. I got into an accident a few months back, and the guy who hit me didn't have insurance. I really could use the cash."

My lips thinned. To be perfectly honest, the woman's candor made me want to throw up. "Tell you what, Phyllis, if you leave now and never come back here again, I won't report you to the police for extortion and fraud."

I apparently didn't have to repeat the offer twice. Phyllis turned on her heel and practically flew out of my office, almost knocking Gary over on her way out. He stared after her, then looked at me. "Dissatisfied customer?"

"Hardly. She tried to tell me the princess was her missing cat Iris."

Gary arched an eyebrow. "I take it the claim was false?"

"She thought she could claim the princess and then sell her for big bucks. I told her if she never came in here again I wouldn't report her to the police."

"That was nice of you. That woman got off easy."

"You can say that again," I said. "I wonder how many more people will pull something like this, just to get their hands on a valuable animal? I don't think I want to find out."

"You can always pull the ad," Gary suggested.

"Good idea." I whipped out my phone and dialed the *Gazette*'s number. A few minutes later I disconnected and looked at Gary. "Done," I said. "June will pull the ad from tomorrow's edition."

"I think that's the smart thing to do."

"So, I guess my next course of action is to see if Gretchen can detect a microchip in the princess. Am I a bad person for hoping that she won't?"

"Not at all. I'm rather fond of that cat myself. She loves my leftovers." Gary walked over and perched on the edge of the desk. "Not to change the subject, but how did your morning sleuthing expedition go? Were my cookies a hit?"

"The cookies were a definite home run. The sleuthing . . . not so much."

I filled Gary in on the morning's events. When I finished, he said, "So, it would seem we're back to square one."

"Much as I hate to admit it, it seems that way," I agreed. "I really need to speak with Melanie. I'm almost positive I saw her pass something to Terrill, and it could have been that business card. If that's the case, I wonder why she did that?"

Gary shrugged. "Who knows. Maybe what you saw has nothing to do with it. Maybe Terrill was just meeting someone there." He cleared his throat and continued, "Olivia and I ran some online searches. We came across an old article in one of those gossip magazines about Noelle Boyd and Terrill. Apparently they had a bit more than just a director-actor relationship."

"Yes, both Mother and Tim hinted that might be the case."

"Well, according to this article they were pretty serious at one point. Even lived together for a bit when Terrill directed her in that play in San Francisco. According to the article, their relationship ended rather abruptly. They hinted at Terrill's roving eye as the reason."

"Terrill certainly was no angel," I said. I couldn't help but think of the note in Taylor's handwriting: *You are a horrible person, and I wish you were dead.* Josh's cousin hadn't seemed the vindictive type. What could he have done to make Taylor write such a thing? As that thought flitted through my mind, I glanced out the back window and saw Taylor hurrying down the alley. "Oh my gosh!" I cried. I jumped up, whipped open the back door and raced outside.

"Shell, where are you going?" Gary called after me.

"Watch the store," I yelled over my shoulder. I raced down the alley, emerging on Broad Street. I looked up and down. No sign of Taylor. Darn! I was just about to turn back when I saw Taylor exiting the drugstore up the street. "Taylor!" I yelled. The girl turned, paused, and then raised one hand in a tentative wave. I jogged quickly over to her. "I'm glad I found you," I said.

"I know. Your mom's probably looking for me. I played hooky today. I woke up with a terrible headache." She opened the bag she held in her hand, and I saw a bottle of aspirin inside. "I just didn't feel like going through all that drama today," she admitted.

"It's drama of a different sort, I'm afraid," I said. I decided not to mention seeing her at the McCloud Building earlier. "Detective Riser is looking for you."

Taylor looked surprised. She turned her hand inward, pointed at her chest. "Me? Why on earth is she looking for me?"

I saw no point in skirting the issue. "I was going through the papers Terrill left in my shed and came across one that said, 'You are a horrible person, and I wish you were dead.' It looked to be in your handwriting."

Taylor met my gaze with a steady one of her own. "He kept that, huh?" she said. "Yeah, I wrote that. He was bugging me about a movie role I'm up for. Production has been postponed indefinitely because the director went into rehab. Terrill wanted me to suggest him for the gig. I told him no way did I want to get involved. So then he said that he'd tell my family just what I did to get considered for that role."

I rose an eyebrow, remembering the conversation I'd overheard in the theater. "Just what is it you did?"

Taylor shifted her weight from one foot to the other. "I had a few dinners with the director. That's all. Nothing happened, but Terrill said my family wouldn't know that. He said he had connections with reporters who could offer convincing—albeit doctored—evidence to the contrary. My relations with my family are less than stellar. I figured they'd probably believe anything Terrill threw at them. I blew my top. I wrote him that note and slipped it under his dressing room door. Childish, I know."

I let out a breath. "Then you need to tell Detective Riser that, Taylor. As soon as possible." I paused. "And it might be a good idea to get a lawyer while you're at it."

She stared at me. "Just because I wrote that he was a horrible person on a note? You can't be serious."

"I'm afraid I am." I hesitated, then plunged ahead. "Taylor, where were you the night Terrill was killed?"

Taylor's eyes narrowed. "You know where I was. I borrowed Josh's SUV to visit my friend. I stayed at her house till one fifteen and then drove back here."

"You weren't back in town earlier? You didn't drive that SUV down my block right around the time Terrill was killed?"

Taylor's eyes widened a bit. "N-no. Why are you asking this?"

"Because Gary is pretty sure he saw Josh's SUV driving down our block right around the time of Terrill's murder."

Taylor lowered her gaze and shifted her weight from one foot to the other. "Really? He's certain?"

"Well . . . no, he's not certain. But he's pretty sure it looked like a Chevy Terrain."

Taylor's head rose, and her chin jutted forward slightly as she answered, "He has to be mistaken, Shell. It wasn't me."

"He seemed pretty positive."

"Well, he's wrong." Her lips thinned. "I'm sure there must be other Chevy Terrains like Josh's around town."

"Maybe so, but not all of them have ski racks."

Her gaze narrowed. "Gary saw ski racks on the SUV?"

I hesitated, then shook my head. "He's not certain of that."

Taylor blew out a breath. "Of course he isn't, because it wasn't Josh's SUV." She glanced at her watch, then put a hand to her head, massaged her temple. "If you'll excuse me, I'll get on down to the police station and straighten this out. Just in case your mother asks if you've seen me, you can tell her I took care of the situation, then went back to my hotel room and to bed. This headache is getting worse by the minute."

Taylor turned and stalked off down the street. I stood there, looking after her. I was relatively certain she was lying. About all of it? Maybe. But most definitely about the SUV.

I just didn't know why, and I sincerely hoped that it wasn't because she *did* kill Raymond Terrill.

Sixteen

I decided to drop by the theater myself and deliver the bad news to my mother that Taylor wouldn't be putting in an appearance today. As I entered the building I spotted Kenny Parsons dragging a ladder over to a light fixture. "Kenny," I called, and walked over to him. His normally somber expression brightened when he saw me. He paused and leaned one elbow against the ladder. "Hello, Sh-sh-shell," he said. "W-what are you d-doing here?"

"Looking for my mother. Is she around?"

He inclined his head toward the auditorium. "S-she's holding court in there, and s-she's not in a real good mood. S-some of the actors haven't s-shown up today."

Great, so apparently Taylor wasn't the only one playing hooky. "Thanks for the info, Kenny," I said.

"I f-f-figure f-forewarned is f-forearmed, ya know. No offense against your mother, Sh-shell, but . . ."

"I know. She can be a handful."

His features relaxed into a grin. "Right."

He started to turn away but I laid a hand on his arm. "Say, Kenny, have you seen Melanie around anywhere?"

"Melanie? You mean the f-food lady?"

I nodded. "Yes. I've been trying to get in touch with her. I went by the deli and they said she took a few days off, but I thought maybe she might have stopped by here."

Kenny shook his head. "Nope. Haven't s-s-seen her."

"Okay. Thanks anyway. If you should happen to see her, could you tell her I'm looking for her?"

"No problem." He paused and then said, "How about what h-happened to that Mr. Terrill? That was a s-shock, huh?"

"It certainly was."

Kenny scratched at his head. "I hate to s-speak ill of the dead, but he wasn't a nice man. H-he gave me the creeps. Kept s-staring at me like I h-had two heads. And he wasn't nice to Miss Taylor at all."

"So I've heard."

I started to turn away but Kenny kept on talking. "I heard he was killed on your property." At my nod he added, "That must have been awful for you. He was renting s-s-space from you, right?"

"In a manner of speaking," I replied. "I still have all of his stuff in my shed."

Kenny frowned. "What's gonna happen to it? Are you gonna throw it out? If you need s-someone to get r-rid of it, I'm always available for extra work."

"Thanks, Kenny, but right now I'm leaving it be. It could be considered evidence. I think I'll just let the police decide."

The corners of Kenny's lips twitched. "Oh, right. Your boyfriend."

"Actually, Josh isn't on the case. It's Amy Riser."

Before Kenny could comment, the auditorium door opened and Garrett Knute came out. He spotted Kenny and me and hurried over to us. "Parsons, just the man I'm looking for. There's a board loose on the stage. Could you get in there and fix it right away?"

Kenny frowned. "I was just gonna f-fix that broken light."

Garrett waved his hand. "The light can wait. I'm afraid someone will take a header on that board and believe me, I do not need that added drama right now."

"S-sure thing."

Kenny picked up the ladder and shuffled off. Garrett turned to me. "I'm glad you dropped by, Shell. Your mother is in a rare mood."

"I gathered that when I spoke with her earlier."

Garrett reached up to rub at his forehead. "I can't say as I blame her, though. First Noelle calls in sick, then Taylor pulls a disappearing act . . . and we've got less than two weeks before the darn play opens."

I looked at him. "Noelle is sick?"

"She called and said she had a sore throat." He rolled his eyes. "Stacey took the call and said that Noelle didn't sound all that bad to her. To tell you the truth, she's been acting rather strangely ever since Terrill died."

"Well, they were supposed to have been pretty close at one point. Maybe his death hit her harder than she figured."

"Hm, maybe so. But I don't think they were all that close. It seemed more like a love-hate relationship to me. Emphasis on the hate." His pocket started to buzz, and he whipped out his cell, looked at the screen and groaned. "Sorry, Shell. I've got to take this. Good luck with your mother."

"Thanks." Garrett walked off, and I turned toward the auditorium.

125

Halfway there I paused to look at some of the new posters that had been hung—okay, I admit it, I was stalling. As I stood there looking the posters over, I heard the front door open and close. I glanced over my shoulder and saw a women enter. She glanced around, saw me, and immediately started to walk right over. I didn't know her, but she seemed familiar somehow. She was tall and slender with auburn hair that brushed her shoulders, and sideswept bangs. I placed her age at around my mother's, maybe a little younger. As she approached I noticed that her eyes were a spectacular shade of blue, and wondered if they might be colored contacts. She paused before me and stood, one hand on her hip.

"You're Shell Marlowe," she said.

"Yes, I am, but I prefer to go by Shell McMillan now."

"You have your mother's smile," she said, and held out her hand. "I'm Kristi Marchall. Your mother and I have worked together a few times."

Now I knew why she'd seemed familiar. Kristi Marchall was a Hollywood talent agent, and for a brief time had represented my mother. The last I'd heard, she'd had a breakdown of some sort and left agenting. "Kristi, of course. How have you been?"

"Much better these past ten years," she said. "I've gotten back into agenting, but it's a bit slow going these days. I lost all my old clients and most of my contacts, but . . . life goes on, right?"

I was glad to see Kristi had such a positive attitude. "What are you doing here in Fox Hollow?" I asked.

"It's actually a charming little town—not what I expected. The Fox Hollow Inn is so quaint." Kristi shifted her bag on her shoulder. "I'm in town to interview a potential new client. Noelle Boyd."

I let out the breath I'd been holding. I'd been certain she was going to name Taylor as her potential new client. "Oh, I am sorry. I just heard that Noelle called out sick today."

Kristi frowned. "That's odd. I spoke with her not an hour ago and she told me she'd meet me here."

"That is odd," I agreed. "Maybe my mother can shed some light on all this."

Both of Kristi's perfectly penciled brows rose. "Your mother? Is she here?"

"Yes, as a matter of fact she is. She's directing the play, actually."

"She is!" Kristi's face fell. "Is that on account of what happened to Ray Terrill?"

126

I nodded. "Yes. She's in the auditorium now. I was headed there to speak to her."

"Fabulous. I'll walk with you." Kristi fell into step beside me. "A shame about Ray Terrill," she said.

I looked at her. "Did you know him?"

She nodded. "Yes. I knew him early on, before he was touched by the bloom of fame. I even placed several clients in his productions." She paused, a wistful look on her face. "He could be a handful, but he could also be sweet, thoughtful and caring."

"You sound as if you were . . . close," I said.

"We were." She paused and then added, "For a while we were very close, if you get my drift. And then I found out his little secret—actually, it wasn't so little."

My ears perked up at that comment. "His secret?"

"Yes, it's the main reason I broke things off with him. I just couldn't abide the fact that he—" Kristi paused again as the strains of "Music of the Night" emanated from her tote bag. She dipped her hand inside, pulled out her cell phone, glanced at the screen. "I'm sorry," she said with an apologetic shake of her head, "I have to take this. You go on in. I'll catch up later."

Kristi moved off, cell to her ear. I stood there for a moment, looking after her. Her words reverberated in my brain: *I found out his little secret.* She'd said it was the reason she broke things off with him. What could it be?

I started for the auditorium. As I reached for the handle, the door burst open and Fannie Adams, one of my best customers, popped out. She saw me and immediately placed her hand on my arm. "Shell, I'm so sorry. Are you all right?"

"Yes, I'm fine. I didn't realize that you were in this production, Fannie."

"I wasn't supposed to be." Fannie pulled a face. "I was recruited by my cousin Ida at the last minute. She begged me to take over her part. She's really busy this month and just couldn't swing it." Fannie grinned. "I hate to see a grown woman cry, so I agreed. I only hope I don't flub my lines. Thank God I haven't too many."

"I'm sure you'll do fine," I assured her. "Is rehearsal over?"

Fannie pulled a face. "For the most part. It's kind of hard to rehearse when no one else shows up."

"No one?"

127

"Well, Taylor was a no-show, and the male leads might as well have been too, for all the good they were. Everyone was off their game today—at least it made me look good." She straightened the silk scarf around her neck and leaned closer to me. "Your mother is fuming."

I grimaced. "Great. I heard Noelle Boyd called in sick too."

Fannie pulled a face. "Um, yeah."

I shot Fannie a look. "You don't think she's really sick?"

"A troublemaker is what I think she is," spat Fannie. She glanced quickly around, then took my arm and pulled me into a corner. "I heard her on the phone yesterday. I don't know who she was talking to, but she was telling them that Taylor might have moved up a notch or two on the suspect list in Terrill's death."

I struggled to keep my expression bland as I answered, "Really?"

Fannie nodded. "I suppose I shouldn't have eavesdropped, but she wasn't talking in a particularly low tone. I heard her say she was struggling with going to the police. Apparently she was out walking by the gazebo the night Ray died. She was by that intersection when all of a sudden this SUV came racing by."

I felt my chest tighten. "SUV?"

"Yes, a dark one. She said it was going so fast she thought it might jump the curb. She had to leap up on the grass to avoid getting hit."

"Did she see the driver?"

Fannie's lips drooped downward. "She claims that she only got a quick glimpse, but she was positive it was Taylor. She told whoever she was talking to that she hated ratting on a fellow actor, but she felt it was her duty." Fannie sniffed. "Duty, my arse. If you ask me, she's jealous of Taylor. Honest, I wouldn't put it past her to be making all this up. Who goes for a stroll at one a.m.?"

I'd done that, but I refrained from mentioning it to Fannie. Instead I asked, "Was that the time she mentioned? One a.m.?"

"I think she said it was somewhere between one fifteen and one thirty."

I swallowed. If Noelle was correct, then that definitely blew Taylor's alibi of being with her friend until one fifteen. Of course, as Fannie had said, the possibility did remain that Noelle could be lying. "Did she say anything else?"

"Yeah. She said that she was trying to give 'poor Taylor' the benefit of the doubt. And then she said, and I'll never forget the syrupy sweet tone she used when she said it, 'cause I almost threw up, 'If she did kill Ray, he probably deserved it.' Did you ever?"

"No, I didn't," I said grimly. "I know Terrill wasn't very well liked, but I just met someone who had a far different opinion of him. Kristi Marchall."

Fannie's eyes widened. "The agent? I heard her talking about her yesterday. She said that she'd just signed on with Kristi, and she was up for some sort of big movie role. If she got it, she might have to leave immediately. Good riddance, I say." Fannie glanced at her watch. "Oops, I've got to get moving myself. Nice seeing you, Shell."

Fannie hurried off, leaving me to ponder over our conversation. I had to agree with Fannie. I had a feeling that Noelle didn't mind at all putting the screws to Taylor. There did seem to be some sort of jealousy on Noelle's part when it came to the other girl, and I felt certain it had to do with Terrill. Noelle had said their liaison was over, but had it really been? And even if she was a royal pain and a bit of a diva, I shuddered to think how my mother might react if Noelle had to pull up stakes and leave the production. I sighed. Even though Terrill was dead, his legacy of being a jinx still seemed to be in full force.

As I started for the auditorium once more, the side door banged open and Melanie hurried inside. She stopped dead still when she saw me. "Shell, hi," she squeaked out.

"Melanie," I cried. "I've been trying to get in touch with you."

Melanie leaned against the wall. She rubbed at the back of her neck with one hand. There were dark circles, like smudges of soot, under both her eyes. She looked tired.

I moved close to her, peered at her face. "You look terrible," I said.

"Thanks." She rubbed at her jaw. "I haven't slept since . . . since I heard the news about Raymond."

"I can believe that." I looked her right in the eyes. No sense playing coy. "You knew him, didn't you? Before he even came here, you had some sort of relationship with him."

Melanie looked startled, and her gaze darted away from me. "How did you know?"

"You mentioned his being a control freak. You said that he still was, which indicated a prior relationship to me."

"I should have known you'd figure it out," she said wryly. "You're really good at this sort of thing, Shell. Maybe you can even figure out who killed him. Lord knows there were probably many people who would have liked to have done the deed—women especially."

I couldn't argue that. I took a quick glance around the lobby. I noticed that Kenny had returned from the auditorium and was kneeling close to where we stood, fiddling with something in his tool chest. I doubted he was eavesdropping, but I wasn't taking any chances. I put my arm around Melanie's shoulders and steered her over to a small alcove with a bench at the far end of the lobby. Once we were seated, I took both her hands in mine. "Melanie, just what was going on between you and Ray Terrill?" I asked.

Melanie ducked her head. "What makes you ask that?"

"I think you know," I replied. "Something transpired between the two of you. I'd like to know what it was. Maybe I can help."

"You're right, Shell. We did know each other—very well." She raised her gaze to meet mine, and I could see tears forming in the corners of her eyes. "We were married," she said simply.

Seventeen

That suspicion had been forming in the back of my mind; still, it was a shock to hear it said out loud. I stared at Melanie. "I'm sorry . . . did you say you were *married* to Raymond Terrill?"

"Yes." She let out a sigh. "It's a long story."

I set my lips. "I've got time."

Melanie looked down at her hands for a few minutes and then said quietly, "It was years ago. We were both seniors at USC—kids, really. We were both in the drama club, but our paths had never crossed until we were both working on a production of Shakespeare's *As You Like It*. He was the assistant director, and I was in charge of costumes. Long story short, we butted heads a few times, and our mutual dislike of each other turned into mutual attraction. We were married a week after graduation."

I blinked. "I never heard that Terrill was married. Every bio or article I've ever read on the guy paints him as single. A ladies' man."

Her lips twisted into a wry smile. "That he was. And that was the main reason our marriage flopped. Oh, he'd always been a bit of a flirt, but like every other starry-eyed woman in love, I thought marriage would change him. Boy, was I wrong.

"Anyway, we'd only been married a short time when Ray got his big break. Assistant director to a major film. Only thing was, it was to be filmed in London, and there was no room in the budget for him to bring his wife along— or so he led me to believe."

"He lied?"

She shrugged. "To this day, I'm not sure. But it took less than two weeks after he was over there for his photo to hit the major gossip columns. Every night, he had some beautiful young starlet on his arm."

I reached out, covered her hand with mine. "You must have been furious."

She nodded. "I was. I packed my bags, went back home. I swallowed my pride and took my family's 'I told you so's' with my head held high. The picture wrapped, and Ray returned. He hunted me down at my parents', tried to cajole me into coming back to him. He said that all those newspaper items were just that—items planted for publicity. He swore those women meant nothing to him."

"And you believed him?"

"I wanted to. Man, did I want to. But the trust was gone. I told Ray that I'd file for divorce." She paused. "That was when he begged me not to."

"He didn't want a divorce?"

"He said that it would look bad for him if I filed at that particular time. He was trying to build up a reputation, and he didn't need to be painted as the 'bad guy' in the public's eye just yet. He asked me to hold off for two years. At the end of that time, he said, he should be established sufficiently so that a divorce wouldn't matter. He offered to cover all expenses."

"And you agreed."

"Yes. By that time I knew that my future wasn't in Hollywood. My parents were both pretty sick, so I stayed around to take care of them. When they passed, I inherited some money—not much, but enough so that I could be independent. I moved to New York, got a job, and made a new life for myself. I was quite happy, actually. And then on what would have been our second wedding anniversary, I got a check in the mail from Ray for five thousand dollars. So I went out, got a lawyer and got the divorce . . . or so I thought."

I frowned. "I don't understand?"

Melanie took a deep breath. "After I got the divorce, my lawyer introduced me to a financial planner who said he could triple my money in six months. What actually happened was he took me to the cleaners. He and my lawyer were in cahoots. I found out later that I was only one of many people they'd swindled." She paused. "I also found out that my so-called attorney had had his license revoked. He wasn't a practicing attorney when he got me my divorce."

My eyes widened. "Oh my gosh! So you were never divorced from Terrill."

She shook her head. "No. I tried to call him at first, but he wouldn't take my calls. After a while I just gave up. I figured if he ever wanted to get married, he'd track me down and we'd make it legal at that point. I didn't want anything from him, and I had no desire to marry again, so I figured what the heck. So you can imagine how I felt when I found out he was coming here to direct that play."

"He sought you out?"

She nodded. "He was far from the Ray I remembered. He was nasty, arrogant. He said he knew the divorce hadn't gone through, but he'd never bothered to contact me because he'd thought staying married to me might come in handy someday."

"Handy? What did he mean by that?"

"He knew I'd inherited property when my parents died. He was going through financial troubles and he wanted a slice of my inheritance since we were still married at the time they died. I explained about how I'd been swindled, but he wouldn't hear any of it. He told me I had to come up with the cash . . . or else. He needed it to settle a score, he said."

I stared at her. "He threatened you?"

She nodded, and I could see tears start to form at the corners of her eyes. "Back when we were in college, Ray took some rather revealing photos of me. Turns out he'd kept them. He threatened to make them public unless I paid him fifty thousand dollars." She raised her hand to swipe at her cheeks. "You know how judgmental some of the people here in Fox Hollow can be. I'd never have been able to show my face around here again. I didn't have fifty thousand dollars, though. I offered him what I did have, every penny I'd managed to save since I returned to Fox Hollow. Ten grand. He laughed in my face."

"What a prince," I said. "So what happened after that?"

"I saw him in your store that day and tried to reason with him. He insisted that I bring the money to him by the weekend, or he'd send those photos to the *Fox Hollow Gazette*. Your interruption was actually quite timely. It gave me a chance to think. I called Ray later, told him that I thought he was bluffing. Before I'd pay him anything, I wanted to see those photographs. He told me to come by your shed at ten that night and he'd be happy to show them to me."

"And did he?"

"No. As it turned out, I never got to the shed. I stopped by the Rusty Nail in town for a shot of liquid courage, and I'm afraid I can't hold my liquor as well as I used to. Fortunately, Collette Pfeiffer was there and she took me home and stayed with me while I spent most of my time worshipping the porcelain god in the bathroom." She tossed me a wry smile. "Hell of an alibi, right?"

I gave her a thin smile. "I've heard worse."

She pushed some hair out of her eyes. "Yeah, well, someone was watching out for me that night. Collette stayed with me till two in the morning. She made several good strong pots of coffee and baked a loaf of banana bread, and the next day I did have one helluva headache." She paused. "I can't say what might have happened if I had gone to the shed. I might have ended up killing him—but as it stands, I never went near your shed, and I didn't kill Ray."

"I believe you," I said. "If I were you, I'd go to Detective Riser and tell her everything."

"I was thinking about doing just that," Melanie admitted. "If those photos should happen to turn up, it would certainly put me in a bad light. I'd be suspect number one for sure."

"I think that's a good move," I said. I paused and then asked, "Could you think of any reason why Terrill might have visited the McCloud Building the day of his death?"

She stared at me. "Ray was at the McCloud Building?"

"To be honest, I'm not sure," I admitted. "I found Horace Wagenstein's card among his papers and thought maybe he went to consult a lawyer." I looked her straight in the eye. "I know you went to see Wagenstein. His secretary spoke highly of you."

Melanie flushed. "After my little set-to with Ray, I felt it necessary to get legal representation. I had an appointment, but Wagenstein got held up in court. I didn't reschedule—and now I guess it's no longer necessary."

"Did you give Terrill Wagenstein's card?"

Melanie's eyes widened, and she gave her head an emphatic shake. "Lord no! Ray has a whole battery of top-flight lawyers. He didn't need to consult with Wagenstein."

"Okay. And one other thing—did you ever hear the stories about Terrill being considered a jinx?"

"A jinx? No, I haven't."

I repeated what I'd found out about the theater fire, the accident that claimed the extra's life, and the bracelet theft. I ended with, "Taylor and Noelle were both in that play as well. I heard that Taylor was accused of the theft."

"If anyone's guilty, my money would be on Ray," sniffed Melanie. "Who knows, maybe he did plot that theft, and engineered it so poor Taylor took the blame. I wouldn't put it past him. Ray could be very vindictive, and he wouldn't have stood for Taylor jilting him. He always had to be the one to call it quits."

I remembered the snatch of conversation I'd overheard between Taylor and Terrill. I had to admit, I felt a sense of relief that Melanie's secret, overall, hadn't been that bad.

I wished I felt as confident about Taylor's. My gut was telling me that whatever secret Taylor was keeping, it was way more complicated.

After Melanie left, I took a quick peek inside the auditorium. My mother was deep into director mode, criticizing one of the extra's performances. I scribbled a hasty note about Taylor not being able to make today's performance and caught sight of Min Barlow, another extra. I had to promise her free food for her gerbil for a month if she'd deliver the note to my mother, and I hightailed it out of there before Min could change her mind.

Out on the street, I paused. Should I return to Urban Tails, or should I go home and have another look-see through the stacks of Terrill's boxes still in my shed. I hadn't gone through them all, so it was possible that the photos of Melanie might still be there. My curiosity won out, and twenty minutes later I was letting myself into the small storage shed. I saw at once that I had company. Purrday and his new friend Princess Fuzzypants were both atop a stack of boxes in the far corner, beneath a small window. I frowned. "How on earth did you two get in here?" I addressed the cats and jingled my key ring in the air. "The door was locked, and so are the windows."

The Persian and Maine coon looked at each other, then back at me. Rather guiltily, I thought.

"Doesn't matter, I guess," I said, sliding my keys back into my pocket. I frowned as I looked at the piles of boxes. Was I imagining it, or had some of the boxes shifted from one pile to the other? I shook my head. "Must be my imagination," I grumbled. I crooked my finger at the cats. "Come here."

Princess Fuzzypants dipped her head at me. Purrday made a sound deep in his throat.

"I'm not kidding," I said. "If the two of you do not get your kitty behinds over here right now, there will be consequences. Serious consequences. Like no treats."

Both cats lifted their paws, gave them a lick. Then Purrday hopped down and started to amble toward me. Princess Fuzzypants, however, lowered her nose to the box and sniffed.

I remembered the cat had done that previously. "You smell Terrill's scent, don't you?" I asked the cat. "I know you liked him. He liked you too."

"Merow." The princess lifted her paw, scratched at the cardboard box. She looked over at me, gave another sharp merow, then jumped down. Her paw grabbed one end of the box as she did so, and the box came tumbling down right after her. She jumped to avoid being hit as the contents spilled out across the shed floor.

"Swell," I muttered. I started forward, Purrday close at my heels. The princess sat back on her haunches. She looked at me with her wide eyes and let out a soft merow.

"I know, it was an accident," I said. I reached out and gave the large cat a pat on the head. She started purring. I turned my attention to the contents of the box. It appeared to be all papers. I picked up a few and glanced at them. They were in Terrill's handwriting, all right. Some were notes on the current production, and others appeared to be notes on past ones. I shoved them into the box and then my eye saw a white envelope that had fallen into the far corner. I walked over, picked it up. I lifted the flap and my breath came out in a whoosh. There were several photographs inside. Could these be the ones of Melanie? I was just about to take a peek when I heard a footfall behind me and then a familiar voice called out. "Shell?"

I shoved the envelope into my inside jacket pocket, then whirled around to face the newcomer—Josh. "Hey," I said. "What are you doing here?"

"I was driving by and saw the door ajar," he said. "Everything okay?"

I swept my arm in the direction of the boxes. "I just thought I'd take another look through all Terrill's boxes. Do you know if Amy was here earlier?"

Josh frowned. "I don't believe so. They're a little short on manpower right now. Why?"

I winced at his bitter tone. I knew he hated that he couldn't participate in the case. "Oh, nothing. It's just that it looked to me like the boxes might have been moved. One pile seemed a little shorter than the other." I waved my hand. "It's probably just my imagination. After all, I didn't measure the piles."

"I hope not," Josh said with a thin smile. "That would border on obsessive." He glanced at the mess on the floor. "I see you've been delving into them, though."

"Not me. You can thank Princess Fuzzypants. She knocked the top box over. I was just about to straighten up."

Josh glanced at the papers, then reached into his pants pocket and whipped out a pair of disposable gloves. "You really should have these on if you're going to be digging through those," he said. "This is all considered evidence, you know. Amy will have ten fits if she thinks you were looking through them without taking the proper precautions."

"Yes, I realize that." I accepted the gloves, pulled them on. "Thank you."

He shot me a hopeful glance. "Want some help?"

I wagged my finger at him. "Oh, no. Not from you."

"Why not?" His brows drew together. "I am a police officer."

"Yes, and one who's taken himself off of this case. I wouldn't want you to do something stupid to put yourself in a bad light with the captain."

He reached up to scratch at the back of his head. "You're right," he admitted. "But before you dig in here, got a second to talk?"

He looked so serious that for a moment my heart skipped a beat. Had something happened? Had Taylor confessed to the crime? "S-sure. What's on your mind?"

"I think you know." He let out a sigh. "We got an anonymous tip yesterday. Seems Gary wasn't the only one who saw my SUV the night Terrill was killed. This person reported seeing a black SUV with ski racks on the corner of Park and Maple at approximately the same time Terrill met his maker."

My eyes widened. "Oh my gosh! Could whoever took the call recognize the voice? Was it a man or a woman?"

Josh shook his head. "It was Marge Paisley, and you know Marge. She said she could barely hear the person, let alone discern whether the caller was male or female."

I did indeed know Marge. A stout seventy-seven, she suffered from poor hearing but often "forgot" to wear her hearing aid. I suspected she'd forgotten it when she'd taken that call. "Too bad," I said. "I've an idea who it might have been, though." I repeated what Fannie had told me about Noelle.

"Makes sense, I suppose," Josh remarked when I finished. "Taylor has a temper, but she didn't kill Terrill."

We were both silent for a few minutes and then I said, "Could Taylor possibly be protecting someone?"

"I thought of that, but I can't imagine who that would be."

I laid my hand on his arm. "Have you spoken to her?"

"I tried. She got angry when she found out I'd been checking on her alibi. She said that I should have more faith in my family and then stormed out."

"Yes, she got a bit defensive when I saw her earlier."

He stared at me. "You spoke to her? What did she say?"

I repeated my conversation with Taylor. Josh listened in silence, stroking his jaw the whole time. When I finished he fixed me with a troubled gaze.

"She's definitely hiding something," he said. "I just hope she's not investigating this on her own. Sue told me she made a remark about detective blood running in the family. To be honest, I wouldn't put it past her." He balled one hand into a fist. "Dammit, maybe I shouldn't have recused myself from this case."

"You had to, you know that."

He hung his head. "Yeah, I do. It's just . . . I feel so helpless."

"So do I," I admitted. "Let me tell you what I've found out so far."

Josh perched himself on the edge of the desk as I went through the day's events, ending with my meeting with Melanie. When I finished, he let out a low whistle. "Wow—you're right, Shell. Melanie's relationship with Terrill would surely bump her up on the list of suspects if it were my case."

"I know. That's why I told her to go to Amy. I know she's got an excellent motive, but somehow I just can't see her as a killer."

Josh shot me a look. "That's why you're in here, isn't it? You're looking for those photographs."

"Guilty." Since he'd called me on it, I pulled the envelope out of my inner jacket pocket. "The princess knocked over one of the boxes and this was in it. There are photographs inside. I was just about to take a look when you came in."

"Shall we take a look together?"

"Might as well."

My heart was pounding wildly in my chest as I opened the flap of the envelope. I slid the contents out and spilled them on the desk. I stared at them unbelievingly.

"Well, for goodness sakes," I said finally.

The photographs were not of Melanie, but rather of a dark-colored sedan. The license plate was spattered with mud so that only the last two letters—AR— were visible. In one photograph a tall, stoop-shouldered man wearing a battered jacket could be seen limping away from the car. The man appeared to be glancing around quite furtively. You could only see his profile, yet there was something about it that struck me as familiar, and for the life of me I couldn't imagine why.

Josh was the first to speak. "Why on earth would Terrill have photos like these?"

I shrugged. "I have no idea. Maybe he was blackmailing someone."

"Over what?" Josh tossed the photograph of the man back into the pile. "Running a red light?"

I picked up the photos and stuffed them back into the envelope. I had the distinct feeling they meant something—but just what, I couldn't say. I slid the envelope back into my inner jacket pocket and turned to Josh. "If you've got some time, want to have a look through some of those boxes to see if we can find Melanie's photos? I've got another hour before I have to go to Urban Tails."

"Sure." He paused. "You do know if we find them, we have to turn them over to Amy, right?"

I nodded. "I know."

We worked in comparative silence for the next forty minutes. By the time I had to call a halt, we'd gone through half the boxes. No other photographs turned up.

Josh swiped at his forehead. "Maybe Terrill was bluffing. Maybe he never had those photos of Melanie."

I set my lips. "Melanie didn't think so. But Terrill didn't strike me as the bluffing kind."

"Maybe so." He was silent for a few seconds and then said, "Shell, have you considered the possibility that maybe Melanie just might have made all that up to get your sympathy? That there are no photos?"

"Oddly, that thought did cross my mind, but I discarded it. You had to see her face when she was telling me the story. She wasn't lying, I'd bet my life on it."

"Well, tell you what. I've got no big plans for tonight. How about if I come by later and we have another go at it?"

"That sounds great. As a matter of fact, why don't you come for supper?"

Josh arched a brow. "Will your mother be there?"

I almost laughed at the fear in his tone. "Sorry to disappoint you, but Mother won't be there. She's dining with Garrett tonight. They're going over some details about the play."

"Whew—I mean, that's too bad," Josh said. He didn't even try to suppress a grin, but he sobered as he asked, "How about Gary? He might not relish the thought of cooking for uninvited guests."

"You're not exactly a guest, and Gary welcomes every opportunity to show off his culinary skills. Plus, tonight's usually pasta night, so an extra mouth isn't all that big a deal." Well, that wasn't exactly true. I figured I'd have to jump through a few hoops, but it would be worth it.

"Well, okay then, as long as you're sure."

"I am."

Josh's phone buzzed, indicating he had a text. He whipped it out of his pocket, looked at the screen, and the expression on his face changed. "Is something wrong?" I asked.

He looked at me, and his gaze was troubled. "It could be," he said. "That text was from Amy. She'd like me to come right down to the station. It sounds urgent."

"Do you want me to go with you?" I asked. I could see that Josh was a bit shaken.

He shook his head. "No, I'll be fine. I'll fill you in tonight," he promised. And then he was gone.

I looked at the cats, who were huddled in the far corner, watching. "Okay, kids," I said. "Time to go back to the house now. We can all go exploring with Josh and Gary later tonight."

That last seemed to satisfy them. We all trooped back to the house, and I put them inside and made sure all the doors were securely locked before I headed over to Urban Tails. Gary looked up from behind the counter as I entered. He glanced pointedly at the clock. "Nice to see you again," he said blandly.

"I know and I'm sorry. I got a bit distracted. What a day!"

Gary glanced around the shop. "Well, we had a rush a bit ago but it's quiet now." He gestured toward the bird aisle, where Robbie was helping a young woman. "Robbie can handle things out here. Let's go in the storeroom and you can fill me in."

I followed Gary into the back room. He settled himself on the edge of my desk while I flopped into the leather chair. I brought him up to date on everything that had happened. Gary was silent for a few moments after I finished, then shook his head. "Curiouser and curiouser, to quote Lewis Carroll, or more specifically, Alice," he said. "What do you make of all this?"

"To be honest, I'm not quite sure," I admitted. "My gut is telling me that in spite of her actions, Taylor's not guilty. And even though she's got an excellent motive, I can't see Melanie as Terrill's killer either."

"What about Noelle? There's some history there, and I'm willing to bet it's pretty interesting."

"Possibly." I nibbled at my lower lip. "According to Noelle, they split on good terms. I heard differently from Tim and my mother. Terrill himself passed a few uncomplimentary remarks about Noelle before her arrival, which leads me to believe their version over hers."

"Noelle's version might well be the truth . . . to her," said Gary. "If she's got a lot of pride, she might have convinced herself that she was the dumper, not the dumpee. It happens all the time in Hollywood, you know that."

I waggled an eyebrow at him. "Yes, I do recall a similar incident on our show with one of the guest stars—Babette Johanssen, if I'm not mistaken. She wasted no time informing everyone on the set what a cad you were."

Gary's cheeks flamed slightly as he replied, "I heard. And everyone knew she was lying. We only went out once, and I was a perfect gentleman. She came on strong to me. And when I wasn't interested, she couldn't wait to bad-mouth me to every gossip rag around."

"Which only served to enhance your fan base. She must really have been pissed after that." I huffed a stray curl out of my eyes.

"Yep. But my point is, if Noelle doesn't think she was at fault for the breakup, most likely she'd twist facts so that she came out smelling like a rose."

"Both Terrill and Noelle seem high-maintenance. It would be hard to say which one might have been at fault."

"I guess the real question is, was Noelle mad enough at Terrill to kill him? Their breakup wasn't recent, so she would have to have harbored that grudge for a while."

"I can't see her as his killer either," I admitted. "To be honest, I keep going back to the argument I overheard between Terrill and Taylor. He threatened to expose her dirty little secret."

"Hm." Gary put a finger to his lips. "I wonder what that might have been."

"I don't know, but Taylor certainly seemed upset over it. She started to say something and Terrill cut her off. He said please don't threaten to kill me, and then passed a remark about having met that quota."

"Sounds like he'd been receiving threats from someone."

"Well, if it wasn't Taylor, Noelle or Melanie, then who? There aren't many choices left, except . . ."

Gary looked askance at me as I paused. "You're not thinking about Tim, are you?"

"I don't want to, believe me. But Tim and Taylor did have a relationship after Taylor broke up with Terrill. That argument between them that day at rehearsal was pretty ugly. And Tim did say he'd do anything for Taylor."

Gary's nose wrinkled. "I somehow doubt that would include murder."

"I hope you're right."

We went back into the store. Robbie had finished ringing up the girl's purchases and was sliding them into a plastic shopping bag. The bell above the shop door tinkled, and Josh ambled in. I took one look at his face and knew that the news wasn't good. I left Gary's side and hurried over to him. "What happened?" I asked.

Josh pulled me over to the far corner of the store, into the niche where we had a grooming table set up. As we hadn't found a pet groomer yet, this area was deserted. "They found what they presume to be the murder weapon." His tone was weary. "A .38-caliber revolver."

"Oh my gosh," I cried. "Where did they find it?"

"Actually a kid and his dog found it. The dog was nosing around a drain about ninety yards from your house. Ballistics is running the bullets now to see if it's a match."

Something in his tone made the hairs on the back of my neck stand up. "That's good news, right?" I asked.

"Not really," he replied. "I recognized the gun the minute Amy showed it to me. It has a distinctive pearl handle. It's Taylor's gun. I gave it to her two Christmases ago."

Eighteen

For a minute I was so startled I didn't know what to say. Finally I blurted out, "Taylor's gun? Are you sure?"

Josh nodded. "Quite. Her initials are carved into the bottom of the handle. It's her gun, all right." He ran a hand through his hair, mussing up the sides. "She never even mentioned to me that she'd brought it along."

"Can she even shoot a gun?"

"She's been taking lessons," he admitted. "There had been a rash of muggings and robberies near where she was working two years ago, so I got her that for protection. I never dreamt . . ." His voice trailed off and he made a helpless gesture with his hands.

"Maybe everything will be all right," I said hopefully. "Taylor's gun might not turn out to be the murder weapon."

Josh cut me a look. "What was it doing in a drain near your house—near the scene of the crime? Why didn't Taylor tell me she brought it with her, and more importantly, if it was lost, why didn't she tell me, or Amy?"

I had no answer. It did look as if Taylor were hiding something. "She was probably afraid she'd get blamed," I suggested.

"Of course she'd have been suspected, but this is so much worse." Josh slapped at his forehead with the palm of his hand. "Why oh why did I take myself off this damn case?"

"You know why. Besides, if you hadn't recused yourself, the captain would have done it for you."

His lips thinned. "Shell, Taylor is my cousin and she's somehow got herself tangled up in Terrill's murder. I-I feel so helpless right now I can't stand it."

"I think it's a very good idea for you to have a talk with Taylor, Josh. But otherwise you need to steer clear of this case."

He pulled his hand through his hair. "You're right. I know you're right. It's just I'm not used to not knowing exactly what's going on."

"I think the first order of business is for you to pin Taylor down and make her be straight with you about what happened that night."

The corners of his lips tugged downward. "You think she's lying about not being in the vicinity too, don't you?"

"I'm trying to keep an open mind," I said carefully. "I like Taylor, Josh, but

143

you have to admit she's gotten pretty defensive whenever anyone challenges her on her whereabouts that night." A sudden thought occurred to me. "Was the gun all that was found in the drain?" I asked.

Josh looked puzzled. "What do you mean?"

"What about a silencer?"

He shook his head. "Just the gun." He inclined his chin. "What are you thinking?"

"No one remembers hearing a gunshot that night. A silencer had to have been used. I was just thinking that maybe the killer kept it and tossed the gun in the drainpipe figuring it would point to your sister."

"If that's true, that's one diabolical person," said Josh. "If he weren't the victim, I'd say it was Terrill."

I looked Josh straight in the eye. "Or one badly scorned woman."

Both his brows rose. "You're thinking Noelle?"

"She acted as if their relationship was no big deal, but everyone else says otherwise. She might be a better actress than people give her credit for."

"Maybe I should put a bug in Amy's ear, have her dig deeper into Noelle's background." Josh stretched his arms wide. "Right now, I think I'd better get over to the inn, see if I can catch Taylor. I've got to impress the seriousness of the situation on her, get her to open up. If her gun does turn out to be the murder weapon, she's going to need a lawyer—a good one."

"Good luck. Call me if you need anything."

"Thanks." He took both my hands in his, pulled me close to him, and gave me a tender kiss on the lips. When he broke the embrace he looked down at me and said, "I appreciate your support, Shell. It means more to me than you'll ever know."

"You don't have to thank me. And we're still on for dinner, right?"

His lips thinned. "We'll see. As of right now, yes."

We hugged again, and then Josh left and I went back over to the counter. Gary ducked down the moment he saw me coming and started to adjust some dog collars in the display case. I went over and tapped him on the shoulder. "I bet you were wishing you had super-hearing, weren't you?" I asked.

He flushed as he straightened up. "That conversation looked pretty serious," he said.

"It was."

I hit the highlights. When I finished, Gary was silent for a few moments.

At last he said, "I feel bad for Josh, but I also think that Taylor is holding something back. I hope he can get her to open up to him."

"Someone must really hate Taylor, to want to frame her that badly," I said. "I'm not fond of Noelle, but I'm not sure she's the killer either."

"Then who's left? You can't be thinking about Tim again?"

I sighed. "No, not really, but as you said, there aren't many suspects left. I saw Tim's face when he talked about Taylor. He's got real feelings for her. I don't think he'd try to frame her even if she dumped him."

"How about that woman who showed up at the play rehearsal? Didn't you say she mentioned she had a past with Terrill?"

"You mean Kristi Marchall? Say, there's a thought," I said. "She mentioned that she broke things off with him when she found out his secret. I wonder if she knew he was married to Melanie?"

"Her forgiving attitude could be an act. Maybe she followed him here with the intent of having it out with him once and for all."

"She said she had a meeting with Noelle Boyd, that she was considering taking her on as a client. I suppose she could have been lying."

"Well, there's only one way to find out, isn't there?" Gary cocked his head at me and made a shooing motion with his hand. "Go on. I don't mind closing."

I cleared my throat. "I was thinking about closing early tonight—like around five."

He stared at me. "Really? Why so early? What's going on?"

"Nothing earth-shattering. I, ah, I sort of invited Josh over for dinner."

"Oh, you did, did you?" Gary arched a brow. "So does that mean you plan on cooking tonight? Or more likely, ordering out?"

I laid my hand on his arm and fixed him with my most ingratiating smile. "I thought that since tonight's usually pasta night, throwing some extra spaghetti in the pot wouldn't be a lot of trouble." I looked at him hopefully.

"You thought that, huh?" Gary huffed. "Well . . . I was thinking of chopping up those extra veggies in the fridge and making pasta primavera. There's more than enough for three people—unless you have more surprises on your guest list?"

"Absolutely none."

"Okay, fine. I'll close up at five. Dinner will be at six." He folded his arms across his chest and gave me his evil-eye stare. "Sharp. And just in case you decide to bring this Kristi along too, kindly give me a heads-up."

I leaned over, gave Gary a buss on the cheek, then grabbed my bag. "I'll make all this up to you, I promise," I called over my shoulder.

"Oh, you bet you will," he called after me.

. . .

Fifteen minutes later I was in the lobby of the Fox Hollow Inn. Lucy Plunkett, a stout middle-aged woman who frequented my shop for food for her rabbit Theodore, sat behind the reception desk. She gave me a wide smile as I approached. "Hey, Shell. What are you doing here?"

"I'm here to see one of your guests. Kristi Marchall."

Lucy frowned. "That name doesn't sound familiar. Can you spell it for me?"

I did so, and Lucy typed it into the computer. She hit the Enter button, then bent over to squint at the screen. At last she looked over at me. "Sorry, Shell. No one's registered by that name."

"Really? I'm sure she said she was staying here. Maybe it was entered incorrectly," I suggested.

Lucy tried spelling both Kristi and Marchall a few different ways. The result each time was the same. Nothing.

An elderly woman came up behind me, rapped her knuckles impatiently on the counter. "Excuse me, miss, but can you help me? I'm having a problem with the faucet in my bathroom."

Lucy nodded. "Certainly. Excuse me, Shell."

Lucy turned to wait on the woman and I moved over to the far corner of the lobby and dialed my mother. To my surprise, she picked up on the second ring. "Yes, Crishell?"

"Mother. I was wondering if you by chance saw a woman named Kristi Marchall today?"

"Oh, yes. She stopped by earlier looking for Noelle. I told her that she was supposedly sick and she was welcome to stop by rehearsal tomorrow. She said she might do that, as she was going to be around for a few days."

"Oh?" That was news. Kristi hadn't mentioned an extended stay in Fox Hollow, but then again, why would she? "Mother, did Kristi happen to mention where she was staying?"

"As a matter of fact she did. The Fox Hollow Inn. Why do you ask?"

"We, ah, had a nice little conversation earlier and I suggested we continue it tonight. I thought she told me she was staying at the Fox Hollow Inn too, but they don't have a record of her registering here."

"She probably registered under her real name," my mother said. "Kristi Marchall is her professional name. Her real name is Christine Blankett."

"Thanks, Mother. I'll try that."

"Wait!" My mother's tone was commanding. "You have a perfectly good agent, dear. If you're looking to get back into show business, I know Max would be happy to . . ."

"I don't need an agent, Mother, and you're right, if I did, Max is excellent," I said hastily. "I wanted to speak to Kristi on another matter."

"Oh, good Lord." I could just see my mother's eyeballs rolling into the back of her head. "Don't tell me you want to grill her about Raymond? Honestly, Crishell, that ship has sailed. At one point they were an item, yes, but that's been a dead issue for years."

"I don't suppose you know why they broke up?"

My mother laughed. "It was one of the best-kept secrets in Hollywood, dear. She caught him en flagrante dilecto with another woman the day after their engagement."

"Wait . . . Kristi Marchall and Raymond Terrill were engaged? To be married?"

"Yes, dear. They were engaged for a sum total of twenty-four hours. And then they weren't. Now, if that's all, I have to get back to Garrett."

"Yes, Mother, that's all. Thanks."

I disconnected and stood, tapping my cell phone against my chin. I certainly hadn't expected to hear that Kristi and Terrill had been engaged. The reason my mother gave for the breakup didn't jibe with what Kristi had said, though. Being caught in the act of cheating didn't seem the same to me as learning someone's dirty little secret. I sighed. I'd just have to ask Kristi myself, when I finally found her.

I went back to the reception area and approached Lucy. "Try Christine Blankett," I suggested.

Lucy typed that name into the computer, then looked up with a smile. "Bingo. She's in room 217. Want me to ring her?"

"Please."

Lucy picked up the phone, punched in a number. A few minutes later she looked at me and shook her head. "No answer. Do you want to leave a message?"

I nodded. Lucy handed me a pad and paper. I scribbled *Kristi, please give me a call,* and left my name and cell number. I handed the pad back to Lucy. Would Noelle Boyd be in?" I asked.

"You mean Fox Hollow's answer to Marilyn Monroe?" Lucy rolled her eyes. "I haven't seen her all day, thank goodness, but I can ring her room."

I stifled a giggle. "Please."

After a few minutes she turned back to me. "Looks like she's out too."

I frowned. "That's odd. I thought she would be in for sure. She called in sick to rehearsal today."

Lucy frowned. "She's not answering her phone. She might not want to be disturbed if she's ill. If you want to leave a message, though, I'll make sure she gets it."

"Thanks, that's not necessary." I paused. "Do you still make complimentary laptops available for the guests?"

"Oh, yes," Lucy said and nodded. "The computer room is just down that hall."

"I see. Is it possible for people who aren't guests of the hotel to use them?"

"Sure. You just need a credit card."

"Thanks."

I hurried down the hall, and sure enough, there was a sign saying *Computer Room* on my right. I pushed open the door and went inside. Aside from one elderly man on a computer in the far corner, the remaining six were unoccupied. I selected the one in the corner farthest from the door and plugged in my credit card information. A few minutes later I called up Google. The incident involving Taylor and the bracelet had happened two years ago. I typed in *Terrill–As You Like It –diamond bracelet–San Francisco* and hit Enter.

A plethora of news articles came up. Most were reviews of the play, which were excellent. A few especially noted Taylor's performance. I weeded through them and concentrated on the smaller papers. I found a small mention of the theft of the diamond bracelet on page ten of the *San Francisco Blaze*. It didn't mention Taylor's name, just that an actress had been accused, then exonerated. I sifted through the other articles. None mentioned Taylor by name.

I decided to go back and look at articles about the play's inception. It seemed like another dead end until I opened up one from the *San Francisco Variety*. The caption read *New Director Named for Shakespearean Play*. A very brief article followed, about how the lead director had "creative differences" and had been replaced by Raymond Terrill. The article chronicled a loud screaming match between the two men the first day of rehearsal.

It was the name of the original director, though, that grabbed my attention.

Timothy Scott.

I read the article twice, then printed it out on the color printer and jammed it into my bag. Tim had mentioned that he'd been the assistant director on that play; he'd never said one word about being replaced as the original director. Then again, perhaps he'd been ashamed of the way he'd acted when he'd been replaced. No doubt it was an incident from his past that he wanted to forget.

Was it possible Terrill wouldn't let him? Was that one of the reasons why Tim had never progressed in his career? Had Tim's resentment finally festered enough so that he was prompted to take serious action?

Tim had certainly seemed sincere when he spoke about his feelings for Taylor. I greatly doubted that even if he'd killed Terrill in a fit of anger, he'd let Taylor take the blame.

I sighed. I was still going to grill Tim on this, but as far as the murder went, it was back to square one. I was just about to continue searching when the door opened and a gray-haired man in overalls stuck his head in.

"Sorry, folks," he said. "Management has an IT person coming in for routine maintenance, so we have to close up now."

The elderly man at the far end grumbled a bit, then picked up his notebook and shuffled out. I slung my bag across my shoulder and followed. I'd just arrived at the lobby when my cell rang. I fished it out of my purse and looked at the screen. Josh. I hit answer. "What's up?"

"Have you seen Taylor?" he asked, his tone terse.

I felt the knot in my stomach tighten. "No, why?"

A pause, and then Josh said in a flat tone, "Ballistics came back with a match. The shot that killed Terrill was fired from Taylor's gun. Amy is out looking for her now."

Nineteen

"Oh, no," I cried. "Is Amy going to arrest her?"

"I can't say for certain, but it seems likely," Josh replied. "I'm afraid I'm going to have to take a rain check on that dinner invitation, Shell. I've got to try and find Taylor."

"I'm at the Fox Hollow Inn now," I told him. "I can go inside and see if Taylor's in her room."

"Oh, Shell, would you? If she's there, please give me a call," Josh said. I could hear the relief in his voice.

"I will. Try not to worry."

"Easier said than done."

Josh disconnected and I shoved my phone back in my bag. I started to turn toward the reception desk once again, when the elevator doors at the far end of the lobby opened and who should come striding out but Taylor herself! She seemed in a big hurry too. I whipped my phone out again and shot Josh a quick text: *She's here.* Then I changed direction and hurried over to her. Her eyes widened in surprise when she saw me, and she blurted out, "Shell? What are you doing here?"

"Hello, Taylor. I was here to pay a visit to a friend when I spied you walking across the lobby." I reached out, took her arm, and steered her over to a small bank of chairs at the far side of the lobby. "Detective Riser is looking for you," I said in a low tone.

Taylor frowned. "Me? Whatever for?" I had to hand it to her, she was an excellent actress. Nothing showed in her face, and her voice was steady. "I've already told her all about that note, just as you instructed me to."

"It's not about the note. It's something else."

Taylor's expression hardened. "Yeah? What?"

I paused, uncertain of just how much I should say. At that moment the front door to the inn burst open and Josh strode in. He caught sight of us immediately and hurried over. "Taylor," he said. "Detective Riser is looking for you."

"Yeah, I know. Shell just told me. But I already told her about the note."

Josh looked his cousin straight in the eye. "Did you bring your gun along?"

Something flickered across Taylor's face—panic? But it was gone in an instant. "My gun?" she said coolly.

"Yes, the gun I gave you for Christmas two years ago. Did you bring it with you?"

"I always take it with me. Why?"

Josh leaned in closer to Taylor. "When was the last time you saw it?"

"I don't know. I know it was locked in my small suitcase the day I checked in, because I put some magazines on top of it and then shoved the bag in the back of my closet."

"It's still there?"

"As far as I know, yes. What is this all about?"

Josh's expression was grim. "Let's sit down."

Josh took Taylor's arm and led her over to a bank of chairs near the fireplace in a secluded corner of the lobby. I followed. Josh sat Taylor down on the love seat and eased himself onto the cushion next to her. I settled into the wingchair directly across. Josh took both of Taylor's hands in his and said, "The police found the murder weapon. A .38-caliber pearl-handled revolver with the initials *TCT* carved into the handle. What's more, they matched the bullet from the gun with the one that killed Terrill."

Taylor stared at Josh. "You mean my gun—but that's impossible. It's locked in my suitcase, and besides, it wasn't loaded. I don't like to carry bullets around with me. I just take the empty gun. It gives me a sense of security."

"It is your gun, Taylor. I identified it," said Josh.

Taylor's eyes narrowed. "Then you made a mistake, cousin. It's not my gun. It couldn't be."

"There's one way to settle this," Josh said in a low tone. "Let's go up to your room right now and have a look in your suitcase."

Taylor's chin jutted out, and then she suddenly crumpled. Her lower lip quivered, and her eyes started to fill with tears. "Oh, all right," she said. "It probably is my gun. I gave it to Ray."

I stared at her. "You gave Terrill your gun? Why?"

Her lips quirked. "You're both going to think I'm a real fool. I loaned it to him because he told me he was in danger."

Josh's face reddened. "What?"

Taylor's chin went up. "He pulled me aside before the read-throughs that day and told me that he needed to borrow my gun. He said that he was in danger from someone and he needed to be able to protect himself. I refused at first. I told him that I didn't want to get involved."

"That was the day I overheard your conversation," I cut in. "The day Terrill got mad at me and accused me of snooping."

Taylor nodded. "Yes. I told him the gun was useless, I hadn't brought any bullets with me. He said he'd take care of that. So I ducked out of rehearsal, got the gun, and brought it to his dressing room. He wasn't there, so I tucked it into a drawer and left him a note. That's the last time I saw it."

"So you don't know for certain Terrill had it in his possession," said Josh. "That was a dumb thing to do, Taylor. Anyone might have seen you with the gun, then gone into Terrill's dressing room and taken it."

"I know, I know." Taylor wrung her hands. "But I wasn't thinking clearly. He'd threatened me, and I knew that he'd go through with it if I didn't give him the gun."

"You need a lawyer," I said firmly. "I'm guessing that Terrill never got your gun. The murderer found it first and killed Terrill with it, and is setting you up to take the fall."

"No, no, no," Taylor said, her words coming out in a whine. "He wouldn't do that."

"He? Who do you mean, Taylor? Tim Scott?" I cried. As Taylor averted her gaze, I added, "You think he killed Terrill, don't you?"

Taylor tossed her head. "I don't have to answer your questions," she said in a low voice.

"No, you don't," I agreed. "You don't have to answer any questions. You can plead the Fifth, but it won't look good for you. You need a lawyer," I said.

"Shell's right," Josh agreed. "I can call Norman Hines. I've worked with him on a few cases. He's an excellent criminal lawyer."

"And expensive, no doubt," mumbled Taylor.

"Hey," said Josh. "This is your life we're talking about, Taylor. Nothing is too expensive for that." He whipped out his phone. "I'm calling him now."

Taylor let out a groan. "Does it have to be right this minute?"

"Yes, it does," said Josh.

As he moved away, phone to his ear, I thought I knew the reason for the urgency. I leaned closer to Taylor. "Getting back to the conversation I overheard," I said. "What was the secret that Terrill threatened to reveal?"

Taylor glanced nervously over toward Josh, then back at me. "It goes back to that bracelet incident," she said. "Ray was in my dressing room afterward, and the bracelet fell out of a box of Kleenex. I told him someone must have planted it there, but he didn't believe me and he said the police wouldn't either. He said that he'd cover for me, but I owed him."

"You let him! Taylor, if you were innocent, why would you do that?"

She hung her head. "Back then I was young and foolish. I believed him when he said he could either get me in real trouble or get me out of it. He-he wanted a relationship with me, and I acquiesced. We were together for nearly a year before his interests went elsewhere, and he dumped me. But he never ceased to remind me that I owed him every chance he got. And I'm sure it was because of him I lost several good acting jobs." She set her jaw. "He's still ruining my life, even in death. Uh-oh. More trouble."

We both looked up as Amy Riser pushed through the inn's double doors and made a beeline straight for us. She came to a halt, nodded at me, then stared at Taylor.

"Hello, Taylor," Amy said. "I'd like you to come down to the station for questioning, if you don't mind."

"She doesn't," said Josh, who'd come up behind Amy. "Her lawyer will be meeting her at the station."

"Fine," said Amy. I could see her jaw clenching and unclenching. I leaned over and whispered in Taylor's ear, "You don't have to say a word until your lawyer is present. Understand?"

Taylor nodded, and then she and Amy walked out to her squad car. Josh laid his hand on my arm. "I'm going to go down to the station as well. I can't sit in, but I can be there to offer moral support."

"I understand. Go on, be with Taylor."

Josh gave me a quick kiss on the cheek and then was gone. I pulled out my phone and texted Gary: *Only 2 of us for dinner. Taylor taken to station. Josh went with her. Be home soon.*

A few minutes later I got a reply from Gary: *OK. Got delayed myself. Dinner at seven.*

I shoved my phone back in my pocket and was just about to leave when Kristi Marchall came bustling in the front door of the inn. She saw me and hurried over. "Did I just see Taylor Tyson getting into a police car?" she asked.

"Yes," I said. "They're taking her in for more questioning."

Kristi shook her head. "They surely can't think Taylor would have killed Ray," she said. "Taylor hasn't a murderous bone in her body. If anyone killed him, my money's on Noelle Boyd."

I raised a brow. "Noelle? I thought she was going to be your client?"

Kristi offered me a thin smile. "I was hoping that might be the case, but she canceled our meeting." Her lips parted in a sigh. "I can't help but think that she's still suffering from what Ray did to her."

"You mean their breakup? Noelle seemed fine with it."

"No, not that. It was early on in Ray's career. He had a reputation for pushing his actors to the breaking point. And if they still didn't perform up to his specifications, he'd get them hooked on drugs."

I almost fell over. "You're kidding. Terrill was a drug dealer?"

"Not a dealer. He just shared what he had. Ray was pretty heavily into them himself back then. A case of too much success and not being equipped to handle it, I suppose. He tried to hide it from the general public."

"So that's the secret you alluded to—that Terrill used drugs?"

She nodded. "That, and he'd gotten Noelle pretty well addicted during her tenure on his play. She was about eighteen then. Ray and I had a date one night and he was late. I figured he got hung up at the theater, so I went looking for him. I found them both naked and strung out in his dressing room. That ended it for me," she said with a catch in her throat.

I reached out and impulsively covered Kristi's hand with my own. "I can certainly understand that."

"Ray came to me the next day, all apologetic. I told him it was over, but for his own good he should get his act together. I told him I had no use for anyone who'd ruin a young girl's life like that. He tried to tell me that it wasn't all him, that Noelle was a willing participant. I told him to go to Hell. A month later I got word Noelle had enrolled in a clinic."

"So she kicked her addiction?"

"As far as I know, yes. But her career suffered for a long time after that. I was glad to learn she finally picked herself up and took charge of her life. When she contacted me about being her agent, I felt I owed her at least a look-see." She glanced at her watch. "Goodness, I have to get going. I booked myself on a red-eye back to LA. It's been nice meeting you, Shell."

"You too."

Kristi took off toward the elevators and I walked out the front door and stood on the sidewalk for a moment, my thoughts in a whirl. Talk about secrets, Noelle had a whopper of one herself. Kristi said that Noelle's career had suffered as a result. Was it possible that deep down she wanted Terrill to pay for what he'd done to her?

I looked at my watch. It was six thirty. I had just enough time to make it back to the house for dinner. As I passed Rory's Tea Shop I glanced in the window and saw Noelle, sitting alone at a table in the back. Impulsively, I pushed through the doors and headed straight for her table. She glanced up and started slightly at my approach.

"Hello, Noelle," I said. "Mind a little company?"

She shrugged, then inclined her head toward the empty chair opposite her. "Suit yourself."

I pulled out the chair and sat down. A waitress bustled over, and I ordered a cup of Earl Gray. Noelle asked for a refill of the same. As she hurried off, Noelle wrapped her fingers around her mug. "I like this place," she said, glancing around the room. "It's nice and quiet."

"Fox Hollow is a quaint town," I responded. "Certainly nothing like LA."

"Oh, don't get me wrong. I like the hustle and bustle of the big city, but there are times when quiet is good." She eyed me. "You lived and worked in LA for years. You can't tell me you don't miss it."

"I do, sometimes," I admitted. "But I'm happy here."

The waitress brought our teas, and we sipped in silence for a few moments. I set down my cup. "Did you always want to be an actress?"

"Since I could walk. You?"

"I never really thought about it. My mother is a classically trained actress, so it was always just assumed I'd follow in her footsteps. I was onstage before I could walk."

Noelle ran her finger around the rim of her cup. "You had a very successful career. To be honest, I'm surprised you gave it up."

"Not if you listen to my mother. It was always a disappointment to her that I didn't take after her and stick to Shakespeare. In her words, I was a sellout."

Noelle let out a snort. "I wish I could have been half the sellout you were. And for what it's worth, I was sorry to see that series end. I liked it."

"Thanks, but honestly, I was ready for a change," I answered.

"Yes, change is good. I think I'm ready for that too, finally."

I leaned in a bit closer to her and said, "I'm glad to hear that. Frankly, I was surprised that you wanted to work with Terrill again, all things considered."

Noelle's eyes narrowed. "What does that mean?"

155

I leaned forward, unsure of just how to broach the subject. "I've heard that you had some difficulties with Terrill early on in your career."

Noelle's lips stretched into a thin line. "Good news travels fast. Who told you? It had to be either your mother or Kristi." She slapped her napkin down on the table. "Not that it's a secret, or anything—nothing's a secret in Hollywood, as you well know—but it's not something I like to advertise."

"Of course," I murmured. "But you got yourself together and got your career back on track. You can be proud of that."

"I'm sure Kristi made it sound like Ray forced me into doing drugs," Noelle said. "He did make the suggestion, but ultimately it was my choice—everything was my choice. I was young, and I couldn't handle the pressure that Ray put me under. I wasn't kidding when I said he was demanding. An excellent director, but he wanted to squeeze the last drop of blood out of you."

"Still, I'm sure you had some feelings of resentment toward him."

Noelle looked at me, then barked out a laugh. "Oh, so this is what this chat's all about? Well, Shell, if you think that I killed Ray over festering resentment, I'm afraid I have to disappoint you," she said. "I did not kill him."

"I don't think you did. But neither did Taylor," I said.

To my surprise, Noelle nodded. "I agree with you," she said. "Poor Taylor doesn't have the guts to kill someone."

We were both silent a few moments, and then I said, "You said that you saw a black SUV driving by the gazebo the night Terrill died."

"Yes. The driver was nuts, that vehicle almost hit me."

"I heard that you thought the driver was Taylor."

Noelle scrunched up her lips. "I did think that at first, but I've since changed my mind. That's why I didn't go to the police."

"Can I ask what made you change your mind?"

Noelle leaned back a bit in her chair. She averted her gaze as she answered, "Nothing in particular. I just had time to think it over, is all."

The waitress returned. "Will that be all, ladies?" We both nodded, and she set down the check. I reached for the leather holder and pushed it in front of me. "My treat," I said. "I insist."

Noelle smiled. "I won't refuse," she said. "Maybe if I had landed that movie role . . . but no sense crying over spilled milk, right?"

I opened my bag to grab my wallet and two young girls happened by at that moment, heading for the table opposite ours. One of them jostled my arm and my bag slid to the floor, spilling out its contents. "Oh, gee, miss," the girl cried. "I'm really sorry."

"No harm done," I assured her. I bent to retrieve the fallen articles.

Noelle bent down as well. "Let me help you," she said.

"It's no bother." I reached for the envelope containing the photos I'd swiped from Terrill's box. The envelope slid from my fingers, and the photographs slid out. We both reached for it, but Noelle got there first. She snatched them up, then her eyes widened a bit and she started to shuffle through them. She glanced at me. "Yours?" she asked.

"Actually, they belonged to Ray Terrill," I said. "My cat found them in one of his boxes in my shed. I haven't had time to put them back yet."

Noelle had been staring fixedly at one of the photos. "Ray had these," she murmured. She gave herself a little shake and looked up at me. "Odd photos for him to have, but then again, we're talking about Ray Terrill. An extraordinary man with a gigantic ego, and a huge pain in the ass."

I silently agreed with her, particularly on the last observation. "I've wondered why he would have photos like that also," I said. "Would you have any idea?"

Her head jerked up and her eyes widened. For a second I detected something there—panic? Fear? It was gone in an instant and she shook her head. "No. None."

I finished picking up the rest of the fallen articles and Noelle handed me back the envelope. Suddenly she scraped her chair back. "Thanks for the tea, Shell. I've got to run."

Before I could say another word, Noelle turned and raced out the teashop door and out into the night.

Twenty

"And she took off, just like that?"

I twirled a forkful of pasta primavera around and ate it while three furry faces followed my every move. I looked over at Gary, who was also stuffing pasta into his mouth. "Yep," I said. "The whole encounter was really strange. First she admitted she was wrong about thinking Taylor was driving that black SUV, and then she seemed mesmerized by those photos I found in Terrill's things, although Lord knows why. Then she just jumped up and hightailed it out of the tea room." I paused for a breath. "Talk about odd."

"Well, you know we actors can be an odd lot sometimes," Gary said with a grin. "Have you heard anything from Josh about Taylor?"

"Not yet. I sent two texts but so far no answer." I popped a piece of broccoli into my mouth, chewed, swallowed, then added, "I'm afraid Taylor might have been arrested."

"Well, you have to admit that gun is pretty damning evidence. Do you believe her when she says that it wasn't loaded, she didn't bring along any bullets?"

"I think she was telling the truth—for the most part. I still think there's something she's holding back."

At that moment a loud knock sounded on the kitchen door. Gary and I exchanged a glance. "Maybe it's Josh," I said hopefully.

"Maybe. Well, if it is, there's plenty of pasta left."

Gary got up and walked over to the door and opened it. It wasn't Josh who stood on the threshold but Gretchen Walker. "Hey, I hope I'm not disturbing you," she said. "I saw your lights on and I figured I'd take a chance and drop in. I had to go over to Denby and use the chip monitor on a Great Dane, so I figured maybe now might be a good time to use it on the princess."

"Thanks, that would be a load off my mind," I said. I explained to Gretchen about the episode with Phyllis McIntyre. "After that incident, I pulled the ad. I didn't want any more people coming around looking to profit from the princess."

Gretchen shook her head. "It takes all kinds. So, where is the princess?"

I glanced around and frowned. "They were all here just a few minutes ago."

"Probably hiding from the big bad vet," remarked Gary. "Animals seem to have an uncanny sixth sense for that sort of thing."

I poured Gretchen a cup of coffee and then Gary and I split up to hunt for the missing Maine coon. I searched the entire first floor and the basement, to no avail, then returned to the kitchen. Gary came downstairs ten minutes later, shaking his head. "Couldn't find her anywhere," he said.

"Cats are very adept at hiding," Gretchen commented. "She could be anywhere."

Kahlua came up to me, twined her tawny body around my legs, and let out a loud merow.

I looked down at the cat. "What's up, Kahlua? Are you trying to tell me something?"

Kahlua blinked her blue eyes, then inclined her head toward the kitchen door. I followed her gaze, and started when I noticed that the door was ajar. I looked at Gary. "Did you close the door after you let Gretchen in?"

Gary looked sheepish. "I don't remember," he admitted. "I might not have pushed it all the way shut."

I opened the door and looked outside. "She could be anywhere," I groaned.

Kahlua let out another loud meow, then started up the path toward the shed. "Or maybe she went back to a familiar place," Gary suggested.

Gary led the way to the shed, followed by Gretchen and me. The shed door was closed, but I noticed that one of the windows was half open. I pointed to it. "She could have gotten in that way."

I opened the shed door and we all trooped inside. The first thing I saw was Purrday. He was lying in front of a stack of Terrill's boxes. When he saw us he rose to his feet and let out a loud meow.

"Warning your girlfriend, are you?" asked Gary. He shook his head at the Persian. "Boy, have you got it bad."

I edged closer to the stack of boxes. "Princess, where are you?" I cooed. "We're not going to hurt you—I promise."

The princess's head popped up from the top box in the stack. "Merow," she said.

"Good girl," I said. "Come on, Princess. Gretchen just wants to see if your former owner microchipped you, that's all."

I reached for the cat. Before I could grasp her, the princess had jumped

159

out of the box, sending it and its contents tumbling to the floor. I jumped back, startled as the cat raced past me. Fortunately, Gary's reflexes were faster. He swooped down and grabbed the princess as she tried to edge past him.

"Come on, there's a good girl," he murmured into her fur. He ran his hand up and down her back, murmuring to her in a quiet tone. It seemed to calm the princess down. She stopped struggling and nestled herself against his chest.

"Gary's fatal charm strikes again," I said.

He grinned. "All women love me," he admitted. He walked over to the desk and gently placed the princess on it. "There, there, Princess," he crooned. "No one's going to hurt you, I promise."

Purrday jumped onto the desk and let out a loud meow. "See, your protector is here as well. You're in good hands," Gary crooned.

The princess tensed, then stretched out across the desk. Gretchen stepped forward and ran her hand along the cat's back. "She's such a beautiful animal. And obviously a pedigree. I can't imagine she wouldn't be microchipped."

"It's definitely a good idea," I agreed. "I should probably get Purrday and Kahlua microchipped."

"You should," Gretchen said with a brisk nod. "It's done with a simple injection. The microchip is implanted under the skin over the midline of the spine, between the shoulder blades. It's a painless procedure."

Gretchen removed the scanner from her tote bag and approached the princess, who squirmed a bit under Gary's hand. "There, there, Princess," she said soothingly. "This won't hurt, trust me."

Gretchen stepped closer and ran the scanner over the cat's head, scanning side to side all the way to her tail. She made several passes over each area. Then, while Gary held her down and murmured to her, she scanned slowly down the sides of the princess's leg, across her neck, along and under her chest and behind her front legs. At last she held the scanner up and looked at the cat. "See there! All done. You were a real champ, Princess."

Princess Fuzzypants looked at Gretchen and gave a loud meow of assent. Gary removed his hand and the princess and Purrday jumped down from the desk. The two of them padded over to the far corner. The princess stretched out full length, as if the ordeal had been a grueling one. Purrday positioned himself right in front of her, and laid one paw on her back.

"Aw," said Gretchen. "That's so sweet."

"Yes, Purrday's grown quite fond of her." I looked at Gretchen. "So? Is she microchipped or not?"

Gretchen frowned. "Not. I'm surprised. Most pedigrees are implanted as soon as possible."

"Maybe her owner was old-fashioned and hadn't heard of getting pets microchipped," suggested Gary.

"It's possible." Gretchen returned the scanner to her bag. "Or maybe she escaped before she could be microchipped. I've asked every breeder within a hundred-mile radius, and no one's reported any cats missing."

"Robbie's asked around as well. Same situation."

"Hm. So what will you do now, Shell?"

I sighed. "I certainly don't want to run another ad and run the risk of another Phyllis McIntyre incident. I'm tempted to just keep her awhile—see if her owner turns up."

Gretchen nodded. "That could be awhile, or it could be never. You might get too attached to give her up, if you had to."

The princess's pink tongue darted out, licked at my fingers. I chuckled. "I guess I'll cross that bridge if and when we get to it. For the moment, the princess stays here."

Purrday lifted his head and let out a loud meow of assent.

Gary and I both laughed. "Someone is happy about that decision," he said. "I'm not sure who would miss the princess more, Shell or Purrday."

"Looks like both to me," said Gretchen. She slung her tote over her shoulder. "I've got to get going. I'll keep an eye and an ear out in case I hear of any missing Maine coons," she promised.

"I'll walk you to your car," Gary offered.

"That's not necessary," Gretchen protested.

Gary shook his head. "I insist. There's still a killer running around town. Can't be too careful." He looked over his shoulder at me. "Coming, Shell?"

"You go on. I want to clean up here."

"Okay. Wait for me to go back to the house. I'll only be a minute."

Gary and Gretchen left, followed by the cats. I bent down to retrieve the articles that had fallen out of the box when the princess had tipped it over. It was mostly papers, a few file folders, and a small teak box. I gathered up the papers and folders and stuffed them back inside the box and then turned my attention to the teak box. It was in the shape of a cat, and the memory of

Terrill's interaction with the princess came briefly to mind. It was still hard for me to think of the man as a cat lover. I turned the box over in my hand. It reminded me of a puzzle box that I'd had as a child. I ran my hand along the side, and felt one of the pieces move slightly. I lifted it up, and the top of the box slid open. There was a folded piece of paper inside that looked like a newspaper clipping. I lifted it out of the box, replaced the lid and put the teak box back where it belonged. I took the newspaper clipping over to the desk and spread it out on the surface. I sucked in a breath at the headline that blared up at me: *Actress Killed in Hit-and-Run.*

The word "killed" was circled in red.

I leaned forward to read the article. It was from the *Kansas City Herald*, dated three years ago, and very similar to the one I'd read in the *Star* about the accident that had taken the extra's life. This one was a bit more detailed. It gave the extra's name—Eileen Cullen—and a list of her credits, which weren't many. There were two photos of the car, which were identical to the ones in the packet of photos I'd found among Terrill's things. The article said that the vehicle had been reported stolen the day before, and there was no sign of the driver, who'd apparently walked away unscathed. Police were working on locating him. No name was given. Eileen was survived by a sister, Diane Malone, of Chapel Hill, North Carolina. There was something else scrawled on the bottom of the page, but I couldn't make it out.

I looked up from my reading and gasped. The article was obviously connected to that packet of photos, and now I knew how: Terrill had a photo of the unidentified man walking away from the hit-and-run! But who was he, and why would Terrill be concerned with the accident? What was there to this that I was missing?

"Penny for your thoughts?"

I jumped and whirled around to face Gary. "Geez, don't *do* that," I said.

"Sorry." He peered over my shoulder at the piece of newspaper. "Where did you get that?"

"It was in a puzzle box in Terrill's things that Princess Fuzzypants knocked over," I said. I picked the article up and handed it to Gary.

He quickly perused the article and his eyes lit up. "This explains the photo. Terrill had evidence of who the driver was."

"Exactly. But what I can't figure out is why Terrill would have kept it all."

Gary shook his head as he handed the article back to me. "Beats me.

Maybe he felt guilty about the accident? Maybe he thought his being a jinx caused her death?"

I shook my head. "From the little I knew of Terrill, I can't see that," I said. "I doubt the man believed in jinxes. No, there's more to this than meets the eye."

"Okay. There's one way to find out."

I stuffed the article back in the puzzle box, replaced it where I'd found it, and eyed him. "And that is?"

He chuckled. "You call yourself a sleuth?" He pointed to the article. "It's early. Let's give Diane Malone in North Carolina a call."

I grinned at him. "You know, you're not half bad at this. Maybe you should open a PI office, after all."

. . .

Fifteen minutes later we were seated in the kitchen, my laptop open on the dining table. There were twelve Diane Malones listed in Chapel Hill. We split the list up and whipped out our cell phones. On my third try I hit pay dirt.

"Yes, Eileen was my sister," Diane said. "Might I ask who you are and why you are inquiring about this three years later?"

I explained about Terrill's death and that he'd had the article in his possession. Diane was silent for a few moments after that, and then she let out a long breath. "I guess the jerk had some feelings after all," she said.

My heart started to pound. "What do you mean?"

I wasn't prepared for her next words. "My sister was engaged to the guy."

I almost dropped my phone. "Engaged?"

"Yeah. He'd given her a diamond and everything. They were keeping it a secret," Diane said. "He'd been going with another actress, and he wanted to break the news to her before they made their relationship public. I thought it was a load of bull, but Eileen was completely besotted with him." She let out a shaky laugh. "You know, for a while after that happened, I was positive that he'd had something to do with it, that it was his way of getting out of a tricky situation. But maybe his feelings for her were on the level. I'll never know for sure, now."

I wished Diane well and ended the call. I'd had her on speaker so that Gary could listen in, and now I turned to him. "Well, if that doesn't beat all,"

I said.

"For the guy to have kept that article all these years—I'd say his feelings for this Eileen were probably genuine," Gary said. "I suppose the actress he was going with whose heart he didn't want to break was Noelle?"

"That's a good possibility, seeing as it was a year before he got involved with Taylor." I suddenly remembered something and grabbed my bag, pulled out the packet of photos. "These slid out of my bag earlier. Noelle helped me pick them up, and I noticed she seemed quite interested in them—aha, just as I thought." I shot Gary a look. "There's one missing."

Gary got up and leaned over my shoulder to squint at the photos. "They do match the one in the article," he said at last. "You said one's missing?"

"Yes. It was of the man. I remember he was tall and he wore a battered-looking jacket with a patch on the sleeve. He had something in his hand, something with stripes. You could only see his profile, which was grainy at best, and yet there was something about him that struck me as being familiar. I just can't place it for the life of me."

Gary eased back into his chair. "You think Noelle took the photo?"

"She must have," I said. "I know it was here before my bag fell. She helped pick up the photos. Right after that she pulled a disappearing act."

Gary put a finger to his lips. "Do you think Noelle might have been in cahoots with that man? That she plotted to get rid of the competition?"

"I don't want to think that, but . . . yeah, maybe it could be that way." I ran a hand through my hair. "I think we should try and track Noelle down. Confront her with this."

As if on cue, my phone rang. I looked at the number, and then at Gary. "It's Noelle." I picked up the phone, hit the speaker button. "Noelle? I was just thinking about you."

"Shell. Listen, I need your help."

"I need your help too, Noelle," I cut in. "I happened to find an article about Eileen Cullen in Terrill's things."

I heard a sharp gasp, and then Noelle said, "Ray kept the article about Eileen's death?"

"I found it in the same box as those photos. You know, the ones that fell out of my bag earlier." I paused. "Noelle, I know you took one of them."

Silence. Then, "I'm sorry. But I had to be sure. That's why I need your help, Shell. I think—I think I know who killed Ray. And Eileen."

Gary and I exchanged a look. "Was it the man in the photograph you took from me?"

"I—I can't answer that."

"Why not, Noelle? Because you and he were partners? Did you hire him to get rid of your rival for Terrill's affections?"

"I can't go into this now, or over the phone," Noelle said. Panic was evident in her tone. "I need you to trust me this once. Meet me later, Shell. The gazebo in back of the theater, where we're going to give the performance of *Our Town*. Meet me there in an hour. I'll tell you everything then."

"Why should I trust you, Noelle?"

"Because if you don't . . . there's a good chance Taylor will be convicted of a crime she didn't commit."

And then the line went dead.

Twenty-one

I tried redialing Noelle several times, but each call went straight to voicemail. At last I set the phone down and looked at Gary. "So? What do you think?" I asked him.

"She sounded sincere . . . and scared stiff."

"My thoughts exactly," I agreed. I glanced at the clock. "I don't want to wait an hour," I said. "I think we should try and find Noelle now. If she's telling the truth and she does know who the killer is, she's in real danger."

"I concur." Gary picked up his phone. "I suppose a call to Detective Riser is in order?"

"Wait." My hand shot out, closed over Gary's. "You know as well as I that if Riser's locked in on Taylor as the killer, she'll want evidence to prove that's not the case."

"We've got evidence," Gary said. "The article, and the photos found in Terrill's things."

I gave my head a quick shake. "All that proves is Terrill had an interest in the case, and his interest in Eileen Cullen explains that. Riser could say Terrill was just keeping mementos of his former love. The real tell is the photo of the man, and Noelle has that."

Gary set down his phone and folded his arms across his chest. "So now what? We have to do something, but for the life of me, I'm at a loss."

A knock sounded on the kitchen door. Gary went over and peered out the side window. He let out a low whistle. "What do you know? It's Quentin Watson," he said.

I pushed my chair back. "Watson? What's he doing here?"

"One way to find out." Gary walked over to the door and opened it. "Well, well, Quentin Watson. To what do we owe the pleasure?"

The newsman flashed us both a toothy grin. "Good evening, Gary, Shell. The two of you are looking well, all things considered."

I moved over to stand beside Gary. "What are you doing here, Quentin?" I asked.

Watson shifted his weight from one foot to the other and clucked his tongue. "Tsk, tsk, how fast we forget. I'm here to impart information."

Gary and I exchanged a puzzled look. "What sort of information?" Gary

166

finally asked.

Watson let out a low chuckle and turned to me. "If you recall our previous conversation, Shell, you gave me a pretty good tip on Terrill paying a visit to the McCloud Building. You also asked me to inform you of what, if anything, I might find out. I'm here to repay you for your tip."

"That's right. I completely forgot." I stepped to one side. "Won't you come in, Mr. Watson? Would you like a cup of coffee?"

Watson stepped into the kitchen and shot me a smug smile. "As a matter of fact, I would."

Gary went over to the Keurig while I ushered Quentin Watson over to the small dining table. He pulled out a chair and sat down, and Gary set a steaming mug of coffee in front of him.

"Cream and sugar?" I asked.

Watson smiled at me. "Please."

I set the sugar bowl and cream pitcher in front of him and pulled out the chair next to him. Gary lounged against the island counter. I waited until Watson had taken a few sips of his coffee before I asked, "So, what did you learn?"

Watson set the mug down. "It wasn't easy getting a bead on him. Terrill apparently was one sneaky devil."

"But you did find out something?"

Watson nodded. "Yes. I finally found one chatty janitor. He recalled seeing Terrill entering the offices of the Skillman Detective Agency on the day in question."

"The detective agency, huh?" Gary leaned forward. "We thought he might have been visiting a lawyer."

Watson nodded. "That's a natural assumption. The building is primarily a lawyers' haven. However, Skillman has been in that building just as long if not longer than most of 'em. Anyway, I went there to check it out."

"And," I said impatiently, as Quentin lapsed into silence. "Did you find out what the appointment was about?"

Watson picked up the mug, took another swallow of coffee, and then continued, "Unfortunately, no. Skillman's out of town, working on a case. He's expected back in a few days, though."

I frowned. "Skillman doesn't have an assistant you could have questioned?"

Watson waved his hand dismissively. "I'd rather talk to the horse himself, if you get my drift. Assistants usually don't have much to offer. Anyway, I plan on visiting him then, see what if anything I can get out of him." He let out a long sigh and ran his finger along the rim of his mug. "It won't be easy."

"Why would you think that? He can't claim client confidentiality, not when Terrill's dead," said Gary.

Watson shrugged. "No, but these PIs are clammy types. Some insist on honoring confidentiality even after death. I might have to grease his palm, if you get my drift."

Oh, ho, there it was. I met Watson's gaze. "I can contribute a hundred, if you need it."

The newsman flashed me another grin. "I'll send you a bill if I do. But maybe we'll get lucky." He drummed his fingers against the tabletop. "In other breaking news, I understand Josh's cousin, Taylor Tyson, has been arrested."

I started. "Where did you hear that?"

"I was passing the police station when I saw the squad car pull up with her in it. I also saw Norman Hines arriving at approximately the same time. He's a pretty high-priced attorney. Specializes in criminal cases. So, putting two and two together . . ."

"You came up with six," Gary finished. "As far as we know, Taylor hasn't been arrested. She was just taken down for some more questioning."

"She might not have been arrested yet, but if Hines is on the scene, it's only a matter of time." Watson took another swig of coffee and pushed his chair back. "I'd best get down there, see what I can ferret out. I need a good headline for tomorrow's paper."

"Take it easy on Taylor, Watson," said Gary. "The kid's being railroaded. She's not a killer."

"I'll agree, she doesn't look the part—then again, she is an actress. You know, just because she's Josh's cousin doesn't necessarily mean she's innocent. She had a pretty volatile history with Terrill, or so my sources tell me."

"So did lots of other women—Noelle Boyd for one. Kristi Marchall for another."

Watson scratched at his head. "I agree, Terrill's history with the Boyd girl does rival Taylor's. Now *her* I could see as a murderess. As for Kristi Marchall— that woman has way too much class. I never could understand her attraction to Terrill in the first place."

"Some women like the bad boys," I said. I shot Gary a sidelong glance and added, "Look at Gary. His whole career has been predicated on that."

Gary wrinkled his nose. "Gee, thanks a lot."

"You know it's true."

"Yeah, but still . . ."

Watson let out a snort as he pushed back his chair. Rising, he faced Gary. "I greatly doubt your public image could compare in any way to Terrill's," he said. He walked over to the door, laid his hand on the knob, then turned to me. "I'll keep you advised on my meeting with Skillman, Shell. Keep that checkbook close." With a brief wave, he pulled the door open and stepped out into the night.

Gary shut the door behind Watson and then looked at me. "That guy is a real piece of work."

"True, but he does have a knack for ferreting out information. I've got a feeling that Terrill went to that detective agency to find out something about the man in the photograph. And if I were a betting woman, I'd bet my house and business that he hit pay dirt and did find out that man's identity."

"The man who killed the love of his life. Hm. Raises some pretty scary scenarios, if you ask me."

"You know, Taylor said she gave Terrill her gun. I'll bet Terrill had a specific purpose in mind when he asked her for it."

"Ah, so now you think the killer acted in self-defense?"

"Maybe. There's still the matter of the silencer. Somehow I don't think Taylor owned one."

"Which would mean the killer purchased one, or brought one with him or her. Which indicates premeditation."

I pulled out my cell, punched in the number of Secondhand Sue's. Sue Bloodgood answered almost immediately. "Hey, Shell. What's up? Do you have any news about Taylor?"

"Nothing yet," I said. "Sue, do you know anywhere around here where someone could purchase a silencer for a gun?"

"Why, sure. Oddly enough, I have a couple in stock. I thought they were war mementos, or antiques. Why?"

"You do! Has anyone bought one in the last few days?"

"Not from me. Let me check with Greta."

A few minutes later Sue came back on the line. "It just so happens that she did sell one a few days ago. To a guy."

"She did!" I gave a thumbs-up to Gary and then asked, "Does Greta remember what he looked like?"

"Just a sec, I'll ask, but you know we're lucky if Greta remembers what day it is."

A few minutes later Sue said, "All she remembers is that he was tall. She said he had a cap on, pulled low, a big puffy coat, and he talked funny, like he had marbles in his mouth or something."

"Did he pay cash? Or maybe a credit card?"

Sue sighed. "I guess I should just put Greta on the phone, shouldn't I. Just a sec." A few minutes later Greta's nasal voice came over the wire. "Shell? He paid cash. I remember that distinctly, because hardly anyone pays cash anymore."

"Did you give him a receipt? Do you have a copy?"

"Oh, yeah. Just a sec."

Another few minutes, and then Greta came back on the line. "He just wanted it made out to his initials: *IKP.*"

"*IKP?* That's it?"

"Yep. Sorry."

"No, no, you've been a big help. Thanks."

I disconnected and looked at Gary. "Well, at least we can narrow it down to a man."

"Maybe. I know some women who can imitate a man pretty well. And in a puffy coat, with a cap, voice disguised . . . I wouldn't rule out a woman yet."

I sighed. "I suppose you're right." I glanced at the clock. "We'd better get over there. Maybe Noelle will be early."

I grabbed my purse and started for the door, then paused as my cell phone jangled. I whipped it out and looked at the screen. "It's Josh," I said, and swiped the answer button, then hit the speaker icon so Gary could hear. "Hey. What happened? Did Amy arrest Taylor?"

"Oh, yes, but fortunately Norman Hines managed to get her out on bail. She was released into my custody."

"That's good, right? So where are you?"

"I'm at the inn. Taylor just went up to her room. I hung back to call you, but now I'm going right up to her room. I'm going to stay with her, at least for tonight. We have a meeting with the lawyer first thing tomorrow morning."

"That's a good idea. Maybe things will be brighter in the morning," I said.

"One can only hope. Once again, I'm sorry about dinner, Shell."

"Oh, no problem. Gary can cook for us some other night." Gary stuck out his tongue at me as I added, "You take care now, and tell Taylor we wish her all the best."

"Thanks. I'll call you after the meeting with the lawyer tomorrow."

I hung up and looked at Gary. "Who knows, maybe after tonight that meeting with the lawyer won't be necessary."

Gary nodded grimly. "We can only hope." He paused. "I thought you might have filled Josh in on our conversation with Noelle."

"I thought about it," I admitted. "But I think he's got enough on his plate right now. I'll call him after we talk to her."

We got in my convertible and Gary drove the short distance to the theater. We parked on the street and hurried up to the walkway behind the theater that led to the gazebo. Usually there were lights along the walkway but apparently they'd burned out and not been replaced yet. Gary called up the flashlight app on his cell, and it cut a bright beam of light down the path that led to the rickety structure. We approached it and stood for a moment, listening. Absolute dead silence.

"Noelle," I said in a stage whisper. "Noelle, it's Shell and Gary. Where are you?"

Silence. Then, a strangled sob, followed by a scream.

Gary and I didn't hesitate. We took the stairs two at a time until we reached the center of the gazebo. Then we stopped and stared at the tableau frozen in the beam of Gary's flashlight.

Noelle lay smack dab in the center of the gazebo. Her neck hung at a rakish angle, and there was no doubt she was dead. Bending over her body, looking pale as wax, was Taylor Tyson.

Twenty-two

For a moment none of us moved. Finally I advanced slowly toward Noelle and Taylor. "Taylor," I said softly. "Taylor, what are you doing here?"

Taylor jumped up as if she'd just suffered an electric shock. "Oh, Shell," she cried. "It's Noelle. She—I think she's dead."

Taylor swayed toward me, but I caught her and held her up. Gary, in the meantime, bent over Noelle's inert form. He touched his fingers to her neck, then looked up at me and shook his head. "She's gone." He rose, pulled out his cell phone. "We need to call the police pronto."

"Do you have to?" Taylor cried. Her voice was muffled against my shoulder. "Riser will never believe me. She'll revoke my bail and I'll have to spend God knows how long in jail."

I shifted so that I could look into Taylor's eyes. "You know we have to report this," I said softly.

Taylor swallowed. "I-I know. It's just—I didn't kill her, I swear."

I gave her hand a quick squeeze. "I believe you."

Taylor's lips thinned. "Then you're in the minority around here."

Gary tapped 911 into his phone and moved away. I led Taylor over to the corner of the gazebo away from Noelle's body. There was a small bench there, and I eased her onto it, then sat down next to her. In a soft tone I asked, "Taylor, what happened? What were you doing here? I talked to Josh and he said he was going to stay with you tonight."

Taylor took a deep breath, exhaled. "I got a text from Noelle. She said that I was to come here at ten, that she'd found information that cleared me of Ray's murder and she'd share it with me. She stressed that I should come alone."

"Really?" I looked over at Gary. "I had a phone call from her earlier. She told me the same thing."

Taylor's eyes widened. "She did? That seems odd, don't you think? Why would she invite you when she told me specifically to come alone?"

"I was thinking the exact same thing," I admitted. "I'm also wondering why she would call me, but text you?"

"I could think of one reason," Gary remarked. "Maybe the text Taylor received wasn't from Noelle."

Taylor paled. "Goodness. I never thought of that. But it was from her phone."

"What time did she send you this message?" I asked.

"It was shortly before I was released on bail. I have to admit, that lawyer Josh got for me is pretty terrific. He called the judge and got me out in no time. When I got my phone back, I had one message. It was from Noelle. She said she had information that definitely cleared me of Ray's murder, and I should meet her here at ten and she'd tell me what it was. She told me to come alone."

Taylor let out a breath. "I didn't know how I was going to shake Josh, but fortunately he said he had a phone call to make and sent me on ahead. I went up to my floor, then snuck down the back staircase and came straight here. I heard your voices, and then I stumbled over her body." Her shoulders lifted in a shudder. "I never cared much for Noelle, but she didn't deserve this. And now she's dead, and we'll never know what she found that could clear me."

I looked at Taylor. "Did Terrill ever mention that traffic accident to you, the one that killed the extra in Kansas City?"

Taylor shook her head. "Not that I recall. I knew about it, of course. Everyone did. But Ray never talked about it—at least, not to me."

The sound of a police siren broke the stillness. Gary walked over to where we sat. "Riser doesn't waste any time," he said.

Taylor rose, wringing her hands in front of her. "What am I going to do?" she wailed. "Riser will never believe me, but I'm telling the truth. She probably can't wait to slap those handcuffs on me and haul me back to jail."

I slipped an arm around her shoulders. "We'll call Josh. Just don't say a word. Tell Riser you aren't going to speak without your attorney present."

"Won't that make me look guilty?"

I raised an eyebrow, and she shot me a sheepish look. "Okay, you're right. I'll plead the Fifth."

"Shell? Gary?" Riser's head appeared at the top of the stairs. Her eyes widened as she caught sight of Taylor standing beside me. "What's going on here?"

Gary stepped forward. "Shell got a message earlier from Noelle to meet her here. She said that she knew who killed Terrill and she'd tell us when we got here."

"I see." Riser looked at Taylor. "And you? How do you fit into all this?"

173

Taylor lifted her chin. "I refuse to make any statements without my attorney present."

"Of course you do," Riser muttered. She turned back to me. "Did Taylor come with you two?"

I shook my head. "No. She was here when we arrived."

Riser turned to Taylor. "You found the body?"

Taylor clamped her lips together. "I have no comment until I can speak with my lawyer."

Riser sighed. She turned to Gary and me. "You two have a problem giving a statement?"

We shook our heads, and Riser pushed her cap up on her forehead. "Good. Shell and Gary, you can give your statements here to Detective Cosgrove. Taylor, I'm going to have to ask you to come back to the station with me. You can call your lawyer from there."

Riser laid her hand on Taylor's arm. Taylor glanced back at me as Riser led her away, and I gave her a thumbs-up before they disappeared down the stairs. Detective Cosgrove touched my arm. "Ready to give your statement, Shell?" he asked.

I nodded grimly. "I am."

• • •

The whole procedure took about forty minutes. It was a little after eleven o'clock when Gary and I got back into my convertible. I'd called Josh while Gary was giving his statement to let him know what happened. As I feared, he'd been frantic when he realized Taylor had left the inn. His mood didn't improve when I told him about finding her bending over Noelle's lifeless body.

"I doubt Hines can keep her out of jail now," he groaned. "Shell, she was released into my custody. I blew it big-time."

"No, you didn't," I said. "Trust me, Taylor would have found some way to elude you and keep that meeting. The killer planned on that, too. Just go down to the station and support her. It's all you can do right now."

I disconnected and Gary turned the key in the ignition and the motor sputtered to life. He shot me a sidelong glance. "Spill it," he said. "I know you've got something on your mind."

"Taylor was set up. Whoever texted her must have known Noelle called me." I sighed.

"I agree," said Gary. "Noelle's body was still pretty warm. She couldn't have been dead too long. I think it's possible that Noelle did text Taylor. Maybe the killer forced her to, knowing Taylor would come and be implicated in her murder."

"It's possible," I agreed. "Noelle said that whatever she found would clear Taylor. Without that information, and based on what happened tonight, I'm afraid she might well be railroaded for a crime she didn't commit," I said. "I want to do something, but what? We've no clues, nothing to go on."

"I wouldn't say that."

Gary reached into his pocket, pulled out a small scrap of paper. "When I bent down to see if Noelle was still alive, I saw this sticking out from underneath her body. I picked it up and stuffed it in my pocket."

I stared at him. "Gary Presser! Shame on you, removing evidence from a crime scene!"

He looked at me, all innocence. "Hey, now, I had no idea it was evidence. For all I knew, it could just have been a scrap of paper that she'd fallen on. And, really, that's all it seems to be."

He passed me the paper. I looked at it. It was a small piece of cream-colored stationery, with the initials *IKP* printed on it. Nothing else.

I let out a cry. "IKP is the person who bought the silencer at Secondhand Sue's. Greta said he only gave his initials."

"I guess that paper could be considered evidence, after all. Maybe I should turn it over to Riser."

"Not on your life," I said. "Riser would throw the book at you or worse. And I need backup."

Gary's eyes narrowed. "Backup for what, exactly?"

"For our visit to Skillman Investigations tomorrow."

Gary stared at me. "Tomorrow? You heard Quentin—the guy's out of town."

"Yes, but his receptionist slash assistant should be there. I'm afraid I don't share Quentin's opinion about assistants. I've always found that they usually know more about the boss's business than the boss, and if they're in the right frame of mind, they don't mind sharing."

Gary nodded. "Good point. Okay—let's get home and get some rest. First thing tomorrow, Skillman Investigations."

Twenty-three

At nine a.m. Gary and I walked through the front door of the McCloud Building. We wasted no time but immediately got in the elevator and went to the third floor, where the offices of Skillman Investigations were located. The office itself looked like something out of a Sam Spade movie. The front office was small and was occupied almost entirely by a massive desk. The woman sitting behind the desk was petite, with creamy skin and long blonde hair that flowed across slim shoulders. She wore a high-necked white blouse and a navy blue jacket and looked very trim and professional. The brass nameplate on the desk gave her name as Liza Pough. She glanced up as we approached and gave us a wide smile.

"Good morning," she said. "If you're looking for Mr. Skillman, I'm afraid he's out of town on a case. If you'd like to make an appointment for next week, I'll be happy to check his calendar."

Gary leaned across the desk and shot her one of his most ingratiating smiles. "We don't need an appointment, Liza. Actually, what we're looking for is information, information you might be able to help us with."

The smile vanished from Liza's face, replaced by a wary look. "What sort of information?" she asked. "I'm not at liberty to reveal details about any of Mr. Skillman's cases. Those are strictly confidential."

"Of course they are," Gary said. "We're not looking for any information about any of Mr. Skillman's cases. We just want to know if you've ever seen this man in here."

He whipped a photo of Raymond Terrill out of his pocket and laid it on the desk in front of her. Liza looked at it and her frown deepened. "Of course I have. That's Mr. Terrill."

Now I leaned across the desk. "Raymond Terrill?"

"Yes." Liza's lips thinned and she regarded us suspiciously. "He's a client. We're not permitted to speak to people about our clients."

Gary leaned further across the counter. "We do realize that, Liza, and we appreciate your discretion. But trust us, this is a matter of life and death."

Her eyes narrowed. "Just who are you and why are you asking about him? Can I see some ID?"

Gary pulled out his wallet, extracted his driver's license and handed it to

Liza. I did the same. She looked at them, and suddenly her eyes widened. "Oh my God. You're Gary Presser! From *Spy Anyone?*"

Gary graced her with his full-wattage smile. "That's me."

"Oh my God," she said again. Her gaze whipped to me. "This license says Crishell McMillan, but I'd bet my life you're Shell Marlowe!"

"I am. Crishell McMillan is my real name."

Liza started fanning herself. "*Spy Anyone* was one of my favorite shows. I cried when it went off the air."

"So did Gary," I said with a laugh.

Liza turned a worshipful gaze on Gary. "Why do you want to know about Mr. Terrill? Are you researching his life for some sort of future role or something?"

"As a matter of fact, that's exactly what I'm doing," Gary said. He leaned across the desk and said in a low tone, "We don't want this to get out, but there are plans to do a movie tribute to Mr. Terrill. I'm in the running for the role, so the more I learn about him, the better my chances will be of snagging the part. I'd sure appreciate your help, Liza."

The girl let out a heartfelt sigh. "Anything I can do to help." She hesitated. "Mr. Skillman is very strict about sharing information on clients, but seeing as Mr. Terrill is dead, I don't suppose it would matter."

Gary threw me a triumphant look, then turned his attention back to Liza. "Well, for starters, do you know what Mr. Terrill was consulting Mr. Skillman on? I'd heard it was a marital situation."

Liza's perfectly arched brows drew together. "Marital situation? Oh, goodness, no. It was nothing like that. As far as I know, Mr. Terrill wasn't married." She let out a self-conscious giggle. "At least, he didn't act like he was."

Gary leaned in a bit closer. "It was something else, then?"

Liza hesitated. "This will stay strictly between us? If Mr. Skillman ever finds out that I told anyone, he'll have my head."

Gary made a crossing motion over his heart. "Just between the three of us, I swear."

I nodded. "I do, too."

"Well, okay then." Liza pushed her chair back, walked over to a small filing cabinet and jerked open the middle drawer. She rummaged around in there for a few minutes before pulling out a manila folder. She came back to the desk and laid the folder in front of Gary. "Mr. Terrill wanted Mr. Skillman to work on a missing persons case. A Leonard Gruber."

Gary and I exchanged a glance. Then Gary asked, "And did Mr. Skillman find this Leonard Gruber."

"Yeah, he did. But it didn't do Mr. Terrill a lot of good. Lenny Gruber is dead."

"Dead," I cried. "Are you sure?"

Liza nodded. "Yep." She tapped the folder. "Obit and everything's in there."

"You wouldn't happen to know just why Mr. Terrill was looking for this Leonard Gruber, would you, Liza?" Gary asked.

She shook her head. "No. All I know is he called Mr. Skillman a few weeks ago from California. He said that he'd gotten a tip that this guy was somewhere here in Fox Hollow and he wanted Mr. Skillman to see if he could locate him."

"So this Leonard Gruber died here in Fox Hollow?" I asked.

"No, he died in Clarendon, Kansas, about six months ago. It's here in his obituary. See."

Liza opened the folder and extracted a sheet of paper. She passed it over to Gary, and I read over his shoulder:

> *Leonard Prestwick Gruber, age 34, of Clarendon, Kansas, passed away at home following a brief illness. He is survived by his mother, Annetta Gruber (née Prestwick), his sister, Isabella Gruber McClellan, and his cousins, Diana Leigh Gruber and Irving K. Prestwick.*
>
> *Relatives and friends are invited to his visitation on Sunday, December 29, from 10:00 to 11:30 a.m. at the McCann-Healey Funeral Home, 851 Monmouth St., Clarendon. Funeral service will be held following the visitation. Interment will be private.*

I looked up at Liza. "I guess Mr. Terrill wasn't happy to learn this," I said.

Liza shrugged. "I thought he wouldn't be, too, but he didn't seem upset in the least. There were some photographs, too, that Mr. Skillman found that were taken at the interment, but Mr. Terrill took those."

"What sort of photographs?" I had a gruesome thought of photos of Leonard lying in his coffin, which I immediately pushed out of my mind.

"Just some photos of the family at the grave site. There was one group shot of the mother and the cousins. Mr. Terrill seemed particularly interested in that one."

Gary handed the obituary back to Liza, who slipped it back into the folder. "I don't suppose there's any way you could get us a copy of that photo," Gary asked.

Liza looked up. "Why would you want that?"

Gary smiled. "You said Mr. Terrill was interested in it. If I could see it, maybe I could figure out why, and it would help me fit into the role better."

Liza brightened. "Oh, sure, if that's the case. I happen to know the guy at the paper who helped out Mr. Skillman. I'll see if he's got another one he could email to me."

"Great. Let me give you my email address. And Liza, you've been a big help to me. More than you'll ever know."

· · ·

Back in the hallway, I turned to Gary. "Terrill must have known that Lenny Gruber was the man in the photograph, the one taken at the scene of the accident that killed Eileen Cullen."

"And he was probably looking for the guy hoping to exact some sort of revenge," Gary said.

"Maybe he wanted to kill Gruber, but Gruber got to him first," I said thoughtfully. "Noelle must have also recognized him in that photograph. That must be why she took it. But the killer can't be Lenny Gruber if he's dead."

"True," Gary said. Then he snapped his fingers. "It fits."

"What?"

"If you recall, the obituary also mentioned a male cousin—an Irving K. Prestwick." He reached into his pocket and pulled out the scrap of paper. "IKP—it fits."

"That's right, it did. So that's why you wanted a copy of that photograph."

"Exactly. Both Terrill and Noelle must have recognized the man in the photograph from the hit-and-run was IKP. Maybe once we see the photo from the interment, we'll get some insight and then we can take it straight to Riser."

"I hope you're right," I said.

Gary looked at his watch. "It's just ten. How about if I take the early shift at the pet shop. You go home and get some rest. You look like you didn't sleep a wink last night."

"I didn't," I confessed. "Everything's been preying on my mind."

"Well, there's really nothing we can do now until we get that photo from Liza. Go on home." He made a shooing motion with his hand. "I'll call you the second I get that photo."

"You'd better."

We parted company at the corner. Gary walked up the block to Urban Tails and I made the left turn that led toward home. The cats all greeted me at the back door when I walked in. "I'd like to think you all missed me, but I know you want food," I said. I filled each of their bowls with kibble and then kicked off my shoes and sat down at the kitchen table. I'd told Gary I was tired, but the truth was I was still too keyed up over recent events to sleep. Two people were dead, and there was a killer running around Fox Hollow somewhere. Sleep was out of the question for now. I had the distinct feeling that there was something I was missing, some obvious clue—but what?

My cell rang. I looked at the screen and sighed. My mother. Well, if I didn't answer it now she'd only call again. I swiped the answer icon and said, "Hello, Mother. What's up?"

"This production is doomed," my mother groaned. "First Raymond, now Noelle. How can I stage a successful production if everyone keeps dying on me?"

"I'm sure it's not intentional, Mother."

"Very funny. And where have you been all morning? I tried your cell a few times."

"Gary and I had an errand to run."

"Oh?" I heard my mother's tone rise ever so slightly. "You and Gary, eh?"

"Yes, Mother. Why?"

"You know, all this just adds fuel to my theory that the two of you are lousy actors."

"Excuse me?"

"You and Gary. Who do you think you're fooling?"

I let out an exasperated sigh. "Mother, if you want to say something, just come out and say it. Don't beat around the bush."

"Fine. You act like you're not interested in him, yet you're always with him. He acts like he's not crazy about you, but any fool can see he's besotted with you."

180

I rolled my eyes. "Besotted? Really, Mother."

"Well, it's true."

"If you must know, Gary and I were over at the McCloud Building, trying to follow up a lead on Terrill's murder."

"See," Clarissa cried triumphantly. "That's exactly what I mean. The two of you continually playing private eye. It's just an excuse for the two of you to be together."

I bit back the angry retort that rose to my lips and said in a soothing tone, "Mother, you're imagining this. Gary is interested in Olivia, and in case you haven't noticed, I'm pretty tight with Josh."

"Not tight enough, apparently," my mother said with a sigh. "I honestly don't know what to do with you, Crishell. Sometimes you just can't see what's right in front of your eyes."

"And you think that's Gary?"

"Heavens, no! The two of you are all wrong for each other. Josh, though, is a different story. Please, Crishell, don't let this one get away."

My mother hung up, and I set my phone down. I hated to admit it, but she was right. Not about me and Gary, but about me not being able to see what was right in front of me. The answer to Terrill and Noelle's murders was there, I knew it.

Princess Fuzzypants ambled over and rubbed her head against my ankles. I leaned down and rubbed her head. "I'm kind of glad no one has claimed you, Princess," I said. "And I think Purrday echoes that sentiment."

The one-eyed Persian looked up from his food bowl and gave a loud meow.

"As for my mother, well, now I know she's nuts. Thinking there's something romantic between me and Gary. I'm nuts about Josh, and Gary likes Olivia. Just because Gary and I make a good investigative team, she's got us paired off like Nick and Nora Charles, or Jonathan and Jennifer Hart, for goodness sakes. I mean, we did play married spies for seven years, after all. Something had to rub off."

Purrday and the princess looked at each other and then at me, then the princess jumped into my lap and started purring. I stroked her head as I thought. I had to get my mind back on the prize. It all went back to that accident, to those photos. There was something there, but what?

I jumped up so suddenly that the princess fell off my lap, landing on all fours. "Sorry, Princess. I've got to check something out. Feel free to tag along."

I hurried upstairs to my office and grabbed a magnifying glass out of the desk drawer. Then I came back downstairs, grabbed my jacket and opened the back door. The princess and Purrday dashed out ahead of me, but Kahlua remained hunched in front of her bowl, determined to finish her kibble and also anyone else's. I made my way back to the shed, and once inside went straight to the box that contained Terrill's belongings. I pulled out the puzzle box, opened it, and took out the clipping. I moved over to the desk and pulled the magnifying glass out of my jacket pocket. I hunched over the desk, examined the photo under the glass. I saw what looked like scraps of paper by the rear tire. It looked like there were some sort of markings on the scraps, but they were so small I couldn't make them out. Darn! If there was only some way to get the photo blown up.

I heard a scuffling sound and glanced up. The princess and Purrday appeared to be fighting over a small scrap of paper. I set the magnifying glass down and walked over to them. "What have the two of you got there?" I asked. The cats stopped, and both looked up—rather guiltily, I thought. The princess lifted her front paw, and I saw what had attracted their attention.

It was a gum wrapper, but not just any gum wrapper. Pink and purple stripes, with yellow dots in between. And across it in bright green were the words . . .

I snatched the wrapper up, turned it over in my hand. "Oh my gosh," I cried. "I know who killed Terrill and Noelle."

"R-really? T-that's t-too bad."

The wrapper fell from my hand as I turned slowly to face Kenny Parsons standing in the doorway of the shed. He held a .45 revolver in his hand, and it was pointed straight at me.

Twenty-four

Kenny moved toward me, his lips curved downward in a sneer. "I've been k-keeping an eye on you, S-Shell. Since you and Gary are s-such m-master sl-sleuths, I knew it was only a m-matter of time before you figured it out."

My heart was beating so hard I thought it might fall out of my chest. Somehow I managed to make my tone remain calm as I said, "You killed Terrill, didn't you, Kenny? And Noelle too?"

He nodded. "They gave me no choice. F-for years I've tried to put that accident behind me. T-Terrill wouldn't let it rest."

"So Eileen's death was an accident?"

Kenny looked almost insulted. "Of c-course it was. I was a little intoxicated that night, I admit it. My cousin Lenny had just passed away, and I was g-grieving. I had a l-little t-too much to drink. I saw that car with the keys in it and thought maybe a drive w-would clear my head. B-but it didn't. Next thing I knew, she was in front of the car. I d-didn't mean to hit her. She startled me so much, I crashed the car. I have no idea how I w-walked away, but I did. And I knew I h-had to get away, before the police came to arrest me."

"So you assumed your cousin Lenny's identity?"

"F-for a while. I didn't know that there was a security camera there, or that it had taken my photo. Things went well for a while. I got a job as a waiter in a diner, and I was making a new life for myself. But T-Terrill was determined to find me. He hired investigators, and someone identified that photo as Lenny Gruber. I remembered one of my customers talking about Fox Hollow and what a nice town it was, so I c-came here, sh-shaved my beard, and got ID under Kenny Parsons. But that Skillman guy—he's a good PI, all right. He made the connection between Kenny Parsons and Lenny Gruber."

"How did he do that?"

Kenny shook his head. "I didn't think anyone would research my real name. Irving Kenneth Prestwick. Skillman did. He traced me from that photo taken at the grave, and he found out that my mother's maiden name was Prestwick. He passed that info onto Terrill. I thought at first when Terrill saw me at the theater I was home-free, but then he confronted me. He said that even though the statute of limitations had run out on my crime, he was going to make sure I paid for taking that girl's life. I tried to tell him it was a mistake, that I wasn't the guy he was after, but he said that he knew 'Lenny Gruber' had a distinctive stutter and I couldn't hide anymore. He said he was going to expose me and make sure I never got another job again. I knew he could do it, too. I saw Taylor put that gun in his dressing room, and I took it. Then I went and bought a silencer. I followed him here that night and took care of him."

I swallowed. "Did you come back here, looking for Terrill's evidence? I thought some of the boxes had been moved."

He nodded. "I did, but then I thought I heard someone coming so I beat it."

That probably explained how the cats had gotten into the shed. "And Noelle?"

"She recognized me from that security photo. Years ago, when she was in that clinic drying out from the drugs, I was working there. I'd told her that I had a secret too but I never told her exactly what. I hinted, though, that it had to do with a car accident. Once she saw that photo, she recognized me and figured it out. She called me, said she knew that I'd killed Terrill. She said that since I'd been nice to her when she was in the clinic, she'd give me the opportunity to flee town, but she was going to tell the police. She couldn't let Taylor get railroaded for a crime she didn't commit." Kenny shook his head. "I followed her to the gazebo, tried to reason with her. She wouldn't agree not to say anything, so . . . it was a simple matter to strangle her with her own scarf. Less messy, too."

"Was it you who texted Taylor to meet Noelle at the gazebo?"

He nodded. "I knew she'd move h-heaven and earth to come, and I knew she'd get arrested for the c-crime. Believe me, I didn't want to frame her, but I didn't have a choice. I c-can't go t-to prison." He reached into his pocket, pulled out a stick of gum, popped it into his mouth. "It h-helps. I s-stutter less when I chew."

I took a step backward. "You don't want to do this, Kenny. You don't want to add another murder to your list."

He shrugged, chewing furiously. "You're right, I don't. But like Terrill and Noelle, you've given me no choice. You won't stay quiet, not when your boyfriend's cousin is the one going down for my crimes." He waved the gun at me. "Take your cell phone out of your pocket. I know you've got one, you wouldn't have come out without it. Besides, you're expecting your pal Gary to call you, right? I guess I'll have to take care of him, too, before I leave town. Now take it out and put it down on the floor where I can see it, then step back."

I hesitated, then pulled my phone out of my pocket and set it down on the floor. I gave a quick glance over at the corner where the cats had been, and noted that neither one was in sight. I took a step backward and raised my chin defiantly. "So, what now? You can't pin my death on Taylor, she's at the police station right now."

"Right. That's why you're going to have a little accident. Come on. Hands in the air."

I moved in front of him, keeping both arms raised. "Where are we going?" I asked. It took a supreme effort to keep my voice from shaking.

"The park isn't far from here," he said. "We're going to go for a little walk." He grinned. "You know that man-made stream, right below the rock mountain? Well, you're gonna be the victim of a slip and fall."

My mouth was dry as I answered. "That's no plan, Kenny. That stream isn't big enough to drown in."

"It is if you hit your head on a rock before you fall in. Which you will." He waved the gun. "This is the night watchman at the theater's gun. I'll have it wiped clean and back before they ever know it's missing. Now come on, let's move. And no funny stuff. I'm a good shot, as you know."

He took my arm and pushed me out the door. We crossed the street and headed for the park. I glanced around at the parked cars and wondered if I could make a dash for them and roll under one of the cars before he could get a shot off.

As if he read my mind, he nudged me in the back with the gun. "Don't even think about it. I see you looking at the cars. Like I said, I'm a good shot. You'd never make it."

We started up the grassy knoll. "I know you're thinking that I'm taking a real chance doing this in broad daylight, but I know this area. Hardy anyone goes by here. Plus, I've got a rental car parked near the back exit. I'll be gone like a shot. To the theater to drop off the gun, and then it's Canada for me."

We were almost at the edge where the grass gave way to a rock wall and the river beyond. Somehow I needed to buy time. If I could keep him talking, maybe I could figure out something. "You know, Noelle was my first choice for Terrill's murderer," I said.

Kenny nodded. "I can understand that. Even though Noelle went to rehab, she still harbored a major grudge against Terrill. Some other actress won a Drama Desk award for a part Noelle had been up for, but didn't get on account of the drugs. She held that against Terrill too. Honest, it would have been so easy to frame her for the murder. If only Taylor hadn't made herself such a target."

I looked over at the rocks piled there, all sharp, jagged edges. About six feet down, off to the right, I saw what looked like a ledge. If I could jump and land on that flat space, I could flatten myself against the rocks so Kenny couldn't see me. I swallowed at the lump that rose in my throat.

I heard Gary's voice in my head: *Honestly, Shell. Sometimes you should just go for it.* And then, before I had a chance to think about the pros or cons of my plan, I followed Gary's advice. I did it.

I jumped.

I flung my arms wide and caught nothing but air. Then I hit the rocks and started to slide. I scrambled for something, anything to hold on to while above me Kenny let out a loud roar.

Suddenly my feet connected with solid ground. I bent my knees and shifted my weight forward, trying to hug the rock wall. My right foot slipped, but the left one held. I felt a surge of panic as I realized there was nowhere to find a handhold—and then my fingers caught the edge of a rock. I dug in and held on for dear life. I eased my free hand down and wrapped it around a large rock that jutted out beside me. Above me I could hear Kenny cursing and calling my name.

I pressed my body tighter against the rock face, then bent my knee and pulled my leg in closer to my body. My hands were trembling, but I had no intention of letting go. I closed my eyes and let my breathing slow to normal. I turned my head slightly to look around. Over the slope of the hill was the business district. If I could get down there without Kenny spotting me, I could get to the pet shop and Gary.

I shifted my weight and started to feel around. After a moment I found a foothold. I loosened my grip on the rock and started to climb slowly down. I tried not to think about the raw palms of my hands or the stab of pain in my right ankle. I must have sprained it when I dashed against the boulder. Right now I was concentrating on staying alive.

A smooth stone pinged off a boulder beside me and into the stream. I looked up to see Kenny, arm raised, launch another rock down the embankment. I knew what he was trying to do—knock me off the rock wall. I held my breath, closed my eyes, and jumped again.

I hit a patch of bushes and grass. My ankle gave way and I landed hard on my left hip. But I was alive, and in one piece. I stayed low to the ground and crab-walked down, finally squeezing myself into a space between a boulder and a patch of tall grass. If only I had my cell phone!

"Thought you could get away from me?"

I whirled at the sound of Kenny's voice. Somehow he'd made it down the embankment and was about twenty yards away from me. He raised his gun but I bent down, grabbed a large rock, and threw it. It hit him on the side of his head, just above his temple. He crumpled like a wet rag. I lunged for the gun, grabbed it. No sooner had I done that than I heard someone calling my name.

"Shell? Are you here?"

Gary. I took a deep breath. "Yes, I'm here," I shouted back. "Kenny Parsons is here too. I've got his gun. He's the one who killed Terrill and Noelle."

Gary's head appeared at the top of the embankment. "We know," he called down to me. "Your mother was in the shop when the photo came in from Liza and she recognized Kenny immediately. I called for Josh and we went to the house. We found Purrday and the princess going nuts in the shed. They must have gotten locked in. Anyway, they were going nuts around a striped gum wrapper. Josh remembered Taylor telling him that Kenny chewed gum that came from a neon wrapper. Purrday and the princess started heading toward the park, but we managed to get them back in the house. Then we came straight here to look for you."

Josh's head appeared next to Gary's. "Hang on, Shell," he called. "I've got some rope. We'll have you up in no time."

A few seconds later, I stepped into a loop of rope and secured it under my arms. I went up, up, up, over the rocky terrain I'd previously scaled, back onto the grassy knoll. Josh and Gary both stepped forward, got me free of the rope.

"Gee, Shell," said Gary. "You took some chance."

I shot him a lopsided grin. "What can I say? I like to live dangerously."

And then I collapsed in Josh's strong, warm arms.

Twenty-five

It was two days later and I was sprawled across the settee in the parlor, my bandaged ankle propped up on an ottoman. Gary came in balancing a large tray, which he set down on the coffee table next to me. "Milady's favorite breakfast," he said with a smile. "Cheese omelet, whole-wheat English muffin with strawberry preserves and three slices of nice, crisp turkey bacon."

At the words *turkey bacon* the three cats, who had been slumbering on the rug by the fireplace, raised their heads in unison. Purrday let out a loud meow.

Gary laughed. "Don't worry. There's more in the kitchen for you three."

"I can share." I picked up a slice of bacon, split it into four small pieces, and set three on the floor. The cats immediately came over to gobble them down, then look hopefully up at me as I popped my own piece into my mouth.

"Come on, guys, let Shell eat in peace. There's more bacon in the kitchen." Gary turned and the cats followed. Gary returned a few minutes later and perched himself on the edge of the coffee table. "Well, they're all stuffing their faces. I see you're enjoying your breakfast."

I'd downed a quarter of the omelet and half an English Muffin. "I sure am," I said around a mouthful of omelet. I swallowed and then added, "I'm sorry you and Robbie have to put extra hours in at the shop."

Gary shot me what I supposed he thought was a stern look. "You should be," he said. "Lucky for us Robbie could use the overtime. Anyway, it won't be for much longer. Dr. James said you should be fine in another week, right?"

"Yep. He also said my injury could have been a lot worse. I was lucky I only had a hairline fracture and not a break."

"Kenny Parsons was pretty lucky himself. He only ended up with a slight concussion from that rock you threw at him. Josh and Riser both said he'll be able to stand trial."

The doorbell chimed. Gary made an exasperated noise and then got up to answer. He was back a few seconds later with Josh in tow. Josh held a bouquet of carnations and roses in one hand. He set it down on the coffee table and bent to brush a kiss across my forehead.

"Hey, Shell. How are you feeling today?"

"Much better. How is Taylor?"

Josh grinned. "Thrilled beyond words and eternally grateful to you. She would have come with me, but your mother is like a crazy person, working the entire cast to the bone so that they'll be ready for opening night."

"She's had tighter deadlines," I said. "So what about Kenny? Is he still in the hospital?"

Josh shook his head. "He was released late yesterday, and Amy arrested him immediately. His lawyer tried to get him out on bail but wasn't successful, thank goodness."

"Kenny is just about the last person I'd ever have pegged as a murderer," I said.

"In my experience, anyone's capable, given the right circumstances," said Josh. "From what I understand, Kenny is claiming he killed Terrill because Terrill was going to kill him."

I wrinkled my nose. "That's kind of a convoluted self-defense, isn't it?"

Josh nodded. "Apparently Terrill had investigators trying to track down Kenny, or Lenny, for quite some time. Once it was established that Lenny Gruber was dead, Terrill had the investigators track down family members. They discovered that Irving went MIA at around the same time Lenny passed, so Terrill had them concentrate on finding him. Skillman got a tip Irving was in this area, so Terrill was planning on coming out here when he got the call from your mother to direct the play. He figured he could kill two birds with one stone. When he heard Kenny talking at the theater he got suspicious, because Skillman had told him Irving had a stuttering problem. Kenny overheard Terrill on the phone with Skillman and confronted him. Terrill told him that he was going to see that he paid for his crimes, and Kenny took that to mean Terrill was planning to kill him. He followed him to the shed, they fought, and Kenny shot him."

"That's pretty much what Kenny told me," I said. "He planned to kill Terrill, though. He bought that silencer from Sue's shop."

"Yeah, his self-defense theory had more holes than Swiss cheese," Gary said with a chuckle. "He'll probably end up with life—a double murder charge and an attempted one on you."

"And Noelle? Kenny told me she recognized him in the photo."

"Kenny had a beard when he worked at the clinic, but when she saw that photograph, she still recognized him and realized that he was the one who was involved in the hit-and-run. He overheard her make plans to meet you at the gazebo. Unfortunately, Noelle was in such a rush she dropped her phone and

Kenny, who was following her, took it and texted Taylor. Then he went to the gazebo and killed Noelle before either of you arrived. He figured Taylor would get the blame and he'd be off the hook and able to leave town."

"He didn't count on Shell's stubborn streak, though," Gary said.

"That's right," Josh agreed. "He knew Shell wouldn't rest until she found out the truth, so he kept a close eye on her. When he saw her find that gum wrapper, he knew the jig was up."

"Well, all's well that ends well, as your mother would say," Gary said.

"Ow-owrrr," said Purrday, who had come back into the room. Kahlua and the princess followed. The princess jumped up and stretched out on the settee next to me.

I stroked her silky fur. "I'm glad I pulled those ads," I said. "I'm going to keep the princess. Purrday's fond of her, and she's a pretty good addition to our detective squad. After all, the princess was the one who unearthed Terrill's secret cache. Without that, this might not have been solved and Kenny would have gotten away with murder."

"And let's not forget those cats pointed Josh and me in the right direction to find you," added Gary. "They're pretty good lifesavers if you ask me."

The princess let out a loud warble, and Purrday joined in. The only one who didn't seem happy was Kahlua. She stretched out on the settee above me and cast me a baleful stare.

I laughed. "Don't worry, Kahlua. You guys will get used to each other."

Josh chuckled. "So how are things going with the play?"

I waved my hand. "My mother is a real die-hard. She called a casting director who owed her a favor and it so happens there's an actress who was just written out of her soap opera looking for work. She's coming here tomorrow to take over Noelle's part. So *Our Town* should still open, but a little behind schedule." I looked at Josh. "I don't suppose I could talk you into accompanying me to the play on opening night."

He reached out, grasped my hand. "I was hoping you'd ask. I've already made arrangements to be off that night." He glanced at his watch, rose. "I've got to get going. I'll check in with you later."

He leaned over, brushed a quick kiss across my lips, and then left. Gary went into the kitchen and then came back out, pulling on his jacket. "Time for me to go to work," he said. "You'll be okay here alone, right?"

"Of course." I waved my hand in the direction of the sturdy cane that rested next to the coffee table. "And if all else fails, you're just a phone call away."

Gary left and I leaned back against the soft pillows, closed my eyes. I'd just started to nod off when the doorbell rang. I pushed myself up, startled. The cats, who'd been sleeping too, also looked annoyed to have their rest disturbed.

The bell rang again. "Coming," I called. I grabbed the cane and hobbled to the door. I peeped out the window, saw a FedEx truck at the curb, and then opened the door. The driver, a young man in his twenties, held out a box to me, along with a computer clipboard. "You have to sign for it," he said.

I scrawled my name and then hobbled back inside, balancing the box as best I could. I went into the kitchen, laid the box on the counter, and got a knife out of the drawer. I slit the box open and looked inside. I saw a slim blue velvet box. I pulled the box out and opened it. Nestled on a bed of cream-colored velvet was a beautiful gold link bracelet. I lifted the bracelet out and held it up. Dangling from it was a charm—the comedy and tragedy masks.

My stomach started to do a flip-flop. I remembered seeing a similar bracelet in someone's apartment, what seemed an eternity ago. "Oh, no," I muttered. "It can't be." I pulled the rest of the paper out of the box and sure enough, at the bottom of the box was a slim white envelope. I ripped it open and out slid a single sheet of paper. My heart pounded in my chest as I unfolded the paper and read:

> *Dearest Shell:*
>
> *I found this while packing for France. I'd been saving it for your birthday and totally forgot I had it. Not a day has passed that I don't regret what happened between us, so I'm sending it to you as a sort of peace offering. Perhaps one day you will find it in your heart to forgive me.*
>
> *Your mother invited me to the opening of her play in Fox Hollow, but I'm afraid I'll have to pass. Another time, perhaps?*
>
> *I've missed you.*
>
> *Patrick*

About the Author

While Toni LoTempio does not commit—or solve—murders in real life, she has no trouble doing it on paper. Her lifelong love of mysteries began early on when she was introduced to her first Nancy Drew mystery at age ten—*The Secret in the Old Attic*. She and her cat pen the Urban Tails Pet Shop Mysteries, the Nick and Nora mystery series, and the Cat Rescue series. Catch up with them at Rocco's blog, catsbooksmorecats.blogspot.com, or her website, tclotempio.net.

Made in the USA
Monee, IL
30 June 2023

38220738R00121